Jerome Chapman

SubSURFACE

UNSEEN QUARRY

For my grandchildren

Abigail, Grayson, John Patrick, Garrison and Mary Claire

SubSURFACE

A
RUSSELL BAKER

DRIFT BOAT
DETECTIVE
NOVEL

By
JEROME CHAPMAN

This novel is a work of fiction. While most locations, cities, and principalities used are actual places, the names, descriptions, entities, and incidents included in the story are products of the author's imagination. Any resemblance to actual persons, events, and entities is entirely coincidental. The opinions expressed are those of the author, only.

Published by Jerome Chapman
Smyrna, GA. USA
WWW.Driftboatdetective.com / WWW.Sandypointtimes.com

Book Design by Jerome Chapman
The Drift Boat Detective Image by Chuck Renfroe
© Jerome Chapman 2017

Printed in the USA
ISBN 978-0-692-87297-0
1. Fiction/Action & Adventure
2. Fiction/ Mystery & Detective / General
17.04.01

In fishing, especially fly fishing, using a fly or a lure that attracts the fish to strike on the top of the water is the ultimate in excitement for the fisherman. The fish can seem to explode on the surface with little or no warning and the moment that one fish hooks up on the top of the water can make the whole day seem a success and set the stage for a lifetime of enjoyment in the pastime of fishing. In a few cases you can see the fish as it speeds toward the fly from its hiding spot, adding more to the adrenaline rush. In some cases, the fish may move up to the fly and seem to sip it in, no explosion and no big splash.

But the reality is that the preponderance of evidence and experience shows that fish feed below the surface over eighty-five per cent of the time, by some accounts. I believe the number is even higher but have done no research though I have spent hours on the water without ever seeing a rising fish.

They feed and live subsurface and can probably do that without ever surfacing. It is that very set of facts that make the top-water strike and catch so unique and thrilling to the angler; an experience that can shape the heart and mind to desire and want the next strike with great anticipation. At the same time, one must learn to enjoy what the river gives them. It may not always be on a top-water fly. It may not always be the biggest fish in the river. Some days, the tiniest fish is the trophy for the day.

In the criminal world, much of the criminal activity goes on below the surface out of view of our daily lives, as well. When we are not looking, expecting, or even realize it, a crime has taken place. Great efforts are made to conceal and cover up the actions, conceal the intentions and deeds, and to prevent detection of the crime and the perpetrator. That world, too, exists subsurface. For years we called it *the underworld*.

Just like fishing, where we would like to catch every trophy on the surface in plain sight, law enforcement has to look underneath the layers of deception and go deeper into the holes where the catch can be made. Under rocks, logs, and on the bottom of the fast moving stream of events. Most catches are made subsurface. Law enforcement has to look into the bowels of society and cyber space to make their catches, too, especially in the mobile and high tech world we live in.

Russell Baker likes to catch trout on the top with a dry fly. But he knows he will sometimes have to use a nymph or a streamer or some other subsurface attractor, working out of human sight. Fishing, as it's called.

Russell Baker is called on to catch big trout and murderers and terrorists and that also may require going deep. And, he knows, the fish doesn't always take the bait on the first try. And, sometimes, the big one gets away.

1

Madison County Sheriff Barry Steinbrenner put on his uniform, warm coat and gloves, kissed his wife and headed out in the cold to his patrol car. It was the night before Thanksgiving and he was going to relieve his chief deputy, actually the Under Sheriff, Wayne Dunkin. It was shaping up to be a night with record snowfall and all the other deputies were off patrol and on emergency standby. If there was an emergency somewhere, the closest deputy would be dispatched and everyone was praying that there would not be one tonight.

Barry keyed the mic on the Dodge. "Madison County Unit One to Madison County Unit Two."

"Madison County Unit Two. Go ahead, Sheriff."

"Wayne, meet me at the courthouse and let's swap vehicles. I think I'll need the Explorer with the four wheel drive and the chains. You can take my car and go home for the evening. We'll be on emergency call basis till this snow lets up. I'll stay on till it looks like the roads are closing down. Have you been seeing much traffic? Over."

"No sir. I haven't seen a car in the past hour. I've just pulled in to Alder Market to get a cup of coffee and I'll head that back way in a couple of minutes. The market is closing now and all the stores closed early in Ennis and in Bozeman, I heard on the radio."

Wayne Dunkin was an Iraq War veteran and was someone the sheriff felt he could always depend on in a pinch. If there was a real problem situation, he wanted Wayne Dunkin to have his six, as they said in the military.

They met at the courthouse and the Sheriff went in and filled a travel cup with hot coffee. Deputy Dunkin said, "After I spoke with you on the radio I did see a car headed north out of town toward Sheridan as I was leaving Alder Market. I couldn't tell much about it because it was snowing so hard. The car was covered with snow and ice like it had been traveling a while. That was the only car I saw in the last couple of hours."

"I hope they make it to where they're going. The county will not be plowing that road anymore tonight. They're trying to keep US 287 open and that is about all they can do now." said Barry.

Barry climbed in the Explorer police vehicle and headed out. "Madison County Unit One is 10-8."

Sheriff Barry Steinbrenner came from a family of sheriffs. His father had been sheriff in Missoula County where the city of Missoula is located and now his brother was the sheriff there. Barry had not gone into law enforcement early on but had attended the Air Force Academy, flown fighter jets and retired to a quiet life in Ennis. Then, he got recruited to replace a sheriff who was ousted for misconduct and won easily.

Most of the time, being sheriff in Madison County was a pretty routine job. It was a lot of square miles, about 7,000 people and very few major crimes. But one case had brought him in contact with Russell Baker, Nancy Freeman and a bunch of bad guys and gals.

During the holidays the Sheriff would take some of the patrol hours so his people could be with their families. The fact that he was willing to do more than was expected of him on their behalf made him highly respected by his department in the tiny county seat town of Virginia City, Montana.

Curious about the car Deputy Dunkin had mentioned, he started out of town on State Route 287. "Madison County Unit One will be headed out Sheridan Road as far as I can for a while to check on the car that went that way," he said into his radio.

Often there was confusion with the State Route and the US Highway with the same number. This was the Sheridan Road to some, The Twin Bridges Road to others, or the Virginia City Road. It all depended on where you were going from.

The Ford Edge with Pennsylvania license plates was also going out State Route 287 trying to get to the Double Barr Ranch. They had been there before but never under these conditions and none of the men in the car had any experience driving through piles of snow. The road was down to two ruts and getting worse. Somewhere between Alder and Sheridan was the long driveway with a lighted gatehouse. It couldn't be far, now.

Cas , whose real name was Kasim Rahmani, was driving when the car hit the hard packed snow and the wheel jerked to the right and before anyone knew what was happening, the Edge spun around and went backwards into the deep snow that had piled up from the snow plows. The center of the car was grounded and both the front and rear wheels had no traction. They were stuck!

After they all got their senses back and managed to get one door open to get out and inspect the situation, they knew they were not equipped to move the car and its several heavy boxes.

The GPS had worked off and on and they knew they were close to the ranch entrance. They didn't want anyone coming along and stopping who might get curious or just accidently take note of their car's contents. They needed someone from the ranch to come get them quickly!

Between their four cell phones they did not have a signal. One of the older men picked up a small bag out of his backpack that was beside him on the seat. He took out an Iridium Satellite Phone and punched in the number of another Iridium phone, both issued to and paid for by an oil industry service company located in Iraq. A voice answered on the other end from someone at the Double Barr Ranch. The person said they would send an ATV to get them but that the road was nearly impassable and even the ATV would have a problem. As for getting the car to the ranch, they would have to see when they got there.

Sheriff Barry Steinbrenner was about to turn around and call it a night when he thought he saw headlights. There were only two ruts on the road and meeting anyone was going to be a problem. To be safe, he turned on his emergency lights and light bar on the top of the car. The blue flashing lights made an eerie sight reflecting off the snow and seeing the police car and all of the flashing lights sent the occupants of the Edge into a panic! A cop was on the scene, emergency lights flashing and they had nowhere to go!

As Barry got closer, he saw that the car had spun out and hit the snow. The lights were shining in his face making it impossible to see what kind of car it was and he could only make out the grill and front bumper. He picked up his mic and called in.

"Madison County One to Madison County. I have a car spun out here just past Alder and I can't tell if anyone is hurt yet. I will check it out and call you back. Please stand by."

"Roger, Madison One," came the response. "Standing by."

The four individuals in the Edge were in full panic and they watched as the door opened on the police car and the Sheriff got out with a big light and headed their way. One of the older men got a .40 Cal semi-automatic out of his bag on the seat. As Barry reached the car the man lowered the window and shot Barry five times with no warning. He fell face down in the snow with his flashlight in his hand and blood started staining the snow.

Kasim Rahmani and Samer Mustafa, two young college students from Salt Lake were frozen. "What have you done!?" yelled Cas.

The shooter sat there silent for a moment. The snow was falling harder and harder. Barry Steinbrenner was not moving.

"Shut up! We could not let that cop look in our car! There is too much at stake. He could destroy everything! Just calm down and shut up! We must decide what to do."

Then they heard the sound of a motor and the lights of a large ATV type vehicle appeared out of the blinding snow. It was a minute before they saw the writing on the side that said Double Barr Ranch. Their help had arrived.

There was an argument about what to do and they now had the Sheriff, his car, the Ford Edge and its contents and the four occupants. The ATV had an electric winch and cable and they attached it to the Edge. They knew they could not leave their car there and have it traced back to them. They also could see that the officer could not have called in any identification on the car as there was no license plate on the front, not even a fake one.

With ATV hooked to the car and all the men pushing, Cas was able to get the car back on the road. The contents of the car, four boxes loaded with AK-47 automatic weapons, were moved to the ATV. Cas and Sam were given no choice but to get back in the car and try to drive back the way they had just come and avoid being seen. The man with the ATV did not believe they could get the car through the snow and all the way to the ranch so the only choice was to drive it back the way it had come in the two ruts that were quickly filling in with snow.

They could not leave their car there with the Sheriff's car and the presumably dead sheriff. The police vehicle was still sitting with the engine running, lights flashing and with the sheriff still lying in the snow. One of the older men walked over and switched off the engine and took the SD card out of the dash cam. He did not see a body cam on the officer.

The ATV headed back toward the direction of the Ranch and Cas and Sam started back toward Virginia City and Ennis. If they had a plan, it did not include helping Barry Steinbrenner.

2

Sheriff Barry Steinbrenner was lying in the snow and his dispatcher was calling.

"Madison County to Madison County Unit One. Come in Unit One. What is your situation?"

After several tries and getting no answer, the dispatcher called Deputy Wayne Dunkin at home.

"Wayne, I'm sorry to bother you but I have lost contact with the Sheriff. He went out State 287 and was past Alder when he called and said there was a car spun out or something. I can't raise him now on the radio and that is not like him."

Wayne Dunkin serves as Under Sheriff making him second in command. He had to make a decision quickly to address the situation. He had no idea what kind of problem he had on his hands, but what he did know was that the Sheriff was predictable in procedure.

"Notify all units to report in. Sound the department alert."

"Are you sure, Wayne? Get everyone out? It may be nothing."

"I will be responsible and if I'm wrong everyone will have a big laugh. But right now, that's my call."

"Roger."

"Get Deputy Hal Smisson on the phone and tell him to get the Sheriff's Department five ton and head toward Alder as fast as possible."

The surplus US Army M-939 truck was a brute but sat high off the ground and could survive difficult situations. Bought with some grant money and county assistance, the truck was good in situations where ground clearance and power were needed. This was just such a time.

"Barry has it set up for winter emergency and it already has chains and is ready to go. We may need it. Tell him to contact me as soon as he is on the road."

"Roger, Unit Two."

"Contact the Public Works Department. We have to have some snow plow equipment up and running on State 287 ASAP! Tell them this is an emergency! And, we need the EMT'S to go toward Alder. Hopefully, we don't need them but we can't wait to see what the situation is out there, that will delay things too long. "

"Roger."

"I am in route to Alder and I'll go as far as I can but I may have to wait on the plows. I will be using my truck since I just have the patrol car with two wheel drive at home."

The emergency calls went out and the Public Works, the EMT's and the entire Madison County force were moving into action. There was some grumbling but no hesitation.

The road back to Virginia City was fast becoming impassable for the Edge and its two occupants, even with the four wheel drive. If they were to meet another vehicle, it would be all over as there was no room to pass.

Ahead, they saw some lights and a sign that said *Motel & RV Park. Bar.* Not a combination you saw every day, but the parking lot driveway to the RV Park had apparently been recently cleared by someone possibly using a tractor. They were in the small town of Alder.

Cas turned in off the road and drove back behind the last car parked next to the building and turned off the lights. He was shaking like a leaf and was sick to his stomach. They were in big trouble and had gotten in with some seriously bad people. People who would not hesitate to kill them if necessary.

Sam had been watching his throw away phone while Cas drove as fast as he could under the conditions. They had about given up but as they parked he saw that he had a small signal. But, they were stuck! They could not drive in any direction due to the snow. In the daylight, they would stand out like the proverbial sore thumb. A once in a lifetime snow and they were in it! A possibly dead cop behind them and prison, or worse, ahead! They needed a minute to think about what to do! Where to go!

They had been there for some time trying to decide what to do and, as they sat in the dark by the building, an answer came. It came in the form of a large truck with a snow blade on the front and pulling a blade behind! It was followed by a large pick up, a large military looking truck, and a police car and then an ambulance. With all the flashing lights and screaming sirens, it wouldn't be but a minute before they woke the dead!

This was their one chance! The road had been cleared and if there were not yet any road blocks set up, they could get back to Ennis and maybe the US Route 287 and get out of there. It was their only chance.

Sam screamed, "Let's go Kasim. Once they get there and find that body, all hell will break loose. We have one choice and that's try to drive out of here."

"Yes. Okay. Our friends from school, Lisa and Laura, are staying near here on their ski trip. Call and see if you can get one of them on the phone. Maybe we could get to their house. Tell them that the road is so bad that we just got here and we would like to stay with them till we can get out to the ranch. No one will look for us there." He drove onto the freshly plowed road and fishtailed out of Alder as fast as he could go.

Sam punched in Lisa's number on the burn phone.

Lisa did not see a number when the call came in and no name came up so she started to ignore it but thinking it might be Sam and Cas, she answered.

"Hello. This is Lisa."

"Lisa. This is Sam."

"Sam? Where are you? I did not see your name on my phone."

"My old phone died and I had to get another one for the trip. I'll see about getting it fixed when I get back. We are almost to Ennis and the road is so bad we have gotten lost two, three times and we are afraid to go any further. We got detoured several miles out of the way. We just wondered if we could possibly impose on you to let us stay there tonight and we will try to find the ranch tomorrow in the daylight or when the road clears up."

After a quick check with her mother, she replied, "Sure. Come on. Call me when you see a road marker but we are out on State Route 287 between Virginia City and Ennis. There is large red wooden archway over the entrance to the drive. My mom will talk you through if you need it."

"We should be there soon," he replied. "Drive, Kasim! We have to get off this road!"

About fifteen minutes later, they pulled into the drive to Miriam's house and the warmth and safety was a welcome sight. The girls met them with hot coffee and big hugs. Now, they would try and keep themselves together and lay low until they could figure out their next move.

Unaware of what was happening in Madison County, Russell Baker had traveled back to Atlanta for a holiday visit with his former in-laws. It was to be the last visit to the house where his wife had grown up in East Cobb County. The McKenzie's were moving to a smaller place. His wife, Sarah, had died unexpectedly and thrown Russell's life into a tailspin which caused him to leave behind his Cobb County Detective job and move to Bozeman, Montana.

A few days before he had been drinking coffee and looking out the window at the oncoming snow storm from his rented house where he was now living near Ennis, Montana when the phone rang. Russ, as most knew him, picked up the phone and recognized the name in the caller ID: *Miriam.*

"Hello, Miriam," he answered, trying to sound calm and speaking softly and refusing to allow himself to reveal the sudden rush he was feeling. "It's nice to see your name pop up here. To what do I owe the honor? I know the rent check is in the mail!"

"Hello to you, Russ. Yes, as usual, your rent check was right on time. If you would just buy that place, you wouldn't have to pay rent. I've wanted to call but I didn't want to interrupt you and Nancy. I hope this is not a bad time to call."

Russ couldn't help but feel a surge of excitement that surprised him. Miriam Alexander was his land lord, but she was more than that: she was a former co-worker and lover and friend who had left Ennis and moved back to Salt Lake City to be with her daughters. She had left him behind and ended their short personal relationship.

Theirs was a relationship that had helped him out his depression over the loss of his wife and job and helped her find her self-confidence after her husband left her for a pretty and rich designer architect

"You're not interrupting anything, Miriam. Nancy is not here. I've just gotten in from a float trip on the upper Madison today. That was after being gone for a few days of personal fishing with some guys from back home," said Russ.

"Where were you on that trip?" she asked.

"You remember Barry Steinbrenner's brother, I'm sure," he continued. "He has a place up on the Blackfoot River past Lincoln and he invited me to use it. Some old buddies came out from Marietta and we fished the Blackfoot, Rock Creek over near Missoula, and the Clark Fork. I did about all the fishing I want to do for a while. And that's just as well, I guess. It looks like we are in for a blizzard tonight. They say it may be a record and more to come the next few days."

"I do remember Barry's brother and I did see that there was a potential blizzard coming your way," she said.

"This Montana weather is surprising," he added. "Bozeman and Ennis get about fifty inches of snow a year. One year, I think they got fifty inches in a twenty four hour period and that set a record. Over at Big Sky, which you know is less than twenty miles away as the eagle flies, they routinely gets two hundred inches and sometimes up to four hundred plus. It makes it a great ski destination. With average low temperatures around Bozeman in the low teens in December, January and February, that's just too cold for me. Some people still go fishing but not me."

Russ thought Georgia or Florida might be better choices for that time of the year. Or, even, maybe the Bahamas. But Montana is a big country, great outdoors and not yet full of people! Open spaces and elbow room.

"They say we could get half a year's worth of snow tonight!"

"So you are still doing some guide trips and detective work?" she asked.

Miriam did not want to say that she had picked up the phone time and time again but had stopped short; not knowing if she could hide how much she was missing Russ. She left Russ and went back to Salt Lake and had all kinds of good reasons including her two daughters who were living there and in college and the fact that she was older than Russ and believed that he would be better off moving on with the Nancy Freeman, the younger local Bozeman beauty. All were good sounding reasons, for sure.

"I still do as much guiding as I want but mostly on a fill in basis. I've only helped Barry at the Sheriff's Office a time or two when he had someone out and he needed help to do patrol. I had to be in court for the trials of the three defendants in that big case we worked on and that has taken some time," he added.

"I was glad I did not have to come back for any of that," she said.

"With the high water temperatures and low water levels, the guides have been working under the hoot owl restrictions on the river and have to be off the water by 2:00 PM. Things have been a little crazy for some of the guides. I helped out in the fly shop a few times, too. I managed a trip to Florida to do some bone fishing with my father-in-law."

Miriam smiled as she thought of a trip she had made to Florida with Russ. It was one of the best times of her life.

Russ did not mention that his relationship with Nancy was pretty cool right now and was not about to tell Miriam it was all because of her. When Nancy Freeman learned how close he had been with Miriam and the fact that he was living in Miriam's house, it was a little too much. They were just seeing each other on occasion now.

"And," he added jokingly, "you know me: I can't hold down a real job."

Russ has not had a steady job since his wife died and he left the Cobb County Police Department. The part time guide work and a temporary job as detective for the Madison County Montana Sheriff's office were about as close as he had come.

"How are things in Salt Lake?" he asked. "I suppose the girls are doing great with you there to keep an eye on them."

"We stay busy in the crime lab. The Salt Lake County crime lab is new and does a lot of work with other jurisdictions to help out the State lab which is always behind it seems. Budget problems over there keep them shorthanded, I think. The biggest problem, believe it or not, is the huge backlog in rape kits," said Miriam. "The girls are busy in school and with their social lives. They live in the dorm but I see them a lot. They're doing something all the time. In fact, that is why I'm calling. They are planning a trip to Big Sky for Thanksgiving break. Big Sky has moved the opening date for skiing up due to the early snow. They usually open the slopes on the 26th. The girls hope to get in some skiing while they are there."

"Russ, they are working with some Middle Eastern refugees here and two of the young men they work with are coming out to a dude ranch near Ennis for an all-boys retreat. The girls thought they could do some things with them while they were in the area. Are you familiar with the Double Barr Ranch?"

"I have seen the sign and the little welcome center by the road and a van or two with their name on it. It's actually up close to Sheridan. I don't believe I ever talked to anyone who has been there," he replied. "They have a little security booth at the entrance to the ranch but you can only see the top of a building or two from the road," said Russ. "I have fished the Ruby River over near there a time or two."

Miriam continued, "I was thinking I might come out for a couple of days with the girls and visit and say hello to everyone and see you and the folks over at Madison County. Are you and Nancy going to be around?"

"Miriam, I'm so sorry. I have made plans to go to Atlanta and see my in-laws. They are moving out of their big house to a town-home and asked me to come one last time for Thanksgiving at Sarah's old home before they move out. Dan wants me to sign some papers to set up a family trust and power of attorney and some other stuff. You know they don't have any other family. I hate that I won't be here any next week."

She did not see the look of disappointment on his face and he was glad for that.

"Well, that sounds very nice. Is Nancy going with you?"

"No. I will be going down alone," he said.

Then he added, "Say. Why don't you and the girls stay here at the house while you are in town? It'll save you a lot of money. Your room is just like you left it. I have been using the guest room and you still have some stuff in the closet."

"Oh, I forgot about those things. I'll bet Nancy doesn't care for having my clothes hanging around there."

"Nancy is not staying here, Miriam. She stays at her place in town. We see each other occasionally but she's mainly dating Dr. Carter from the school."

"Oh. I did not realize that," said Miriam. "Are you okay with that?"

"That's the way it is. I'm okay."

Miriam could not help feeling glad about the news and she felt a pang of guilt for feeling that way. She still had strong feelings for Russ and she had not found anyone in Salt Lake to take Russ's place. He had been there when her husband had walked out and left her. It was difficult to explain their relationship. Not just an affair but it had been a safe harbor for them both: a harbor that seemed at the time to have no tie downs or encumbrances.

"Are you sure about that Russ? It would be nice to stay there, I think, and I could clean out the rest of my things. It would be a lot nicer if you were going to be there but maybe you can come to Salt Lake and visit us soon."

All those reasons to not see Russ suddenly did not seem too important.

"We'll make a point to make that happen! I would love to come out there!" he said. I'll call you when I get back and we'll set up some dates."

3

Russ's flight had taken him from Bozeman to Salt Lake and then from Salt Lake to Atlanta. With the time difference and plane changes, he had spent the better part of the day traveling when they finally touched down at Atlanta's Hartsfield-Jackson Airport.

He had told his in-laws Dan and Doris McKenzie that he would rent a car but they would not hear of it. They were standing at the luggage carousel with smiles and hugs waiting.

When Russ's wife, Sarah, died, he became all they had left and they treated him like a son and not an ex-son-in-law. The feeling was mutual. He was looking forward to spending some time with them over the holidays and reflecting on the good days he'd had with Sarah. He was finally able to think about Sarah and remember the good things and not the fact that she had died with little warning, leaving Russ a wreck.

They got into Dan's Range Rover and headed the 30 miles to their home in Cobb County. There was no snow on the ground in Atlanta and that was a good thing. Two inches of snow in Georgia is enough to wreak havoc on the roads and businesses. It took a lot of years to add up 50 inches of snow fall in Georgia. But it was really good to be home. Maybe, he thought, he had been gone long enough.

Miriam Alexander had grown up near Salt Lake in Burley, Idaho where her father and grandfather had been beet farmers. She was the first in the family to go to college and had attended the University of Utah in Salt Lake. She got married her senior year but went on to graduate although she had to wear what she laughingly called a maternity graduation gown.

Her two daughters, Lisa and Laura, were born there and now were in their freshman and sophomore years but they were going to the private, expensive, Westminster College thanks to Miriam's ex-husband and his new rich wife who had made that part of the divorce settlement. Both girls were as pretty as their mother and had immediately gotten involved with some of the programs at the school.

One of the programs was working with the college and the City of Salt Lake assisting refugees and through this they had met two young men from Iraq who were enrolled in school with some financial assistance and were themselves working with other young refugees at Westminster. They were handsome, polite and did not seem particularly religious and, after all, were attending a Presbyterian college. In spite of any concerns in the beginning about cultural differences, Miriam had come to like both of them.

Kasim Rahmani was called "Cas" by his friends and Samer Mustafa was called "Sam". The nicknames seemed to make them more local when they were introduced. More American sounding. They always appeared to have money and both had fairly new cars, although not BMW's or Mercedes. Both had jobs with one working in computer store and the other a phone store. They fit right in with the other kids from more well-to-do families attending the school.

The boys had already made a couple of trips to Montana to the Double Barr Ranch. It was a 7500 acre working ranch with some actual cattle being raised there, but was mainly billed as a dude ranch and spa. It was a few miles outside of Ennis near Sheridan.

The ads said it had horseback riding, snowmobiling, and cross-country skiing, sporting clay and skeet shooting, massages and hiking. In addition, guests could be involved in certain activities of a working cattle ranch. There was skiing at Big Sky which was not too far away and there was a large enclosed and heated pool. Something for everyone.

The ranch was at one time part of a much larger operation owned by a family named Barr that had all moved back East to Boston and New York and were filthy rich, according to local legend. Not quite on the order of Ted Turner and Robert Redford, but never-the-less, people who had worked there at the ranch building cabins and gymnasiums and barns and amphitheaters came back with stories of a huge operation with lots of people coming and going although no one locally really knew anyone who worked at the place or who had ever spent a weekend there. People who called for a reservation always found the place booked solid.

Lisa and Laura had told the boys that they had once lived in the area for a while and would like to go to Ennis with them when they went. The boys seemed excited about them coming but had said it was booked up for a guy weekend and there were no vacancies at the facility. That's when the girls decided to try to get in on the season opening at Big Sky. That sounded reasonable with the snow coming in early this year. They could spend some time in and around Bozeman with the boys and visit with some high school friends as well. Staying at their old house was icing on the cake and cash in the bank. The boys were driving to Ennis with friends and the girls would fly to Bozeman with Miriam and they would meet up there. They were all set.

Nancy Freeman stood at her desk at her clothing store in Bozeman. The calendar on the desk in front of her had a day circled and a little note that she had written in with a pen. It just said, *Russ in Atlanta.* Looking at it a few days before Thanksgiving made her sad as she thought about Russ's call asking her if she would like to go to Atlanta with him.

"No, Russ, I don't believe I want to go to Atlanta with you. Besides, it's my busy season at the store and I need to get as much business from it as possible. You go and have a great time. Maybe I'll see you before Christmas and we can get together. I am pretty booked up for the holidays, though. Give my regards to the McKenzies."

Why had she made such a mean statement to Russ? He was trying to be nice and she had trashed his idea and deliberately tried to make him feel bad. But looking at the calendar, it was she that was feeling bad.

She had felt hurt when she learned how close Russ and Miriam had been before Miriam had moved back to Salt Lake. But, as her brother kept reminding her, she had continued to date Dr. Carter so Russ was free to do as he pleased. She wondered if Russ was missing her down in Atlanta.

Miriam decided she would get everything together and have a traditional Thanksgiving dinner with her girls, and the two boys, at the house she had rented to Russell Baker. After they got their rental car they headed for Ennis and she picked up everything she needed at Madison Foods in Ennis for Thanksgiving lunch. She would get up early Thanksgiving and they would have a great meal.

"Girls, let the boys know that we are having Thanksgiving lunch about 1:30 at the house and they are welcome to come join us."

4

Russell sat down with Dan McKenzie to get an update on his investments that Dan had been handling. Russ had sold the house and gotten some insurance money after Sarah's death. He had made enough most months to cover his bills and had not spent much except for a new RO drift boat and a new Silverado truck to replace the Tahoe that had gotten shot to pieces by a guy who was trying to kill him.

"Russ, we have done very well with your money we invested. With the money from the house, the insurance proceeds and some stock growth you now have almost a couple of million in cash and stocks. You can live most anyplace you choose and you don't have to scrimp unless you want to. I also want you to know that Doris and I have close to five million in stocks and cash plus the house, cars and some jewelry. I have set up a trust to handle all of this and you will be the administrator as well as the beneficiary of all remaining monies after we are gone. All I ask is that you make sure that Doris is well looked after if I should die first."

Russ sat silent for a moment. Then he said, "I will do my best and will consider it an honor. Beyond that, I am somewhat speechless." Dan McKenzie was a fine man-with or without any money.

"Great! Then let's go find some fun stuff to do!" said Dan. We want you to see the new place up on Lake Lanier. We are also going to have a small condo at Mexico Beach in Florida so we can go down there and bum around when we want. When I say we, I mean you and us. I'll make sure you have keys and codes and such. Maybe you can come down and meet us there after Christmas."

Russ decided to call the Cobb County Detective Bureau and see if he could speak to Chief of Detectives, Alan Schreiber. They gave him the usual line about the chief being unavailable and was asked if someone else could help him.

"If you don't mind, please tell him that it's Russell Baker and I'd like to speak to him for a moment," said Russ.

"Just a moment, sir," was the reply.

To his surprise, the next voice was Alan Schreiber's.

"Russell! This is unexpected! How are you? Are you in town?"

"Yes sir, Alan. I'm visiting for a few days and was hoping I could stop in and say hello. I understand if you are too busy," said Russ.

"Could you come on by now? I was planning on leaving this afternoon for a couple of days' vacation squeezed in around Thanksgiving."

"I can be there in fifteen minutes, if that's okay."

"That will be just right."

The place looked about the same as when Russ walked out his last time following Sarah's death. He was in a bad state of depression and self-pity that day. Alan Schreiber had understood and been supportive but in the end, Russ had decided to walk away from the job and the work he loved. He had packed up a U-Haul trailer and headed to Montana with Marietta in his rear view mirror.

Russ went in to his old workplace with some mixed feelings. He saw a few old faces and several new ones. The person at the reception window invited him to come around and buzzed him in to see Alan Schreiber.

"I heard about your big case in Montana, Russ. You did a great job out there."

"I am surprised that anyone here would have known about that, Alan." said Russ. "How did you hear about it?"

Alan picked up a file that was on his desk. Opening it, Russ saw a letter on Madison County Sheriff, Madison County, Montana letterhead. Alan handed it to Russ to read.

Russ stood for a moment with his mouth open in disbelief. The letter was to Alan Schreiber from Sheriff Barry Steinbrenner and gave a glowing report on the performance of Russ in the Madison River murder investigation and subsequent arrests of a key crime boss in Montana. In conclusion, Barry Steinbrenner had offered his opinion that if Russell ever wanted to come back to work for the Cobb Police Department, they should jump at the chance. Also noted was that he would hire Russ full time but that they had no place in the department at the time and no money to hire him full time. Russ had no idea that Barry had sent such a letter.

"I thought it was a nice letter from a small town sheriff but I did a little checking on Sheriff Steinbrenner and that changed my opinion. He has quite a resume. He's a pretty high level guy. Are you ready to come back to work?" asked Alan.

"Alan, that is tempting. Are you saying you have a job for me?"

"I have room for another detective. I have some issues related to promotion and advancement policies but they could probably be resolved."

"I hate to always be undecided with you on everything, Alan, but I did not see this coming. Can I think about it?"

"Sure. But, whatever you decide, it's good to see you back to your old self again."

Cas and Sam, the two students, spent a lot of time at the Student Center at the college and seemingly had no friends outside the group other than the two Alexander sisters. But on one occasion, they had received a call when the four of them were at a restaurant and the two boys had become very serious. They had walked off and had an agitated conversation and then came back and Cas said, "We have to run to the dorm and pick up some papers take them to my uncle who is passing through town. It is important that they do not see your faces as they have strong feelings about how women should dress in public. They are believers in the old ways and will be unhappy that we are not adhering to them. Okay?"

They had rushed to the dorm as if it was a big emergency and Sam ran in and came back in a few minutes with what looked like a shoe box. They then hurried to the Wal-Mart parking lot on S 900 E. where a car was waiting. One of the men came to their car and Sam handed him the shoe box.

"Who are these?" he said referring to Lisa and Laura and looked in the window at them.

"These ladies are taking us to dinner tonight, *Kahli*. They work at the Student Center. Everything you asked for is in the box. We must run now."

Cas hurriedly drove off as the man looked at them and went back to the waiting car. The girls noticed Cas and Sam seemed anxious to get away from the Wal-Mart. The girls thought it was because of their religious views. Later, they discussed how scary the man had looked.

The man had gotten back to his car, loosened the tape holding the lid shut and took out the cash. Some hundreds, some fifties, and some twenties. About $40,000 in all. Enough to cover the expenses of the two men in the car for a while. Most would be spent on women.

The driver asked, "Was there a problem?"

"There were two American women in the car and they saw me but we all look alike to them." They both laughed. Then the man with the money said, "He called me *Khali*, so all is well."

Kahli is the word for *my uncle on my mother's side*. A code word to let the other party know that there is no threat. The two young students had some very dangerous associates and they were not uncles.

Before leaving to go to the Double Barr Ranch the day before Thanksgiving, the students had been instructed to pick up the same two men they had given the money to in the Wal-Mart parking lot. The students only knew that they were very dangerous and skilled members of their group.

On Wednesday morning in Salt Lake, they all piled into Cas's dark silver Ford Edge and headed for Ennis, Montana and the Double Barr Ranch. They chose the Ford because it was roomier and all-wheel drive. They thought they might need the extra traction in the weather conditions they saw online. They also needed room for some items the passengers were bringing along. They did not look like the types to be headed to a Montana Ranch with their striking Middle Eastern features.

Just before leaving Salt Lake, Cas changed the license plate on the Ford to a Pennsylvania plate and the tag frame was changed to show a Pennsylvania car dealer. There was no discussion. They left to make the drive of 370 plus miles.

They would take turns driving, pay cash for everything and use 4 disposable burn phones that Sam acquired from the phone store where he worked. The ride in the harsh weather conditions would probably take them close to 7 to 8 hours and would put them there in the late afternoon or early evening. They would stay within the speed limits and try to avoid attracting any attention. They were not on any particular time table but needed to be there by Friday. Thanksgiving was of no interest to them.

The snow had been coming in waves for several days and the temperatures were staying below freezing so the accumulated snow was not melting. The snow plows were working overtime and people were being advised to stay off the roads unless absolutely necessary.

It was a holiday week and plans were being canceled and postponed. It was going to be a record year for snow, no doubt.

Miriam and the girls made it to the house and were glad when they were able to get inside, light a fire in the fireplace and fire up the pellet stove in the den. Russ had left everything in perfect shape and it felt good to Miriam to be there and to be able to feel that Russ had been there. She only wished he was there at that moment. God, she had missed him! She couldn't help but wonder if he was feeling the same.

Miriam had no idea what the week being back in Ennis and the days following had in store for her and her daughters.

5

The Madison County snow plow had done a pretty good job under the conditions and Deputy Wayne Dunkin was right behind it in his personal truck and his handheld radio. While he could not reach the courthouse or maybe even one of the repeaters, he could communicate with the snow plow and the EMT's as well as his other deputies who were nearby.

The snow plow operator got on his radio: "I see flashing lights ahead. It looks like we have found the Sheriff's car."

Deputy Wayne Dunkin of the Madison County, Montana had been to Iraq and seen lots of bad things. He never talked about his experiences in the military or what he did over there although Sheriff Steinbrenner had a pretty good idea. But when Deputy Dunkin got out of his truck on Highway 287 outside Alder, Montana his heart almost stopped. He immediately recognized the form lying in a mixture of blood and snow as his boss and friend, Sheriff Barry Steinbrenner.

He yelled into his radio, "Where the hell is that ambulance team! Get your asses here! NOW!"

"We have you in sight Deputy. Be there in a few seconds!"

"This is bad! Real bad! He has lost a lot of blood and he may be dead now."

Sheriff Steinbrenner had installed a sophisticated radio repeater system to help his few officers cover a lot of miles and always be in contact. His small radio message had been picked up and retransmitted to Madison and Gallatin County, who participated with Madison County in emergencies. In a matter of seconds, the word was out: "Officer Down!"

The snow plow moved ahead and cleared way for the ambulance and then turned around to head back the way they came. The Five Ton also went by and the ambulance crew went into action.

In a matter of less than 5 minutes, they had the Sheriff in the Ambulance and were on the radio to the trauma center in Bozeman. They were having difficulty getting any vital signs. The strange looking group of rescuers headed back the way they came, on their way to Bozeman with Barry Steinbrenner where a surgical team was being readied, if it was needed.

Deputy Wayne Dunkin stood looking at the scene and two other deputies had arrived as they tried to sort out what they saw before them. Dunkin realized he had a major crime scene and between the snowplow, the five ton and his own truck plus the ambulance, and the continued snowfall, a lot of his crime scene had been obliterated!

The sheriff's bullet proof vest was lying on the passenger seat of the Explorer. His service weapon was still in his holster when they arrived on scene. Clearly, the Sheriff had not seen this coming.

Thanksgiving morning came and people across the country were celebrating with family. Russell Baker and the McKenzies were in Marietta for a last dinner at the family home where he and Sarah had enjoyed so many good times with her folks

Instead of football on TV, Dan McKenzie had set up an afternoon on the Soque River for a couple of hours. Doris would go and sit on the screened in porch and read a book while he and Russ waded and cast to the monster rainbows.

The lady and her husband who owned this half mile stretch managed it for trophy trout. The big rainbows tested the 3X leaders and tippets and were not a sure thing, either. But today, the two fishermen, stuffed with turkey and dressing, were casting in a beautiful stream at 66° using a Hare's Ear and a San Juan Worm dropper. The San Juan Worm was the fly of choice today and they landed and released a dozen fish in the two and a half hours before it got dark.

"I believe you have about gotten this fly fishing thing down, Russ," said Dan.

"I owe it all to you, Dan. I learned from the best!"

Then, it was back home to some leftover turkey, some sandwiches and then some rest on the couch. Maybe a nap. Friday was to be mostly looking at the new townhouse and helping Doris get things organized for the move and seeing what would be used in the new lakefront townhome and what might be kept for the Florida condo.

Miriam and her girls were enjoying the smells and the table was set. No TVs and the snow had all but stopped. It was turning into a beautiful day in Montana, at least weather wise. Cas and Sam kept looking out the window, expecting any minute to see a police car pull in. But things were quiet outside. Russ's drift boat sat in the shelter, with the snow piled up on the sides, looking like a cocoon about to burst open.

The house phone had rung a few times but the phone was Russ's and so Miriam told everyone to just let it go to voicemail. No one she knew would be calling her on that number.

Cas went out to the car with a trash bag to clean out the water bottles and trash from the drive over from Salt Lake. The four passengers had made quite a mess and he needed something to do. Lisa yelled from the door, "Do you need any help?"

"No, thank you. It's cold out here."

"Thank you! I really did not want to come out there!" she said with a chuckle and a flick of her hair.

Cas rounded up the trash and his eyes got fixated on an object in the space between the seat and the right rear door: a .40 Cal SW cartridge hull!

"Oh my God," he thought. He had not thought about the shell casings from last night.

He could not let the girls see these and start asking questions. He had to round them up and dispose of them and not in the trash to be spotted by someone. Frantically he searched for the others and found another one under the seat but he really did not know how many there were. Certainly, more than two.

He walked to the door and called Sam who was pretending to be helping in the kitchen. "Samer, can you come out here for a minute? You helped make this mess and you need to help me clean it up," trying to sound cheerful.

"It's your car, Kasim. You clean it up!" Samer replied jokingly.

But he saw in Kasim's face there was a note of seriousness. "But, because you are my friend, I will do it."

With that, he bolted out the door leaving the girls laughing.

Cas said, "We have a problem! Look what I found in the car!" he said as he held out his hand with the two cartridge hulls. "I found two but I do not know how many there are! We have to make sure all of them are found and done away with. How many do you think there are?"

Kasim said, "I have no idea. It happened so fast. Maybe four or five. Could even be six."

Cas said, "Help me go through the car but we can't look like we are panicked. We don't want the girls coming out here. Those shell casings could send us to the electric chair or the gas chamber!"

After several minutes of searching and convincing themselves they had covered every inch of the car, they found two more spent cartridges. Cas took the four shells and put them in his pocket until he could decide how to best dispose of them where they could not be found and connected to them or the shooting.

Laura yelled out the door, "Are you fellows through yet? The turkey is ready! Let's eat!"

Thursday morning, when a lot of people were getting ready for their Thanksgiving meal with their families, the Madison County Sheriff's office, along with state investigators were at the crime scene on State Route 287.

The day light answered Deputy Dunkin's greatest concerns the night before: the place where the car had probably been in the ditch had been covered with snow from the snowplow. No tracks, no forensic evidence, no nothing.

Metal detectors were being used to try and locate shell casings but so far had turned up nothing. There were no houses close by and there was only the entrance to the Double Barr Ranch about a quarter mile down the road which he had observed was closed last night with a sign that said to call from the call box for admittance.

A man from the Double Barr ranch had ridden down to the on a large ATV early in morning to see what was going on and had ventured too far into the crime scene before anyone stopped him. He said there had been no coming and goings from their ranch last night although they had expected some people who were apparently held up by the weather. He had ridden down after hearing about the Sheriff on the TV.

Dunkin and the other officers would start out in both directions from the scene and question anyone they could find, hoping someone saw something. The lab folks would go over the Sheriff's Car but Dunkin did not expect to find anything there. There were no notes, dash cam videos or anything they had found helpful yet. The video SD card from the dash cam was missing and no one knew for sure if there had been one in the unit at the time of the shooting.

Sheriff Barry Steinbrenner was alive.....just barely. He had four serious wounds in the chest, lungs and abdomen and a slight nick on the top of the head that was believed to be from a fifth round. He had been in surgery all night in Bozeman. The doctors believed the cold and snow may have saved his life by reducing the blood loss but most just said it was a miracle he was still alive.

There would be a news conference at 3:00 and Deputy Dunkin would not have much to tell the reporters. Neither would anyone else. No motive. No gun. No witnesses. No suspects.

Nancy Freeman got a call from her friend Dr. Carter and he asked, "Did you hear about the sheriff over in Madison County getting shot? I have heard you mention him before. Apparently he is in real bad condition."

"No, we have not had the TV on here today. My brother and his family are here at our house. Thank you for calling and letting me know."

Nancy dropped down on a chair in disbelief. She had dealt with the sheriff on the murder case involving her fishing guide friend and had great respect for him. Crimes of this nature did not happen often in Montana and now she knew two of the people involved in two of the worst the area had seen in years.

Nancy dialed Russ's home number but got no answer. She dialed his cell and it went to voicemail. She left Russ a brief message: "Barry Steinbrenner was shot last night while on patrol and they are not sure he will make it. He is in the Bozeman Trauma Center. That's all I know at this time and I am sorry to ruin your holiday with such terrible news." She sent him a text with a similar message.

6

Russ had enjoyed a great couple of days and knowing he could come back to his old job if he wanted it was some unexpected news. He had not told Doris or Dan McKenzie as he did not want to build up any false expectations. But, it was an offer he would have to give serious consideration.

The fishing on the "Sock" as the Soque was referred to by some of the locals, was an unexpected surprise. He would have not chosen to go fishing since he had just been fishing for several days, but there was no way he would tell Dan he did not want to go. Besides, they landed some nice rainbows.

His phone was left in the car at the river and had no signal, anyway. When they got back to the house in Marietta, he saw the text from Nancy. For a moment, he could not do nothing but stare at the message. It was unbelievable that anyone would shoot Barry Steinbrenner or that he gave someone the chance to do so as he was a vigilant officer. He called Miriam's number.

"Hello, Russ. How are things in down in Atlanta?"

"We've had a couple of really nice days but it was all spoiled by the news I just got on Barry. Have you heard what happened?"

"No, Russ. We have not had any TV on today. The weather was so bad last night that we stayed in and it ended up that the boys from Salt Lake stayed with us last night because the roads were so bad. They helped me cook Thanksgiving lunch and finally just got through and everyone had a nap. What's happened?"

The news about Barry was shocking and unbelievable and she was choked with emotion. Barry had been a great boss when she worked at the Sheriff's Office and had helped her become a skilled and sought after forensics lab technician. He treated her with kindness, respect, and gave her credit for the work she did. But, that's how he was with everyone.

"I called the hospital and they would not tell me anything, Miriam. I tried to call his brother but I only got his voice mail. But I called Sheriff Charlie Neilson in Bozeman. He is providing around the clock security. Barry is in intensive care and they will not let anyone in but his family. They still have more surgery and it's not clear yet if he will survive. I tried to call Wayne but I know he is tied up with all that's going on. Charlie Neilson said the State DCI is all over this so at least Wayne won't have it by himself. But, according to Charlie, they have nothing to go on yet."

"Apparently, Barry called in on the radio and told the dispatcher there was a car spun out over past Alder. They didn't hear any more and Wayne went looking and took half of Madison County with him. Charlie said Wayne's quick thinking got help to Barry just in the nick of time. If he survives it will be because Wayne handled it so well. I'm scheduled to come home Tuesday. I guess I'll leave it like that. If you hear anything please call me. I can change my plans. Of course, I have no role in any of this. I'm not actually on the department roster. I just help on a part time, as needed, basis. I won't be butting in on Wayne."

"Do you mind if I stay over a day or two extra, Russ? I can move to the motel if you think that is best. I have a few days' vacation and would like to see Barry when he's able and speak to his wife."

"If anyone goes to the motel, it'll be me. Stay as long as you want, Miriam. See you late Tuesday."

Laura and Lisa saw their mom's reaction. "Mom! What on earth is the matter?" asked Laura.

"My old boss, Sheriff Steinbrenner was shot last night several times and may not survive. I just can't believe it could happen here and to someone like Barry." She went on to tell them what Russ had told her.

Cas and Sam said nothing but just looked the other way. The events of last night were coming closer to home and now had become even more personal. The girls did not notice. Cas and Sam were accustomed to death and dying and this was not all that unusual for someone growing up in their homeland.

The two young men were sleeping in Lisa's old room and the girls were staying in Laura's room for the time being. Miriam had spent the first nights in her old bedroom which was just the way she had left it when she moved back to Salt Lake. But tonight, after everyone settled down, Miriam quietly went into the main guest room that Russ had been using. She laid down and pulled the covers over her head and she could smell his presence in the cool bed sheets. She would finally admit it to herself: she loved Russell Baker and did not have any idea what to do about it.

There was a room in a building at the Double Barr Ranch used for business meetings, and other activities. The man at the table had a look about him that said he was in charge and was a religious man. In fact, he was the Imam and was head of the mosque at Double Barr Ranch. In the room were the two newly arrived men. Men that had been brought in from a road accident the night before and had been picked up by a large ATV. They had brought with them four cases of Kalashnikov AK-47 rifles, a gun designed in the 40's and the most popular gun of all time. Over one hundred million AK-47's are said to be in use today. Made in various versions in over twelve countries. Deadly and reliable, they are the choice of terrorists worldwide. These had made their way to the US in shipments of cocaine and heroin courtesy of some Mexican cartel. Money is money, even if it comes from a Middle Eastern terrorist group.

The men were not there to be congratulated or thanked for bringing the guns. They were there to explain how they managed to shoot the local sheriff just down the road from the entrance to the compound that had been so fiercely kept off the radar screen.

The leader wanted to know about the driver of the car and his companion. Why were they allowed to leave? Could they be trusted? Where did they go? Would they keep their mouths shut or would someone have to shut them....permanently? Who else knew about them that might be considered a problem? One of the men replied to the questions.

"Kasim and Samer have been here twice before. They came to us with papers saying they were from Iraq and were sent to be activated at a later date. In the meantime, they are in school in Salt Lake City and have been accepted as Iraqi refugees."

"They are loyal and dedicated to the Jihad. They know these girls from the school refugee program and these infidels are trying to help all the downtrodden refugees by providing food and assistance to our people so we accept all their generosity. The girls and their mother know nothing of Kasim and Samer's real mission and dedication."

"Where are these men now?"

"We don't know. We needed to get the car away from the scene since it could be traced back to Kasim although it had fake plates. The news has said nothing about them or anyone else and they seem to have no clues. I shot the law officer before he could see us or the boxes or the license plates. The front of the car with the headlights shining in his eyes was all he saw."

"I do know that the young women lived here for a while and their mother owns a house that they were planning to stay in while here. Kasim and Samer may have gone there. But the women live full time in Salt Lake City. We know where they all live."

Another man, who had been silent, said," We will find out where they are staying here and know where to find them should we need to silence them."

The man from the car asked, "Do you mean the women or the two young men."

"All of them and the mother too, if necessary. And if trouble comes to us from all this, you will suffer the same fate as well. "

Miriam, Lisa and Laura now had a target on their backs without even knowing it. So did Kasim and Samer. Or whatever their real names were.

Double Barr Ranch was a training camp. The so called gymnasium was just that when workers from town or anyone that had to be let in was there. But it was used daily for prayers and religious instruction. It served as a mosque and place for other combat type exercises. The amphitheater in the compound hid from satellite and aerial views the shooting training and other activities that might look out of place on a dude ranch. Stables had some horses and some bomb making facilities with hay stacked on them. They had a fireworks show for the so called guests on Friday nights and this was when bombs and other explosives were detonated.

The cabins served to house all the people there for training. This was a well thought out training site hidden in plain sight in Madison County Montana.

When someone called the ranch wanting to come out for the spa or other activity, they were thanked for calling and politely told that they were booked up for the foreseeable future but their name would be taken and if there were any cancellations, they would be called. There were never any cancellations and no one was ever called. People came in cars and vans usually marked with such names as Portland First Baptist or Seattle United Methodist. Nothing too threatening to anyone who might be looking.

7

The meeting at the court room at the Madison County Court House went on for about an hour. All of the various law enforcement agencies were there, the District Attorney, and the three County Commissioners. Deputy Wayne Dunkin was in charge to review the shooting of Sheriff Barry Steinbrenner. Little was accomplished other than to confirm what they knew when they started: there was nothing yet to go on.

Their best hope was that Barry Steinbrenner would make a miraculous recovery and would be able to shed some light on what happened and could provide them with some suspects and a motive. Right now, that was looking like a long shot.

More surgery was needed to remove one bullet but he was too weak to go through it and they would have to wait.

"The scene of the crime has been gone over and over and the clearing weather and warming temperatures have helped in searching for any evidence left behind. We used generators and propane powered space heaters to melt the snow from the area where we thought the vehicle would have been and nothing has been uncovered."

"The Sheriff's car has also been gone over in a garage with the help of the FBI and the Montana DCI along with Madison County personnel and as of yet, nothing that seems to be linked to the case has been found," said Wayne Dunkin addressing the group.

"I know that a vehicle went out of Alder heading north just as I was going in to the Alder Market for a cup of coffee but it was snowing so hard I did not get a look at it.

I didn't see any more cars on the way back. They were closing the market when I left due to the weather."

"I was driving the same vehicle the Sheriff was driving when he came back out that way because we switched back here so he would have the four wheel drive and chains."

Wayne continued, "My dash cam card would have been the one that was missing when we found the car but I can't say for sure the Sheriff did not remove or change the card."

Wayne surprised everyone in his professional and poised handling of the meeting. Barry would have been proud of how far Wayne had come.

Russell Baker's plane came in to Bozeman Yellowstone Airport and taxied over to the terminal. Only a fraction of the size of Atlanta's, the Bozeman facility was not hard to get in and out of. Russ could see the hanger where Ted Turner's plane was kept when he was in town and Russ tried to imagine what it was like to be one of the country's biggest land owners. And, he wondered what it was like to be Barry Steinbrenner who was now in a medically induced coma and still clinging to life. Did he know what was happening around him, Russ wondered. Did he know who shot him and why?

Russ drove from the airport over to the Bozeman Deaconess Hospital to see if he could find out anything about Barry or see someone that he might know there. There was no one in the waiting room and Barry was being allowed no visitors except immediate family. All the family had gone home to get some rest after being up several days in a row.

Russ turned on E Main when he left the hospital and drove down to where he could park and go into Nancy's. He wanted to try and say hello and see what she was hearing about Barry but, again, he struck out. She had gone for the day and if they knew where she was the ladies in the store did not say.

He called Miriam.

"I'm back in Bozeman and am headed that way. Do you want me to pick up anything?"

"No. I went up this morning and got some things and left some flowers for Barry. We have all we need right now."

"I'd like to come by the house for a few minutes and see you and the girls and I'll pick up some clean clothes and go over to the Reel Me Inn tonight."

"We can't wait to see you, Russ, but the girls and the boys are over at Big Sky and haven't gotten back yet. But they'll be coming back at some point. The boys are supposed to go to the Double Barr Ranch tomorrow so they will be staying out there for the rest of the time they are here. The girls are going back Thursday evening. They have some Christmas parties in Salt Lake these next few days."

"Okay. I'll be there in a few minutes then."

Miriam ran to the bedroom to find a fresh outfit and set about making herself as beautiful as possible. Russell was coming and she was acting like it was prom night.

Russ scrolled through his phone and found Wayne Dunkin's cell number and hit the dial button.

Wayne Dunkin answered on the second ring. "Hello, this is Deputy Dunkin."

"Hello, Wayne. This is Russell Baker. I have been gone several days and was so sorry to hear about Barry. I just went by the hospital but they would not let me see him, which I understand. But how is he and how are you?"

"They are not sure about Barry yet, Russ. He lost so much blood. They have no way of knowing yet how much damage that may have caused. His body is healing slowly and they still have a bullet to take out if he gets strong enough to endure the operation. I thought he was dead when we got there."

"As for me, I'm okay but I am very frustrated. We have a dozen people working on this with no leads. We started out with about 30 people but the FBI has pulled back some and so has DCI. Since we have no leads there is little to follow up on. I really want to get this guy or whoever it was."

"I know if anyone can do it you can, Wayne. I have talked to Miriam and Nancy and some others and they tell me that you saved his life the way you handled things," said Russ.

"Well, Russ, that remains to be seen. But thanks for saying it."

I'll talk to you again soon Wayne. Goodbye."

"Goodbye, Russ."

Miriam was watching out the front for Russ to drive up. As soon as he drove in the yard, she sat down in a chair by the fireplace, trying to look very casual. She expected him to just come in since he was, after all, the tenant and it was his house to use. But Russ, instead, knocked on the door and that blew Miriam's planned greeting and welcome out the window.

She got up and opened the door and before she could stop herself she had thrown her arms around him and was holding him as tightly as she could. Then, she burst into tears. The emotions of the week and seeing Russ had now overwhelmed her. He held her for a few minutes and neither said a word.

Finally, she said, "I'm sorry Russ. I did not mean to lose it like that. Being back here, having this mess with Barry and now seeing you just got the best of me, I guess."

"I'm having the same problem, Miriam. I don't really know what I'm supposed to be doing right now. But, it's wonderful to see you and have you here."

Miriam filled Russ in on what she knew and about her visit with Barry's wife. She had also been by the courthouse and talked to her friends there about Barry.

She said, "There is a sense of gloom over everyone and Wayne Dunkin feels that all his help is slipping away and he will soon be down to just the local department in Virginia City to solve the case. Barry's brother from Missoula has been over and involved, but he is also losing confidence in finding the shooter. There is no direction and no evidence unless by some miracle Barry can provide a clue when, and if, he comes around. The shooter could be out of the county by now."

The next day would be a week since the shooting. A trail that started out in the cold of the winter snow storm was even colder now.

Russ was tired from traveling since early that morning and went to his room and rounded up a few clothes.

Russ called the Reel Me Inn and rented a cabin. Miriam followed him out to his truck and it was then that the Ford Edge came into the yard with the two boys and Lisa and Laura Alexander returning from skiing.

They pulled over to the side parking pad and for no particular reason other than having been a patrol officer so long, Russ noticed the Pennsylvania plates on the car and the license plate holder with a Pennsylvania auto dealer's name.

It was not of any real interest other than Miriam had said they all lived in Salt Lake. The four piled out and showed the tired look of people who had been out in the weather on ski slopes all day.

Miriam introduced Russ to Cas and Sam. The boys stood there for a minute and then waved as they went on into the house.

Russ chatted with the girls for a minute or two more and told them he would probably see them tomorrow. He got in his truck and left for the motel and some rest. There'd be no fishing tomorrow and he did not know when he would be back on the water. He had no bookings lined up and the snow and cold had probably dried up the client pool. And, he really did not mind at this moment.

8

Russell Baker woke up at the Reel Me Inn and sat on the edge of the bed looking at the floor. He was not sure what he should do, if anything, regarding the shooting of Barry Steinbrenner. He wasn't sure what to do about his relationship with Nancy or how to handle seeing Miriam again. And, he wasn't sure what to do about the possibility of moving back home to Marietta and going back to work at the Cobb County Police Department. The fact that he still called it home seemed to suggest something and Dan and Doris McKenzie were counting on him down the road.

He wished he could take his drift boat and find a warmer spot and just take a slow float to somewhere. Maybe the Holston River in Tennessee would be a nice place or even the Toccoa or the Chattahoochee. Sitting around Ennis for three months doing nothing did not sound too exciting but Dan had asked him to come to Florida.

Russ had called Nancy's number on the way to the motel the evening before and had gotten her voice mail. He left a short message: "Hi, Nancy. I got back from Atlanta today. I went by to see Barry but I was not able to see him. I came by the store to see you and missed you there, of course. Hope to catch up with you soon." He hung up.

She had gotten in a little late to call him back and had sat in the bed and played his message over several times and somehow it made her sad.

His phone rang and he saw it was Miriam. "Russ, the girls want me to go over to Big Sky and ski a while today. Would you like to go and ski on all the fresh snow with us?"

"It's tempting, but somehow I'm just not in the mood for skiing, Miriam. You said the girls were going back tomorrow so why don't you go with them and I'll take you all to dinner tonight in Bozeman. That way you can have a girls' day with them."

"Great. We will try to get back and be ready about 6:00 if I've not broken anything. We'll probably be pretty tired and hungry by then," she said.

Russ got in his truck and drove to downtown Ennis and parked in front of the Bear Trap Grill and went in and ordered breakfast and coffee and found a booth with a Bozeman Daily Chronicle newspaper that had been left behind. It was now a week gone by and the story about the shooting of Barry Steinbrenner was now on page three and only a short story saying there was no progress in the case. It would soon be just old news and Barry was still clinging to life in a hospital intensive care. That made Russ angry but he knew that was the reality.

He looked up to see Deputy Wayne Dunkin walk in and the deputy spotted Russ and waved. He walked over to Russ's table. "Mind if I join you, Russ?"

"That would be great, Wayne. Have a seat and breakfast is on me."

"Anything new on Barry?" Russ asked.

"No. I get my info through Janet, his wife. I'm sure you know her. One tough lady. But they still have him on life support and in an induced coma. She believes that may go on for another few days and the hope is he'll get to where he can breathe on his own and get strong enough to get that last bullet out."

"I do know her," said Russ. "I met Janet at their house once or twice and we went to dinner once. She's a very impressive person. I hate what she and the family are going through. I guess you are not sure yet if there was more than one shooter?"

"The first three bullets were from the same gun and were .40 Cal S&W's. The fourth we are not sure about, yet, till they get it out. He was struck a fifth time but that bullet glanced off the side of his head and kept going so we can't draw any conclusion from that. There were no shell casings at the scene which means they picked them up, which is doubtful with all the snow, or they shot him from inside the car and the casing stayed in the car. Of course we do not know how many rounds were fired but Barry did not have his gun out and was not wearing a vest. It is clear he did not see this as a hostile situation. Barry was the victim of an ambush and attempted murder!"

Russ leaned back in his seat and sipped on the hot coffee and tried to visualize what Barry had gone through.

"Wayne, Barry did not call in an ID on the vehicle. Make, model, tag, anything?"

"No. I believe the car may have been off in the ditch with the front facing back at the road and the snow was deep out there after two days of heavy snow and the plows had piled up a lot on the sides of the road out that way. I've never seen as much snow since I've been here."

"Wayne. If the car was stuck before Barry got there, in such deep snow, how did they get the car out and leave the scene? Someone had to help them, didn't they? And with the road almost impassable further on, where did they go? I suppose they could have been in some big vehicle like a Hummer or a large Jeep."

Wayne replied, "The tracks were snowed over by the time we came on-scene, Russ. It was almost white out conditions for a while. Then, the plow was in such a hurry to clear a path and leave room for the ambulance and me and the other vehicles, it went a couple of hundred feet down the road and turned around at a field road drive way and so did the five ton. By the time we got Barry in the ambulance and checked out the immediate area, all tracks up the road were gone. The next morning, the guy from the Double Barr Ranch came down in a large machine. It is actually a Snow Cat type unit similar to those used to maintain on ski runs at ski resorts and it does not leave deep tracks but would have covered any signs at least up to their entrance. It seems an unusual machine on a ranch but they are not a typical ranch. But one thing for sure, it would be capable of pulling most vehicles out of a ditch."

"We interviewed the guy who manages the ranch about three times and he is very cooperative. Came in to the office twice. He's from France, I believe, and runs the Spa part of the operation. They have a Hispanic fellow who looks after the cattle operation and we interviewed him, too. Both had similar stories: they closed the main entrance due to the weather and no one came or went all night. Most of the people who come and go use vans or buses from somewhere else and there are not a lot of cars going in and out."

"You have a tough one, Wayne. And, before I forget, I just wanted to say again everyone thinks you did a great job getting out there and getting Barry to the hospital. And, so do I."

"Thanks. Well, I have to get to the courthouse for a conference call. I have been talking to Charlie Neilson in Bozeman, Barry's brother in Missoula and the DCI office in Helena every morning. But so far, that hasn't produced any results. See you later. And thanks for the breakfast." With that, he was gone.

Russ suddenly felt helpless and useless. His drift boat was parked and he was back to square one on his relationships and had zero love life. The only thing he had going was he had enough money to live and he could be a failure at anything he wanted. At least, that was how he was feeling at the moment.

Since Miriam and the girls were off skiing and the guys were supposed to be gone to the ranch, he thought he would go to the house, go through his mail, wash clothes and regroup.

He had accumulated a lot of laundry by being gone to Lincoln for several days and then turning around and going to Atlanta. He also needed to clean out the boat from all the use it had gotten lately. Besides, he liked looking at the boat that he had named *SASSY,* his nick name of his first wife, Sarah. So he went by the motel and then drove out to the house. He hoped to be gone when the girls' got back from skiing. He'd go back and pick them up at 6:00 and he would make dinner reservations from the house.

Miriam's husband was a lousy husband and so-so father. But, he was a master builder and it showed in the house he had built in Ennis for him and Miriam when they moved there. She got the house as part of the divorce settlement when he went on to marry a very successful architect/designer who was building houses for wealthy movie stars and tycoons.

Five bedrooms, a large game room and a separate den. Plenty of bathrooms, a three bay enclosed garage, an outdoor cooking area in the back and, something Russ really liked: a pull through boat storage house. There was no having to back a boat and trailer in.

You could just pull through and either leave the truck attached if you were leaving early the next day or unhook and just back up to the trailer the next time you were going out and you could come in from either end. Miriam's husband liked power boats and had one when they were living there. Russ had no need for a storage building in town to keep the boat in anymore.

The garage bays opened to the back of the house and no one coming in the long driveway from the road ever saw a garage door, much less one open. In addition, there was a semi-circular drive up to the front with room to park about three cars if they had guests. Russ drove to the front as he did not expect to be there long and it was convenient.

As Russ walked up to the door, he could see that it was not closed fully. "The last people out must have left in a hurry. The door is not closed all the way," Russ thought.

Russ had seldom used the alarm system but had purposely turned it off since there would be people in and out who did not know the new codes. A lot of people did not even lock their doors in the area although Russ usually did having previously lived in a larger metro area. At that point he did not think too much about the door other than being annoyed at the carelessness.

He went into the main guest room that he had been using and immediately noticed all of his mail that he had left neatly stacked on the small corner desk was strewn around and his computer monitor was missing.

Desk drawers were in disarray. The closet was open and clothes were scattered on the floor and the storage shelves on top had been ransacked. It looked like he had been robbed!

He hurried to the other rooms and found that they had all been gone through the same way. Miriam's suitcase was thrown all over the floor and so were those in the girls' room. Someone was looking for money, or something.

He went back to the front door and saw no sign of forced entry there. He retrieved his .45 Cal semi-automatic from the truck and went around back. The garage doors were fine and so was the boat. But as he went on around he saw the patio door was completely shattered. Looking closer he could see they had used a pry bar to open the door but had applied so much pressure that it shattered the glass. They had come in the back and gone out the front.

From Russ's experience, that suggested more than one person had been there and one waited in the vehicle out front as a lookout.

"Hello. Madison County 911. What is you emergency?"

"This is Russell Baker on State Route 287. I have been burglarized and my house broken in to. The house is clear and the perpetrators are gone."

"Russell, this is Don Walton. Sorry to hear about this. I'll get a car out there ASAP. But there is no danger to you or anyone else: correct?"

"That's correct."

In a few minutes, Deputy Wayne Dunkin drove up with lights flashing. "Wayne, I didn't expect you to come out here for this with all you have going on," said Russ.

"I heard the call come in and I took it myself. I owed you for breakfast," he added almost with a chuckle. "We still have to do the day to day business, you know."

The deputy did a report, took some pictures, as did Russell, and they talked briefly about the crime wave that had hit in Madison County. The chance of finding the people were slim. When the alarm was off so were the security cameras. Maybe that was the one flaw in the design of the house.

"Can you tell if there is anything else missing, Russ?"

"I have to check more closely but the TV's are still here and I don't see anything obviously missing. It looks more like someone was looking for something in particular."

Wayne said, "It does look that way."

"Well, you don't happen to have a new sliding glass door in your car, do you Wayne?"

"Just used my last one. Sorry."

A little humor to lighten up the mood never hurt. Wayne Dunkin was not known for his quick wit, however.

As Wayne Dunkin drove off, Russ called a guy he knew who worked part time at the fly shop and also did some home improvement work. He agreed to come out that afternoon and get a door to replace the broken one and Russ set about getting the mess cleaned up. He wanted to have it done before Miriam and the girls showed up. Then he thought of something that was bugging him. He dialed Miriam's number and to his surprise she answered.

"Hello. This is Miriam. What's up Russ?"

"Just checking in to see if you were doing alright and hadn't done too much damage to yourself."

"I'm actually in the lodge by the fire. The girls met up with a family from Los Angeles and they are going up and down and up and down. I'm drinking hot chocolate and waiting for them to have enough."

"I did have one question, Miriam. Were the boys gone when you left this morning?"

"Oh, yes. They left real early. Probably an hour before us. Why do you ask?"

"Don't be alarmed, Miriam, but someone broke into the house. I came over to get some clothes and do my laundry and found where someone had broken in through the patio door. I don't think anything was taken but they rummaged through all our stuff. I just thought I'd make sure that no one was here when they showed up."

"My goodness. Russ, that's scary. I have never known anything to be bothered around there."

"Me either. A crime scene person is on the way from Madison County to dust for prints but I do not expect them to find any. I'd keep the girls away to let this person finish so the girls don't get too excited. The tech will want prints from the three of you and me, as you know. We may want the boys to come back to leave some comparison prints, too. They could go by the courthouse at their convenience."

"Dinner is still on as far as I'm concerned. We will set the alarm and cameras when we leave."

"Sounds good. I may want you to stay tonight in the guest room, if you don't mind. The boys cleaned up their bathroom and wiped everything down before they left this morning. It was spotless. I don't believe you'll find much in the room they used or the bathroom," she added.

"Sure. I can stay if it won't bother Lisa and Laura. Well, the prints we want will likely be in your room or mine or the girls since that is where they seemed to be looking for whatever they were looking. It did not look like a typical robbery of TV's and electronics as none of that was missing. But, I'll see you when you get here."

"See you in a bit, Russ."

9

There was another meeting at the Double Barr Ranch. This time, it was the security man named Hussar and the Imam.

"What did you find in the house? I hope you were careful not to leave any trace of your being there."

"The men, Kasim and Samer were right that the alarm was not on but when I was prying open the patio door I broke the glass, so they will know there was someone there. I took photos of mail and other ID's and I looked up the property online. The house is owned by a woman named Miriam Alexander who lives in Salt Lake. Her two daughters Lisa and Laura live in Salt Lake and go to the college with the young men. The woman worked for the Sheriff's Office when she lived here. She now works for the police lab in Salt Lake. Her identification was in her room."

"As best I can tell, the house is rented by a man who lives there alone and does little except take people fishing. His name is Russell Baker. All this is much as the men told us. There is no evidence that these people pose us any threat at this time."

"These two men know the Alexander girls through the school's refugee assistance program and think of themselves as do-gooders. The women thought nothing of the men calling and asking to stay during the storm and there is no evidence the police have inquired there."

"Very well. They can stay. It may be useful in knowing someone in the police department in Salt Lake. They will be easy to find should we need to."

The meeting was over.

6:00 PM and Russ showed up at the house to pick up the three ladies.

Miriam said, "Russ, the crime tech from Madison County just left. Whoever was here was a pro and did not leave any prints. It appears everything in the rooms was wiped down and even our prints have been erased."

Russ could not imagine anyone who would be checking him out like that and did not consider that it might have been Miriam and the girls. That would certainly make no sense because they did not live there anymore and no one knew they were going to be there. Or, did they?

Miriam and her daughters were dressed up for dinner in their best clothes. They were three beauties that would have stood out anywhere and they were sure to stand out in the Daryl's on Main Restaurant in Bozeman.

Russ had dressed in his nicest pants and pullover sweater and with his athletic build that he kept in shape by rowing a drift boat around. They were a fine looking group.

They were seated at their table right in the center of the restaurant when they arrived and every eye in the place was on them. Every male was staring at the three ladies and every female was staring at Russell Baker.

Many knew him from the newspaper accounts of the murder case he had been involved in and many knew him from his guiding service. Russ was a local hero for a while but most people had forgotten about all that now.

At another table further back was another group celebrating a birthday. Nancy Freeman was there with her brother Chad and his wife and two kids and their mom. It was a milestone birthday for their mom and a happy occasion. And, it seemed like every time there was some struggle in their personal lives they ended up running into each other in situations like this.

Russ did not notice them but they sure noticed him! Nancy Freeman *really* noticed him. Nancy had a rush of every emotion run through her all at once: anger, jealousy, hurt, betrayal, and envy. Envy for the beautiful lady that she recognized as Miriam Alexander, a former lover of Russ's and the owner of the house he lived in. Envy that Miriam was there with Russ and not her.

She had lost her appetite for cake and ice cream. Her bother Chad, also a local fishing guide who often worked with Russ, could see the change that came over Nancy and could only shake his head. Russ had lost a wife and Nancy had lost a fiancée and both were afraid of lightning striking twice.

Russ and Miriam and the girls had a great dinner even though Russ was still thinking about the break in at the house.

Miriam had not enjoyed a day like this in a long time in spite of the business with the intruder. A day skiing with her daughters and a marvelous dinner with a man she adored. It did not get any better. Unknown to her or Russ, Nancy Freeman did not have the same kind of evening. She regretted even more the way she had reacted to Russ's invitation to go to Atlanta. It just might have been the worst decision ever.

The girls were worn out from the long day and trip after trip down the slopes. Miriam was tired too and they all thanked Russ for a good evening and Miriam explained to her daughters that Russ was staying in the guest room as extra security because of the break in. They all disappeared to their rooms.

Russ laid down on his bed and started trying to think about the reason for the break in and who might have been behind it. Before he realized it, he was sound asleep.

Sometime during the night, against all her best judgement, Miriam had gotten awake and could not get her mind off of Russ who was in the room at the other end of the house.

She slipped on her robe and stepped into the hall. There were no lights on and no sound but the heavy sleep breathing of her daughters in their rooms.

She quietly walked down the hall and opened the door to Russ's room. She would still be there when the light started coming over the mountains in Big Sky Country in the morning.

It was the end of the perfect day in Miriam Alexander's life. She would worry about any consequences another time.

Kasim and Samer had gotten approval to come to the Ranch to receive more training and indoctrination. It seemed that no one was looking at them as being connected to the shooting of Barry Steinbrenner.

The mission of the Ranch to handle training and recruitment was too important to let a couple of spoiled kids or their spoiled infidel girlfriends muck it up. Anyone who brought trouble there would find a new home under the Big Sky of Montana....under a few feet of dirt.

The woman would be going back with the daughters in a few days and the unemployed trout bum would be doing some part time work to make ends meet and the public would see about getting a new sheriff. It was amazing what a good blizzard could do for your operation. All was well with the world. Allah be praised!

Miriam was up early and got breakfast started. Lisa and Laura would be heading back to Salt Lake and they could not understand why their mother was so happy this morning.

Russell had gotten up and driven in to Ennis to let Miriam have the last bit of time with the girls before they went back and, in fact, he wasn't sure he could look them in the eye this morning after waking up with their mother in his bed so he decided coffee at the Bear Trap and breakfast with the newspaper sounded like the coward's way out.

He was sitting there trying to sort out Miriam, Nancy, break-ins and Barry Steinbrenner in the hospital when his phone rang. He could see it was Deputy Wayne Dunkin.

"Hello, Wayne. You found the people who broke into my house yet?" Russ thought that would be a good ice breaker first thing in the morning.

If Wayne got the humor that was intended, he did not let on that he did. "Yeah, sure. You probably know where that is on my priority list!"

"Right, Wayne. But you could at least give me the politically correct answer and tell me how you have all your resources trying to get my video monitor back."

"I'm not much of a politician Russ, if you hadn't noticed."

"Someone may have mentioned that to me, Wayne. Why are you calling me when you could be having breakfast at the Bear Trap with me and this time you could buy?"

"Sorry, buddy. But I just got off the phone with my morning conference call. DCI is all but written this thing with Barry off as a random shooting. They don't see any hope in finding the shooter unless Barry has some info and wakes up to give it to us."

Wayne continued, "Charlie Neilson says he will keep providing security for a while at the hospital but that is causing him manpower problems. And, Barry's brother over in Missoula wants to know when I'm making an arrest in the case. That same question is being asked by the Commissioners and everyone down at the Bear Trap. I may have to make my own coffee for a while."

Russ softened his voice to a more understanding tone. "I know you have a load right now. Maybe Barry will be able to help and soon."

"Russ, I need you to come in and take this case and see if you can get a focus on something that will lead to getting these dirt bags. Barry's brother and Charlie suggested this morning that I should ask you to come on board to take the case as lead detective. Badge, gun, car, and even a little paycheck. I won't ask you to shoot anybody. Just point them out to me and I'll use my .338 Barrett to handle that part."

Russ was stunned. He knew this was a hard call to make for Wayne and if anybody wanted to solve this case on their own it was Wayne. He could tell that Wayne was not joking about the shooting part.

"You telling me you have a .338 Barrett, Wayne?"

"I might," replied Wayne. Russ knew that meant: "You bet your ass I do!"

Then Wayne added, "And I might know how to use it!"

Russ remembered Barry saying something about Wayne being the guy you needed in a tough situation and he was beginning to understand more about what he meant.

"Can I let you know tomorrow, Wayne? I am not sure that I want to take on that responsibility."

"Sure. Call me tomorrow." With that, he was off the line.

Russ had barely laid the phone down to sip on his coffee when the phone rang again.

This time it said Jerry Steinbrenner in the caller ID box.

Jerry was Barry's brother and sheriff of Missoula County. He was also the guy who had let Russ and his friends use his cabin over at Lincoln for several days, free. His real name was Gerald but no one called him that and he preferred Jerry.

"Hello, Sheriff," said Russ.

"Good morning Russ. I'll get right to the point. Charlie Neilson and I discussed with Wayne Dunkin the possibility of getting you to take that Special Investigator role on again and dig into this thing that happened to Barry. The State hasn't solved it in a week and they are about to throw in the towel. Wayne is a great deputy and a good man but he needs some help on this. Will you do it?"

"I talked to Wayne just before you called and told him I'd let him know tomorrow."

"Screw tomorrow, Russ! You let him know today or I'm going to bill you $250 a day for using my cabin."

"In that case, Jerry, since I don't have $250 times about six days, I guess I will do it."

"It was seven days and you damn well know it!" said Jerry.

Then in a soft and very sincere voice he said, "I can tell you it will mean the world to Barry's wife Janet, to me and it will mean a lot to Wayne. Not to mention Barry when he gets back on his feet."

"Alright, Jerry. I will call Wayne back and let him know. I have things going on today and I'll get started in the morning."

"Thank you, Russ." Jerry Steinbrenner was gone from the line.

Russ ordered another cup of coffee and sat for a long time wondering what he had gotten in to.

Then, he got in his truck to go to the house and tell Miriam what he had just agreed to do, not that it would affect her since she would be headed back to Salt Lake in a day or two. He would call Wayne Dunkin on the way.

The rear door was now replaced and Miriam had called to say she was on the way back from the airport after seeing her daughters off. Russ sat in the cool air on the patio and kept looking at the door and wondering what the break in was about. Who did it? Why? He did not have anything going on that would cause this type of thing to happen as far as he could see.

Miriam was no longer around on any regular basis and it was unlikely anyone with a grudge would have followed her from Salt Lake City. If she was working on a case that could affect someone there, it would be much easier to bring harm to her there or to pry into her affairs.

Her ex-husband certainly had no reason to bother her. He was living in the lap of luxury with his new wife.

That left the girls, Lisa and Laura, and the two boys from school, Kasim and Samer. There, again, was no practical reason for anyone to follow the girls from Salt Lake.

It did not seem reasonable in the case of the boys either. So, maybe it was just a random thing with some people driving by and thinking there may be some easy pickings. But, if that was the case, why did they not steal anything. He had not come up on them nor had he met a vehicle coming out to the house.

But, they could have gone the other way. Out toward Alder! Out toward where Barry was shot! Surely there was no connection but his suspicious cop nature was rearing its ugly head, again.

The only other thing out that way was the Double Barr Ranch where he had never had any dealings and neither, to his knowledge, had Miriam. Neither, he felt, had the two girls. But....the two young men from Salt Lake had!

Another option would be that they came back looking for something themselves and were locked out of the house. But whoever it was had wiped the place free of prints and the two guys would have had no need as they had been all over the house and their prints would have naturally been eliminated from suspicion. Unless that was the whole purpose of the break in! To erase the record of their presence! Now, that was something that made sense but what did they have to hide?

"Calm down, Russ," he thought. "You're letting your mind play tricks on you."

In a little while Miriam arrived with some sacks of food and some bottles of wine. She set up a little serving tray full of cheese and some gourmet crackers and the wine on a table in the den by the fire. She put a blanket on the floor and they sat there in the glow and warmth of the fire and sipped the wine. They stayed here in front of the fire until sometime in the early morning when they got up and went back to bed in her bedroom and stayed there till the sun came up.

"I know I'm not supposed to say this Russ but I have missed you terribly. I thought I would get over you and move on like I did my husband when he left me. It just hasn't happened," she whispered.

"I know, Miriam. I know exactly what you mean because I have had the same problem. I had thought I'd connect with Nancy but something kept getting in the way of that."

"Was that something me, Russ?"

"Yes."

"What do we do now, then?" she asked.

"I have no idea," he replied.

They got coffee and sat at the table and he asked her about the boys. Something was nagging him and he laid out the thoughts he ran over in his mind the night before.

Miriam could not conceive of the boys being involved in anything like a break in and certainly not Barry's shooting. They were at her house with her and the girls. They were exemplary kids with hearts of gold helping other refugee kids in Salt Lake. Russ knew that they had a pretty good alibi at the moment and he had nothing to refute it.

"When did they move out from Pennsylvania, Miriam? Do you know?"

"As far as I know, Russ, they have never mentioned Pennsylvania. It was my understanding they came to Salt Lake City from Iraq. Why would you think they came from Pennsylvania?"

"Their car had a Pennsylvania license plate and the frame around the plate was from a car dealer somewhere in Pennsylvania. I don't recall the city," Russ answered.

"I never noticed that before. I'll ask about that when I see them," Miriam said.

"It's probably nothing," commented Russ. "Hold off mentioning anything until I get to snoop a little. I don't want to spook anybody unnecessarily."

"Since you are going to be working on the case and Barry does not seem to be coming out of the coma anytime soon, I may go back to Salt Lake tomorrow and then come back when he is able to have visitors."

"Sounds good," he said.

Russ drove to Virginia City and walked into the historic courthouse and into the Sheriff's office. He was greeted by some familiar faces and Wayne Dunkin waved him into his office. The local judge was in with Wayne Dunkin to swear Russ in and make things formal since, as deputy himself, Wayne could not swear in a deputy. The procedure took about three minutes and the judge left. Wayne closed the door.

"Here is your gun, badge and keys to the patrol car. I had your old photo ID so we will just use that one for now. You're official and good to go."

"Wayne, I hope that everyone has not set the expectations too high. If all the Federal, State, and local cops have not found anything it seems a big challenge."

"I know. But I need to have someone working full time on this and while this is now not front page news it's still my number one priority and Barry's family's too."

"But understand one thing: I don't want a dead cop on my watch. You call me and keep me informed and don't get in any threatening situations without backup. Am I clear?"

"Understood, Wayne. I am not a hero looking for a shootout, I can tell you that. I think all of us want to put the people responsible in jail. And I know we have to be looking for more than one person."

"You can use the Grand Jury room for your work room and any meetings. Any help you need you will get and I briefed everyone first thing this morning. You can expect full cooperation from Gallatin County if your investigation takes you there. Just let Charlie Neilson know what you are doing and what you need. If I have to go off the grid on this, I will. Do you understand?"

"I believe I do. You couldn't be clearer."

"I know the respect you have for Barry and his for you. Just understand I'll afford you that same respect and give you the benefit of the doubt. I'll expect no less from you. But in the end, I'll make any final decision until Barry comes back or I am relieved of duty here."

Russ listened and was hearing a side of Deputy Wayne Dunkin he had not heard before and he knew one thing: Barry had hired the right man and made him a good law officer. One who you could count on when the going got rough.

"I have all the case notes on the table in the jury room and here is a key. Keep it locked at all times. Where do you want to start?"

"I want to ride out to the scene. Can you go with me sometime today?"

"How about right now?" Wayne replied.

Russell Baker had parked his drift boat. Again.

And he was behind the wheel of a police cruiser. Again. And, he was looking for a killer. Again. He was now Detective Russell Baker, Special Investigator for the Madison County, Montana Sheriff's Office. Again.

The job offer in Cobb County would have to wait.

10

The weather was clear and the last few days had been in the low 50's so there were only patches of snow here and there in the shade. It was a quick ride out to the scene where they had found Barry and crime tape was still draped around some fence posts and some stakes driven in the ground. It did not look like a kill zone or a place where a man had come close to losing his life, and may yet do so, at the hands of persons unknown. Wayne Dunkin pointed out the area where Barry was lying in the snow and the place where he thought the spun-out car might have been. Then he stood by the patrol car and let Russ look around.

Russ looked up the road to the field gate drive where the snow plow and the other vehicles had turned around. It was, like Wayne had said, a couple of hundred feet past the crime scene. Russ walked up to the spot and stopped. He turned and looked back at Wayne and then on up the road where he could see the sign and entrance to the Double Barr Ranch. The small security gate or welcome center or whatever they called it was there and a car was parked there indicating someone might be on duty. He had left his handheld radio in the car so he waved for Wayne to drive on down to where he was and pick him up to go on to the gate.

But, when Wayne got there Russ opened the door and said, "If you don't mind, drive on up to the gate and I'll walk up there from here. I want to see what I can see between here and the gate."

Wayne drove on up to the gate and was stopped by the lift arm and the security guard. He told the guard he was waiting on his partner who was walking up.

The guard walked back in the small building which looked to have a small sofa, TV and closed circuit monitors and a small bathroom. There was a coffee pot and microwave and what looked like a mini fridge. All the comforts of home. The car had a sign on the side that said USA Security Service, Bozeman, Montana.

So they apparently used an outside service for the gate. The guard immediately picked up a phone, rather than his radio, and called someone.

Russ could see the slight impressions of what looked like a wide tracked crawler tractor. He remembered that Wayne had mentioned that someone had come down to the scene in some type of snow cat vehicle and this was likely what made the imprints. It appeared the vehicle had been that way more than once and may have been all the way back to the crime scene since the snow melted. He reached the guard house.

To the guard, he said, "We'd like to talk to whoever is in charge and maybe go up to the main building."

"I called the manager and he is coming down. They don't like to have people in there unescorted. Liability, they say," said the guard.

A standard Polaris ATV side by side came down the paved gravel drive. Wayne saw that it was the Frenchman he had talked to at least three times before.

Wayne got out and was standing by Russ when the man walked out through the pedestrian gate.

"Hello, Sheriff. I hope you have found your criminals by now," he said in his French accent.

"Not yet. We are still working on the case and following some leads." That was a standard cop answer for *we don't have anything to go on, yet.* The man could read between the lines.

"This is the Russell Baker, the detective that we have assigned to the case."

The man extended his hand and Russ shook hands with him and as he was doing so he asked, "Why did you say criminals instead of criminal, singular? Do you have reason to believe there was more than one person involved in shooting Sheriff Steinbrenner?"

The question took the man by surprise and it took Wayne Dunkin by surprise as well.

"It was just a manner of speaking, Detective Baker. You can be certain that we have no knowledge of how many people were involved or if it was a single person."

"Would it be possible for us to go up to the main house and look around?"

"We could arrange that but today we have most of the people out on activities and there is not much to see. But, if you call me back and set up a time, I will gladly give you a tour."

"I did not realize that would be a difficult request."

"Not difficult at all, Detective. Just inconvenient at this time and I have been more than cooperative with the officers that have been out here and I have been to the courthouse for statements twice."

"Of course. But I'd like to ask you a couple of questions if you don't mind.

"I think I've answered a lot of questions already," he said.

Russ could see he was getting under the guy's skin and that sometimes caused stories to change. He pushed on. "You haven't answered any for *me*, yet."

"What do you want to know?"

"You seem very concerned about security yet you closed the guardhouse on the night in question. Right?"

"Right. The road was impassable through here and no cars could get here anyway. We usually don't keep the entrance open all night."

"I'm aware that the roads were bad and Deputy Dunkin and the ambulance had to use a snowplow to get out here. That makes me wonder where the car that was in the ditch went and how it got freed from the ditch. If the road was impassable, where did they go? Could someone have assisted them from the ranch?"

"Absolutely not! We did not know there was a problem until we saw it on the news the next morning. The security company did not get here until about mid-afternoon because we advised them about the road conditions and we all agreed to delay their arrival until it was safe. Should anyone have shown up, there is a call box as you see there and we could come down?"

"The sheriff's car had all the emergency flashers and strobes going when Deputy Dunkin arrived. Is it possible someone would have seen them from the house?"

"I don't believe anyone could have seen them from the house especially in the snow."

Russ nodded, and asked one more question: "Do you ever close the guard house other than last week in the storm and do you have video surveillance tapes?"

We close it every night at 12:30 AM. When the guard leaves he closes the big iron gates behind the arms. The call box is still on and is twenty four hours a day. The cameras face up the hill and show vehicles after they pass through the gate, unless manually moved to show the outside of the gates, and cars are seen as they come down the hill to exit. We keep the tapes usually no more than seventy two hours and they are a continuous loop. We have never really had a need for them. Anything else?"

"That'll be all. I may need to come back and take that tour sometime. But we will be on our way and thanks for your time."

Russ and Wayne walked to the car and started turning around and the manager sped up the hill on the ATV.

"Hold it one minute, Wayne," said Russ and he jumped out and went back where the guard was still standing.

"I just wanted to ask about the ranch house and facilities. Are they pretty nice?"

The guard's response took Russ by surprise. "I guess they are. I have been coming out here about eight months and I have never been up there. We are not permitted past the gate house. They say they don't want the guests to be concerned by having guards around. They have private security up around the house I'm told in plain clothes."

"What did you ask him, Russ?" Wayne asked when he got in the car.

"I asked him about the ranch and he said he'd never been past the gate. Not allowed."

"That's strange, don't you think?"

"Very," replied Russ. "And what's stranger is they say the road was impassable and the security guards could not get in or out but Barry Steinbrenner calls in a car in the ditch a few hundred yards below their gate and, not only does it get out of the ditch, it disappears somewhere. That's strange, too"

"Where to now? Have you seen enough?"

"Yes. Let's go and I will go through all the case notes. Miriam is going back tomorrow so I might take her to dinner tonight. Would you like to join us?" asked Russ.

"No. I'm in the doghouse now for being gone so much. It will be home tonight for me."

"And I thought you would be working on my break in."

"You can do that in your spare time, Russ." That gave them both a laugh.

On the ride back to Virginia City, Russ asked Wayne, "You saw a car going out from Alder on what turned out to be an almost impassable road. If that was the car that Barry encountered, where could it have gone?"

"I've asked that over and over and we checked every field road and drive and cattle gap between the scene and back to Virginia City. We had plenty of help those two days and we could find no sign of recent activity at any side road exit." was Wayne's reply.

"We did see where someone went up your driveway but we learned from Miriam that some boys came out from Salt Lake and spent the night with them because the road was so bad. There had been some traffic in Alder. Apparently some idiot had tried to drive his Airstream on Route 357 out from up near Ruby Dam and got stuck in Alder right after I left. The guy at the RV park took his big tractor and front end loader and cleared out enough to get the guy back to the park with his truck and camping trailer. So that was clear right there at the RV park and we checked that but found nothing."

"No security cameras, I suppose."

"No. They have a monitor in the bar that shows the parking area and the entrance to the RV park but it is only a live feed inside to keep an eye on comings and goings. They were closed when my deputies came back through and no one saw anything unusual."

"How about we pull in there as we go by if you have time."

"Sure," said Wayne.

Wayne pulled in beside the bar and they parked and look over the area. "So, Wayne, this area might have been clear for a while between the time you left town and came back looking for Barry?"

Wayne thought about the question for a minute and said, "Yes. That sounds right."

"So, if the car got free somehow, it maybe could have come back this far and pulled in where the area was cleared off. If they had just gone out that way, it may have been passable enough to do it." Russ said, mostly thinking out loud.

"That would seem possible. Hard, but possible," said Wayne.

"I'll come back out and re-interview everyone around here tomorrow or the next day after I finish the case notes."

They left for Virginia City and Russ spent some time with the case notes before Miriam called. "I got the girls off on their way and if it works with you, I'll fix some dinner at home. Is that okay with you?"

"Sounds great to me, Miriam."

Miriam had driven her daughters to Bozeman to catch the plane back to Salt Lake and she knew she probably should have gone with them. But the thought of having one more evening with Russ without anyone else around was too strong. She didn't know when she would get that chance again.

All in all they'd had a nice time with the skiing and seeing Russ and dinner at the nice restaurant. She had seen Nancy and her family at dinner but had not pointed them out to Russ, who had not seen them in the back or who had not let on if he had. She wanted Russ all to herself that night.

The girls were upset that they had not been able to say goodbye to Kasim and Samer. Their phones had changed and they were not answering. They had indicated that they would be hard to reach at Double Bar Ranch and sometimes cells did not work there but they still would have liked to say goodbye. But they would see them back in Salt Lake in a few days.

Russ's phone rang again and he saw it was Chad Freeman, Nancy's brother. He was was a popular river guide in Bozeman. "Hi, Russ. I wanted to see if you wanted to do a drift tomorrow since the weather is looking reasonably good. I got two sets of people who want to give it a try."

"Chad, I am tied up right now. Madison County has asked me to help with the Barry Steinbrenner case and I am doing some investigation on that. I may be tied up for a while."

"Oh, Man. When did that happen?"

"I started today."

"Have you told Nancy?"

"Chad, Nancy and I aren't talking too much right now. I had hoped to see her before Christmas but she did not seem too interested the last time I talked to her. I invited her to go down to Atlanta and she made it pretty clear she had no interest in going anywhere with me."

"Hell. She doesn't know what she wants, Russ. She's the same way with that Carter fellow. He leaves scratching his head every time they go out. I know because he called me a couple of times and wanted to know what he's doing wrong. He's head over heels for her and she treats him like crap. Just like you. If you ask me, she keeps hoping you'll grab her by the hair of the head and drag her off."

When Russ didn't reply he said, "You might try that. I'll let her know you are back packing a gun and I'll call someone else for the float. Be careful out there."

"Thanks, Chad. Goodbye."

Russ hung up, and just looking at the phone, thought how sometimes he would like to drop it in the deepest hole in the Madison.

Chad called his sister Nancy. He knew she was smarter, prettier, and more successful but sometimes he wanted to strangle her!

"Hello, brother Chad."

"Hello, Nancy. Two things: Russ won't be doing the float trip I have for tomorrow and I have to get someone else in a hurry. He has signed up as of today to investigate the shooting of Sheriff Steinbrenner and won't be doing any floats for a while."

"What!? He's signed up again to possibly get killed? He almost made it last time!" she interrupted. A shudder went through her as she remembered looking at his shot up car after his last involvement with the sheriff's office.

"Well, you have to take that up with him, Nancy. Oh, that's the second thing: he says you don't seem to want anything to do with him. So I was just going to say; you are an idiot! I love you dearly but you are an idiot when it comes to relationships with men."

"And I have two things to say to you, Chad Freeman: Go to hell! And, you can get somebody else to do the float shuttle tomorrow," she yelled into the phone as she was hitting the end call button.

Drift boat fishing requires moving trucks and trailers around from the place the boat is put in the water to the place it is going to be taken out. Nancy had done shuttles long before she got her dress shop up and going and she still did it when she could for Chad and others and Russell Baker. Russ had been her favorite because she was crazy about him and he tipped better!

She threw the phone across the room and pieces went everywhere. If Russell Baker wasn't bad enough she had to deal with her meddling brother, too!

Russell Baker was having a much better evening than was Nancy Freeman. Another beautiful woman who was also crazy about him had prepared dinner, bought wine, put on some music they liked and the sexiest outfit she could find. She was leaving tomorrow but she was there with Russ tonight and he would not be forgetting her soon.

The next morning, Russell and Miriam said their goodbyes and she was all smiles as she waved and drove off to go to the airport in the rental car. But she was in tears almost all the way there: What was she going to do about how she felt about Russell? She thought he loved her in some fashion but probably not the way she loved him. She would stay with him forever if he asked her to.

That was probably not going to happen and she wasn't getting any younger. Right now she could compete with the Nancy Freemans of the world but soon nature would take its course. The thought of losing Russell was just too hard to think about.

11

Russell Baker got into high gear that morning at the jury room full of notes, photos, and forms. All of them clearly stating the obvious about the shooting but nothing pointing to a suspect. He started putting post-it notes up on the easel and a map of the area with all the points of interest he had to look at and tried to make sense of the vanishing car.

As much as he kept thinking about the ranch and its proximity to the crime scene he could not believe that they would be stupid enough to be involved and then take the car to their ranch. It would make sense that someone could have committed a crime and then showed up there as they were expected and no one would know of their involvement. But how did they get the car out. Maybe it wasn't stuck just spun out and they got it going with no assistance.

He was curious about the way the security was handled and the fact that they did not want anyone up at the house other than guests. He might could get a search warrant but there was no connection to the ranch that would sway a judge, probably. And, the guy had seemed to be cooperative from the start.

Maybe the car made it back to Alder but the information about the Airstream Trailer made it clear they could not have gone out to Ruby Dam. The Airstream had to have a front end loader to make it a few hundred feet. They did not go to Ennis while Wayne and the emergency people were in route as they had not met anyone.

That did leave one far out possibility: they pulled in at Alder after the entrance to the RV park was cleared. But where did they go from there?

The ranch manager had said they could not see anything happening on the road from the house.

Russ wondered about that. He thought he might test that theory.

Russ's was sitting in the booth at the Bear Trap eating a burger and fries and sipping on a cola when his phone rang. It was a number that he did not recognize and wasn't in his phone. He resisted the urge to ignore it and swiped the phone to answer.

"Hello. This is Russell Baker."

"Russell, this is Janet Steinbrenner. I just spoke to Wayne Dunkin and he said you agreed to come on board and try to help get the bastards that shot Barry. I just wanted to let you know how much I and the family appreciate you doing this. Barry has always spoken highly of you."

"It's nice of you to call, Janet. I hope I can be of some help but I also hope everyone doesn't get their expectations set too high. There are not many clues."

"If you do the best you can do, we won't ask more than that. Barry may be strong enough for the doctors to bring him out of the coma tomorrow or the next day. That's some good news. We still have a long way to go, though."

"That sounds wonderful, Janet. I hope he will get stronger and get out of that place. Of course, we need to talk to him when he is able and see what he can tell us about the night he was shot."

"I will call you as soon as I get any word on that. You can count on it."

"Thanks for calling Janet."

He had no sooner hung up than the phone rang again and he was surprised to see it was Nancy. It had now been several days since he last spoke to her. He suspected that Chad had told her what he had said earlier. He almost swiped to answer then decided to let it go to voice mail. He wasn't up to a contentious conversation that would only make matters worse.

Nancy had managed to put the pieces of her phone back together and decided she would call Russ but she was struggling with what to say. She knew that Miriam had been in town and may still be for all she knew. Maybe that's why he did not answer. Maybe he just did not want to talk to her now. Or ever. She hit the hang up button without leaving a message and was relieved he did not answer.

They both felt badly about the way they had handled the call. But neither was inclined to do anything about it at that moment. Russ had a woman that was crazy about him and Nancy had a guy that was crazy about her and yet they were both miserable. Who could figure?

Russ drove to the house and sat down in front of the fire with notes he had made so far on the case. He turned on the TV and it was apparent he was much more tired than he realized and when he woke up it was midnight and he was still dressed and sitting in the chair.

He went to the kitchen and splashed some water on his face and put a coffee pod in the coffee machine and made himself a cup. And as he stood looking out the window at his boat under the shed, he had an idea.

Russ remembered that the manager at the Ranch said they closed the gate security office at 12:30 and he also said they could not have seen the emergency lights from Barry's car up at the main house. He thought he might do a little test of that since the security person would be gone by the time he drove out there.

Russ got his Beretta M9, 9 mm and checked to see that it was loaded with a full clip. It had been a while since he'd fired it. He also did the same with his S&W .45 Cal Compact and he made sure he had his bullet proof vest and high intensity flash light. He threw all of the gear in the car, took his coffee and headed out toward Double Barr ranch to test his theory.

They had assigned him his old Radio ID Number at Madison County. He picked up the mic and called in. "Madison SO this is Madison Unit 8. I am 10-8 and going out State Road 287 to the recent crime scene location. Be advised."

"Madison SO to Madison Unit 8. Understand. Do you need assistance at that location? Over."

"I don't require assistance. I will report in every thirty minutes. 10-4?"

"10-4 Unit 8. Be careful out there."

In Cobb County an officer automatically gets back up. The dispatcher sends a second unit to confirm the situation, even in traffic stops.

If it appears it is a non-hostile situation, then the backup can continue with their patrol. But when you have three or four cars covering 3603 square miles that is a luxury Madison County cannot afford. Russ would be in the middle of nowhere by himself.

Shortly after passing through Alder, Russ saw a car coming from the opposite direction. He guessed he might be meeting the security guard in the Ford Focus with the emblem on the side and as the car passed that was what he saw. The guard had left on the minute to get home, it appeared.

Russ approached the spot where Barry was shot and he could still see some of the tape. He pulled off and called in on his radio: " Madison County Unit 8 is 10-23 my location. Over."

"Roger, Unit 8. Understand you are 10-23. Is all well out there Officer?"

"Yes. I will report back in thirty minutes. I will be 10-7 for thirty minutes but will have hand held. Out."

Deputy Wayne Dunkin was listening and wondering what Russ was up to. Wondering if he should go there, too.

Russ got his light, vest and guns and turned on all the emergency lights on the police cruiser and left it running as he exited and walked up the road for several hundred feet and found a low spot on the opposite shoulder from the Ranch House and compound. He crouched down and waited.

The blue and red lights from the cruiser were lighting up the area and lights were casting a hue over the darkness. He was about to end his experiment when he heard the sound: The sound of a diesel engine coming from up near the Ranch.

He saw the bright lights before he saw the machine. Then it appeared as it came over the rise from area of the ranch.

It made it to the area and remained inside the ranch fence and approached the spot where the car was parked on the road. It had tremendous lights that illuminated the area and the operator had a spot light that he was using to work the ground around where the car was parked and now the Pistenbully snow cat was clearly visible in the lights of the patrol car. This machine could easily move a car from a snow drift.

The big machine was impressive with a blade and wide tracks and a cab where the operator was. Russ could tell there were at least two people in the cab.

They sat for a minute and then turned the machine slowly around so that the road was illuminated back toward where Russ was hiding and he got further down so he could not be seen.

The big snow cat moved slowly back up the fence line toward the security gate.

Russ wasn't sure what they intended to do and if they were coming outside the fence to the road and then come back but he did not want a confrontation.

He had what he came for. Someone had seen the emergency lights from the house.

Russ sprinted to the car, threw in his gear and left the scene as fast as the car would go. The wide track crawler was good for a lot of things but it would not catch the patrol car. He maintained speed until he got to Alder and there he pulled in beside the Bar and backed in and turned off his lights and waited to see what would happen next. He expected to be followed but after a few minutes he left for home. He radioed in that he was calling it a day and off for the evening. He had more to think about tomorrow.

"What did you learn last night, Russ?" asked Deputy Wayne Dunkin.

"I learned that they have security at the ranch and they can see emergency lights from the house. Whether that was possible on the night in question with all the snow, I don't know. I learned they have people who go investigate when something is going on, even at 12:30 at night. The snow cat could have been used to move the stalled car from the ditch. But, of course, I don't know that they did any of those things."

"I left the scene and came back and parked where we parked in Alder by the bar to see if I was followed and no one came by so I left after about twenty minutes. Probably a wild goose chase but I had to salve my curiosity."

Then Russ continued, "I don't know if you talked to Janet Steinbrenner but she called yesterday and said they were possibly going to try and wake up Barry today or tomorrow."

89

"She called this morning and said it would be tomorrow, Russ," said Wayne.

"I need to interview those two boys who were here with Miriam and her daughters. They might give us some insight on what's going on out there at the ranch," said Russ.

"Russ, if there is anything going on, the boys are probably part of it or they wouldn't have been allowed in."

That gave Russ a chill down his back. Could that be the case? If so, Miriam and her daughters could be in real danger.

"But that is a wild supposition, I know," said Dunkin.

"Wayne, how do you feel about going back out there and going to the ranch complex and looking around? We might be able to put some of our concerns to rest. Do you think they will just let us in and look around?

"I'll call the French guy and see. I can say we are looking for a car that might have some damage because we found some evidence that the car at the scene was damaged. That might get us in for a look-see."

Wayne made a phone call to the ranch and the manager told them to come around 1:30 PM and they could look all they wanted.

That surprised both of them, but they were at the gate at 1:20 and were allowed to drive up to the house.

The house was old but well maintained. A big porch on the front and benches around for sitting in the huge expanse of yard. There was an equipment shed full of tractors, haying equipment and other farm implements as well as the big snow cat. There was a huge building that said Gym on the little sign and some people were in there playing basketball. A lot of money had been spent there from somewhere.

The pool had a few people swimming and splashing water. There was a horse stable but the horses were mostly gone. The manager said today was equestrian day and a lot were on the mock cattle drive. They would spend the night out and food would be prepared by the chuck wagon. There was a parking area with some cars and two out of state buses that looked like they might carry thirty people each. Cas's Ford Edge was in the parking lot but showed no signs of being wrecked. There was no sign of either boy.

The amphitheater was very nice and had removable and fold up bleachers. Russ thought that odd. There was the smell of gunpowder in the air as if some shooting had been going on but they did have a sporting clays set up, too.

They thanked the manager for letting them see the place and left, disappointed that nothing showed up to tie the ranch to the shooting of Barry.

"Well, Russ. What do you think?" asked Wayne.

"It was almost too perfect, Wayne. It was like a script and everyone was playing a part for us to see. Not nearly enough people and very few cars. Not a hair out of place, as they say."

"I got a little of that but all in all we did get in, they were openly cooperative, and we didn't see anything to follow up on. We couldn't get a warrant with what we have."

"I agree," said Russ. "So, I guess we look somewhere else."

The Imam was in the small meeting room when the manager and the security officer came in. "Were they convinced enough to leave us alone?"

"It appears their curiosity was satisfied. The group did an outstanding job especially the basketball. But we will keep out eye out, just in case."

"We have already had too much attention this past week and I wish no more," said the Imam.

After two weeks in the hospital, Barry Steinbrenner was now breathing on his own. That was a major step but he was still weak and unable to talk with more surgery on the calendar.

In Salt Lake, Miriam and her daughters were now looking forward to Christmas. Cas had called Lisa from the ranch and said everything was fine there; they were having fun, and would be home in a couple of days.

Miriam went back to work and life was looking good. She was talking to Russ again almost every day. Somehow that put a lift in her step.

The people at the ranch were resetting the gym to serve as a mosque so they would ready in time for evening prayers. They had a drill on how to reconfigure the setting quickly when needed and that had worked fine today and the two country sheriff department officers had been easily fooled. Or, so it seemed.

Russ was tired from the all-nighter he had done the night before and headed home. He was ready for a sandwich and bed and anything that he was working on could wait until tomorrow. He was asleep in no time. But it was not meant to be. The phone rang and it had to ring several times before he managed to get oriented and answer. He swiped he phone without looking to see who it was.

"Hello. This is Russell Baker."

"Did I wake you Russ? I'm so sorry," said Nancy Freeman.

"That's no problem, Nancy. No one should be in the bed at 10:00 anyway but old people," he said as he looked at the clock on the nightstand. "It's nice to hear from you."

"Russ, I want to apologize. I don't know why I keep being so difficult to get along with. I guess some of it is being afraid of losing someone again after my fiancé died in Iraq. Maybe its jealousy. Maybe I'm just a mixed up woman where you are concerned."

"We were so close then all of a sudden we are angry and mad and hurt. Then, I know I started spending so much time with Steve and that was not a way to be treating you. Steve is a nice man and he doesn't tie me up in knots like you do. Then I see you with Miriam and it starts all over again. Is she with you now?"

"No, Nancy, she is not here. I know you called trying to be nice, I think, but whether she is here or not is none of your business at this point in our relationship. I am not asking you if Dr. Carter is with you. If I did you would hang up the phone."

There was silence and the sound of what Russ thought was crying on the other end.

"If you want to be friends, I guess that is doable. It would be tough, but doable. If you want to date occasionally, maybe that will work, but I doubt it at this point. And, Dr. Carter is not likely to want to be part of that kind of relationship, either. You may end up back at square one. Alone."

Russ waited for a response but got none.

"You say that Dr. Carter doesn't tie you up in knots. Great. I suppose he's in love with you. The question is do you love him or are you just comfortable with him. I don't know if comfort is enough. When I was married to Sarah it was more than comfort; I respected her. I loved her. She couldn't do anything that would make me stop. And, she loved me the way I was. She loved me as a cop. She would have loved me as a mechanic or anything else. She wasn't ever trying to remake me. Nor I her."

Nancy still did not say anything.

"You have Dr. Carter and I have Miriam. But we can't just use them and discard them when we are through with them. At least, I will not do that to Miriam. I think she would move here with me in a heartbeat and Dr. Carter would probably do the same with you. I don't know him but I know Miriam and she is a fine person."

Still no response from Nancy.

"So you have to decide first, Nancy, if you can be nice to me or not. I will not tolerate being hung up on, ignored, and being generally kept at arm's length so you can avoid the possibility of being hurt. I was a mess when I came out here and you were nice to me then and I guess you saw me as non-threatening but I am back on my feet, emotionally, I think."

"I appreciate what you did for me and I thought we were going somewhere. For the life of me, I don't know why we haven't. But any future we have is in your hands at this moment. But that won't last forever. I will move on without you. If it's security you want, I suspect I have as much money as Dr. Carter. If he has something else that you want that I don't have, then you should be with him."

"Good night, Russ. Be careful and don't get killed out there," Nancy said softly. With that she hung up before he could say anything else. Her soft reply was like a dagger in his heart.

He sat there on his bed in the dark, surprised that he had been so harsh with Nancy. She sat on her bed surprised that he had been so harsh to her. Both lay awake the rest of the night, unhappy.

12

Morning found Russ back in Alder interviewing everyone about the night of the blizzard and the shooting. People heard the emergency equipment but most thought it was a snow plow operation to clear the road. None saw any car and none could offer any help.

He went into the Alder Market and learned they did have a security camera on the gas pumps to prevent drive offs. No one had asked them about it when the first investigators came through and the owner had not considered it important. They gave him what they had but did not know if the discs went back that far as the recorder worked off a motion sensor and eventually started recording over itself. At least it was something he could work on. He needed a lead on the car!

It seemed clear to Russ that the car had to either go to the ranch, which they had no evidence it did, or it came back toward Alder and Virginia City or somewhere in between. Ruby Dam was out of the question and there was nowhere else. The Alder parking lot at the RV park was a possibility but, again, he had no evidence. No empty shells. No tracks. No witnesses. No finger prints. And nothing being done about the break-in at his house. His first week had produced exactly zero so far. And, he had pretty well made sure that Nancy Freeman would never speak to him again. Best described as a lousy week.

Russ took the disc from the security camera at Alder Market and put it in the player at the court house and started watching and hoping. The owner said it was motion activated and Russ soon saw that it picked up some passing cars on the road in front. Because of that the disc got used up and looped back much quicker than he would have thought. Another dead end. There was nothing from that far back on the disc.

He sat and looked at the chart he had drawn on the easel and trying to link all the dots. The link he needed was indeed a missing one and he could not tie any place or event to another except for the blizzard and the shooting. Nothing else seemed to fit. But there was one thing he had not explored: interviewing the boys. He picked up the phone.

"Well, hello Russ," said Miriam. How are you doing this fine morning and how is Barry?"

"I'm doing great and Barry may be awake today. We are keeping our fingers crossed. I called to ask a favor. Can you give me the phone numbers for Cas and Sam? I want to interview them before they go back and see if they may have seen anything that can help me. No one actually interviewed them as far as I can see in the case notes."

"Russ, I don't have the numbers. They had different phones when they got there. Something about getting a phone wet and having to get a throw away for the trip. But Lisa and Laura have the numbers. The girls had a hard time connecting with them and I guess they have bad cell service at the ranch. Should I just tell the girls to call them and give them your number to call before they leave town? My understanding is they are leaving to come back here tomorrow."

Russ thought a moment. "Sure. That'll probably be fine. It's probably a wild goose chase, anyway. Tell them they can call anytime."

"Will do Sir," she said in a lighthearted manner. "Good to be working with you again, Sir."

"And you as well, Madam." Russ hung up.

It was always nice talking to Miriam. She seemed to always be the same. But there was a definite change in her tone when he talked to her. She was beginning to sound more and more like the way Sarah had always talked to him.

After a meeting with Wayne Dunkin, Russ rode to Bozeman for lunch at Betty's and some good hot dogs. He might stop by the River's Run Fly Shop to say hello and Merry Christmas. That was bearing down on everyone and he had to do a little shopping but he had a short list and getting shorter. He would be right up the street from Nancy's but that may be off limits now.

Somehow, Russ felt that if they did not have the shooting solved by Christmas, the shooter or shooters would be long gone. When the New Year came, everyone would be moved on to other things. The days were clicking off with no new leads.

Russ ate his hot dogs at Betty's and did not see any of his friends there. Nancy's brother often ate there but Nancy rarely did. "A thing about hot dogs," she'd said.

A swing by the fly shop and seeing John and the gang was nice. They had one of the nicest shops in the West. To Russ it was a pleasure to see the new items they were always bringing in.

He drove by Nancy's, where he did not stop, and then he was back to Ennis and Virginia City. And, more frustration.

The next day came and went and about seven o'clock in the evening, he realized he had not heard from Cas and Sam.

A quick call to Miriam and she said she'd told the girls to call. She would find out what they did and call him back.

She called back in a few minutes. "The girls did not actually ever get the boys on the phone but they did leave voice mails for them asking that they call. There was not much else they could do."

More frustration. And still, he had no idea why anyone would have broken in his house. Were they looking for something from Russ, Miriam, the girls or the boys?

The next day brought a bit of good news. Barry Steinbrenner had opened his eyes and was able to at least squeeze his wife's hand. To her, that wasn't a step, but a leap, in the right direction.

They hoped he would come out of the mental fog in another day or so and he might get to where he could be interviewed. Maybe he could help find the missing link.

Russ was looking at maps, side roads, driveways and houses along the stretch of road back from the shooting and he saw something that caught his eye. It was his house. Any outside investigator would have had it on the list from the beginning. It offered one of the last places to exit the road coming back from the crime scene.

The other option was that they may have gone on to Ennis and then on to Bozeman if the road had been open. Was the road open?

"Wayne, do we know if the roads out of Ennis were open that night? Could someone have just come back from out there and headed out US 287 and gotten on Interstate 90?"

"The state guys were keeping US 287 open but mostly only one lane to I-90. Then they had a lot of equipment working to keep 90 open. The State DCI guys interviewed the crews that were working locally and none recall seeing any traffic going out of town after it started getting dark. All the news people were saying stay home."

Kasim Rahmani and Samer Mustafa were glad to be getting out of Montana and back to Salt Lake. The two men that had accompanied them on the trip over did not return with them. The men were not friends but the students had funneled money to them on occasion in Salt Lake. They didn't know where the two were now and didn't care. They were probably doing the will of Allah. And, they didn't know that the two men had come to the US through Mexico, were on watch list and no fly lists in the US. There were a number of arrest warrants for them in France, England, and The Netherlands.

Master bomb makers and trainers of terrorists around the Middle East and Europe, they had come to Salt Lake and then on to Montana. They were wanted all over the world and willing to kill anyone who got in their way, including a small county sheriff in Madison County.

The two students had been called and told to pick up these two men and some boxes and bring to them to Double Barr Ranch. They had not counted on the weather and they had not counted on one of the men pulling out a gun and shooting anyone.

Violence was not new to the students and they were training to participate in more when they were called on, but the shooting had come as a total surprise and put them in the middle of a major investigation. It messed up their plans to have some fun with the naive Alexander girls, the pretty brunettes with a beautiful mom who fixed them good meals and took them out to nice restaurants.

They would like to stay below the surface until they finished school in Salt Lake. A good education would serve them well in the future.

They had chosen to ignore the voice mails from the girls and would think of some good excuse. They were not going to talk to the Detective Baker if they could avoid it. And, besides, he had nothing on them. They had targeted the Alexander girls because of their mom's affiliation with the Salt Lake Police. The fact that they were pretty and liked to party while helping the refugee community was a real plus.

They did not know how close they had come to disappearing after the incident. They were loose ends that needed tying up, the ranch security man thought. But the Imam did not want any more dead people around that had told everyone they were coming to the ranch.

The ranch used a few Hispanic workers and the security service to help put an everyday American look to the world they encountered but nearly all of the visitors and recruits were from some place in the Middle East or Africa. Places like Somalia with cells in Minnesota. They were from Afghanistan, Iraq and Syria and with cells in nearly every area of the US and growing.

They came using the cover of being Middle Eastern immigrants that had gone to Germany, France and Belgium. These were places where they who could find their way to the US fairly easily. Plenty of work and training and indoctrination. They were the so-called radicalized segment that wanted to bring America and the West to its knees. The two men the boys had carried to the ranch were known by many names but to the people at the Double Barr Ranch, they were Nabil Mussan and Mahdi Shamah.

So, the students got to leave walking upright and able to drive. No, they did not know how close they had come to being casualties for just being in the wrong place when a cop showed up. It was their passengers and their cargo that mattered and sacrificing the two students was a calculated risk. And, they were easily replaced if necessary.

They were out of there and that was all that mattered to them at the moment. They drove by a big trash dumpster in front of a garage on the outskirts of Salt Lake City. They stopped and removed the SIM cards and batteries from the throw away phones and they did just that: threw them away. No one could track them now. Certainly no hic cop that was a fishing guide a week ago.

They thought they knew all about Russ because they had helped stage the break in to provide the Double Barr Ranch security man with the info on the people they had ended up staying with after the shooting. Including the girls' mom. They had seen his pitiful little check book with a few hundred dollar balance in the First Madison Bank and a deposit here and there for guide services. Nothing regularly. From what they saw, he had not amounted to much. They did not know about the accounts at Wells Fargo in Atlanta and Fidelity managed by Russ's former father-in-law.

Cas called Lisa and let them know they were back in town. "We are so glad you made it back. We have a lot of holiday parties lined up. Let's get together soon. I'll text you with the info on the party tomorrow night," said Lisa.

"Sounds real good, Lisa. Do you want us to pick you up?"

"Oh, that would be nice. Say 7:30?"

"7:30 it is."

"Oh, Cas. Did you call Mr. Baker before you left Ennis? I left you several voice mails. Mom said it was real important."

"I'm sorry, Lisa. I did not get any voice mails and I have turned in that phone. They got mine fixed. What did he want me to call him about?"

"About that sheriff that got shot, I think."

"Well, in that case, it won't matter because we don't know anything about that."

"Oh, I know. But you know how moms are."

"Yes. Certainly. See you tomorrow."

Cas thought about calling the security man at the ranch but decided to let the matter drop for now. The cop was almost 400 miles away and they would not likely be hearing from him again.

Barry Steinbrenner had finally gotten awake enough for some exchange of information. Other than the understandable confusion about what had happened to him and where he was, he knew his wife, and seemed to be past the critical stage. Maybe another day or two in ICU and he would be able to go to a room and be interviewed by Russ and Wayne.

Miriam was miffed at Cas and Sam for not calling Russ but she had to accept the fact that they may not have gotten the voice mails. When they came to pick the girls up she would impress upon them the importance of calling Russ. They probably did not understand the urgency.

The boys showed up right on time to pick the girls up and they were invited in so Laura, who was always late, could finish getting ready. Miriam arrived home and their car was in the drive way: the silver colored Ford Edge with a Utah License plate. "That's odd," she thought. "Russ mentioned the car had Pennsylvania plates and I believe he said the tag bracket was a Pennsylvania car dealer. This car now has a Utah plate and shows a dealer in Salt Lake."

When Miriam went in she was her normal cordial self but she immediately mentioned the conversation with Russ to Cas and Sam. "I know you may not feel this is important but please call him. We have some dangerous people out there and Mr. Baker is trying to find them."

"Yes. We will call him tomorrow, Madam Alexander."

"Thanks. You all have a good time." She went to her room to call Russ.

"Russ, this is Miriam," she said when he answered his phone.

"Hi, Miriam. Some good news today. Barry is awake and seems confused but knew his wife and it looks like he is out of the woods."

"Oh, that is good news. I spoke to the boys about calling you and they promised to call you tomorrow."

"Thank you for following up. I wish you were here to help on this case."

"Russell Baker, don't you wish too hard. I might just come running."

"But, then, I might not get any work done. You may can help me from there with less distraction," he said, as he tried to make a serious comment sound like a joke.

"Russ. Didn't you mention that the boys' car had a Pennsylvania tag and license plate frame?"

"Yes. That's right."

"That's funny because I just noticed the car in the driveway and it has a Utah plate and a Salt Lake dealer name on the frame around it."

"Why would they have changed the plate this quickly since they got back to Salt Lake, Miriam?"

"I have no idea. Should I ask them? There is probably a simple answer."

"No. Don't ask them yet. I did not have any reason to write down the number of the Pennsylvania tag so I don't have it. Could you get the Utah plate number and we can run a check on who actually owns the car."

"Russ, you don't really think these boys are suspects in anything do you?"

"Miriam, I need some suspects from somewhere. Salt Lake is as good a place as any. Do you mind?"

"Not if it might help find the people who shot Barry and help my favorite fly fisherman, uhh, detective. I will try to get it when they bring the girls back tonight."

"Thank you."

"Should I be worried about the girls?"

"Let's you and me get the facts and then we can worry if it seems necessary. I may be way off base even looking at this. But we will get to the bottom of it. It is odd."

"Good night, Russ." She hung up.

So, two good things had happened today: Barry was awake and they had a lead to follow up on.

The girls got back late but they did not come back with Cas and Sam. They got dropped off by a girlfriend that lived nearby.

She was watching out the window and decided that she did not want to go into why she was up waiting on them so she went to her bedroom and closed the door.

The girls had a dorm room at the Westminster College Residence but were spending time with their mother during Christmas and she did not want to appear to be spying on them. She'd have to figure a way to get the license number some other way.

13

Morning at Russ's brought an early phone call from Wayne Dunkin. Barry's wife had invited them to come and talk a few minutes to Barry who was being moved to a private room and was still under guard by a deputy from the Gallatin County Sheriff's Office. "Do you want to ride together, Russ?"

"I may want to go by the fly shop while we are in Bozeman, Wayne. Why don't I just meet you there?"

"No problem. Do we have anything new on the case?"

Russ answered, "I'm following up on a curiosity, I guess you could call it. The car driven by the two boys that were here visiting, and who later went out to the ranch, had Pennsylvania plates when it was here and I mentioned it to Miriam. She wasn't aware the boys were from Pennsylvania but we did not ever say anything to them about it. Then, when they got back to Salt Lake, she noticed the car had Utah plates. And the tag frame had been changed as well."

"That is strange. Sounds like they are trying to hide something. People don't usually change the license frame, if they even have one. What are you doing about it?" asked Wayne.

"Miriam is trying to get the number on the car now. I did not see a reason to write it down when they were here so I do not have the Pennsylvania license." Russ said.

"See you at the hospital in one hour, Russ."

"Roger that."

Barry Steinbrenner had survived combat in fighter jets and been shot at by surface to air missiles and never got a scratch. But his luck ran out on a cold and snowy night in November on Route 287 in Madison County, Montana.

Barry looked like death warmed over to Russ when they entered the room. He was pale and there were numerous fluids and tubes and wires attached to him. His faithful wife was holding his hand.

Barry had jokingly told Russ once that his wife was a crack shot with a gun and he never wanted to get on her bad side. Russ could see a toughness in her and somehow he knew not to get on her bad side, either. No one was coming in that room unless she said it was okay.

Barry's throat was raw from days of a breathing tube and feeding tubes. He spoke barely above a whisper. "Hello, fellows. Janet told me you were coming and that we had an old team member back with us."

"Russ waived his hand and smiled and waited for Wayne to speak. "Yea, Barry. You may have some budget problems when you get back but we all decided to get Russ to come on board and work on this full time until we get the people who did this." He looked at Russ expecting him to say something.

"Good to see you Barry," said Russ. "We've been worried about you. We hope you'll be able to shed some light on what happened as we don't have a lot to go on."

"Right. Well, I don't have a clear memory yet of what happened. I remember seeing a car and I think it was off to the shoulder in the snow with nothing but the front end showing. It was just a car that had spun out," whispered

Barry. "It didn't look like a threat. I started walking over to see if anyone was hurt and the last thing I remember was someone lowered the window on the left side and here I am."

Any idea on the car, Barry. Make, color, anything?"

"I just don't remember. I do remember a lot of snow. Maybe in another day or so more will come back to me."

"Then, Barry, we will get out and wait for Janet to call us. We'll come running." Wayne gave a little goodbye wave.

That was Russ's cue that they were leaving. As they walked to the door, Barry whispered, "Thank you fellows."

They nodded and left.

"Well if we don't get more from him than that, we may be up that creek, Russ. No boat or paddle."

"I hope to hear back from Miriam on the car registration, today. That may give us something. And, to tell you the truth, I would really like to make a surprise raid out at that ranch with a search warrant," said Russ.

"I can try to get one if we can get any kind of probable cause but with what we have, I doubt a judge will give us one."

"Okay Wayne. Maybe an anonymous 911 call saying there is a shooting or a fire or something and we just go charging in."

"I'd have to say, Russ, that might seriously foul up my retirement. Spending a few months on unpaid leave in the county jail would not do my finances any good."

"But, Wayne, think of how much fun we could have! I guess we'll save that for plan C. I will be on back that way in a couple of hours. Call me on the radio or my cell if you need me."

"The same here, Russ."

Russ scrolled through his phone and found Chad Freeman's number and hit the dial button. He wanted to get a read from Nancy's brother about how Nancy felt about their last conversation. Chad was one of those guys that you'd better not ask him anything if you really did not want to know his opinion. Chad never got Diplomacy 101 training. He went to the *Tell It Like It Is* class.

"Hello, Mr. Baker. And before you ask, yes, she is mad as hell!"

"Have I been around you so much you can read my mind already, Chad?"

"When it comes to you and my sister a first grader can do that. You are mad or she is mad, all the time. But this time, Buddy, you screwed the pooch! She said she never wanted to see you or hear from you again. And that goes for shuttle service, too. She told me to tell you that. She said she called to eat some humble pie and you blasted her good."

"Yes I did do that. That's how she treated me a few days before and I guess I was trying to get the last word. A bad idea, huh?"

"Russ, I think you succeeded on that. The last word part, anyway. I believe she is pretty serious this time."

"So you wouldn't recommend me stopping in the shop and throwing my hat in first?"

"If you happen to have that Kevlar vest, it still might not be safe. But she isn't there today. She went to Butte with mom to see some specialist today. Mom has some medical issues."

"Thanks for the info, Chad, at least about your Mom. She is one nice lady and I hope she'll be fine. How has the fishing been?"

"If you can get down in the holes and any cutback around the bank you can drag some nice fish out but not in droves. That heavy snow and cold changed things quite a bit. It has all been subsurface these past few days."

"How is the detective stuff going or can you say?"

"Chad, I can tell you all I know, which is about nothing. Like the fishing, everything seems subsurface right now. Nothing rising to the top. Do you have time for a hot dog at Betty's?"

"Sorry. I have to meet my wife about some Christmas stuff for the kids. Maybe the next time you are around give me a call."

"Well, see you later then." Russ ended the call. He would just go to Ennis and get something to go at the Bear Trap and go on home.

The news wasn't good on the Nancy Freeman front, at all. He may have burned that bridge.

"Hi, Mom. I just wanted you to know that we are over at the Shaw Student Center and our little refugee help group is having a meeting and we will not be home for dinner," said Lisa Alexander as she called her mother.

"Well, Sweetie, that will probably be better than being here for dinner. I was just going to order pizza or something, anyway. Are Laurie and the boys with you over there?"

"Sure. Why do you ask?"

"I just wondered if you were out by yourself," said Miriam.

"Love you, Mom, but you worry too much."

"That's what moms do," she replied.

Miriam sat down at the computer and pulled up a map of the campus at Westminster. She had attended the University Of Utah and had not been on the campus around Westminster that much.

She found the Shaw Student Center and she saw there were four parking lots around the Shaw Center that the boys' car might be parked in and one was a parking garage. She also knew it might not be in any of them. The students had student parking stickers but she had no idea where to start looking.

Miriam had a County of Salt Lake Unified Police card that allowed her to park in no parking zones and other places when on official police business. She was declaring this trip as official business.

She drove to the Shaw Center and entered the first lot. She would try all the outside lots first. A drive through the Foster Charleston lot did not turn up anything as she drove through quickly hoping she would not be spotted by her girls or the boys and have to explain what she was doing there,

She went around to the Dumke Field Parking lot and it was packed with cars but no silver Ford Edge. She had to drive all the way around to the other end to the last open lot called Lower Nunemaker and there she saw the car she was looking for. She stopped and walked over and she saw a familiar backpack that her daughter used for a book bag so she had no doubt this was the right car. It only took a minute to write the number down and she walked around to the front and wrote down the vehicle's identification number as well. She quickly left the lot for home.

Miriam sent a text message to Russ with the license plate number and the registration number that was on the decal. They would know soon who owned the car and she was hoping it was Cas or Sam. Miriam decided to swing by her office where she worked in Support Services for the Unified Police Department, headed up by the Salt Lake County Sheriff.

Salt Lake City and County authorities used the National Motor Vehicle Title Information System known as NMVTIS. It is a collection of title and vehicle information that shows vehicle history, flood damage, salvaged and ownership of automobiles, There is also the Utah Motor Vehicle Registry and the National Insurance Crime Bureau that helps show if a car stolen using its VIN. Many states interchange information and share with each other.

Miriam headed back to her office to access the information on the car and see for herself and not have to wait on Russ. She entered the search on the Utah Department Of Motor Vehicles by both the license number and the VIN and she quickly got two responses.

The tag was registered to a Daniel Bernhart in Salt Lake City. The NMVTIS showed that it was a car that had been totaled in an accident several months before.

The VIN number check showed a similar Ford Edge from Harrisburg, Pennsylvania that had been totaled in a wreck there earlier in the year. The same insurance company had paid claims on both cars. The Pennsylvania car had belonged to Wilson Proxmire in Harrisburg. The car had two identities!

By all accounts the car that Cas was driving around in did not really exist but a quick look on either the VIN or the license would show a silver Ford Edge and probably would not be noticed in a traffic stop on the highway under normal conditions. But, it could be that the car was a salvaged car and someone had put them together but since one was in Pennsylvania and one in Utah, that did not seem likely.

 It could have been the boys bought a car that had false papers. But, in any case, something was not right.

Miriam thought she would wait for Russ to do his check from Virginia City. Then they would have verification and could decide the next course of action. Staying calm was her biggest concern now as she was getting very worried about these boys her daughters were mixed up with.

Russ made it in to the office early and with the help of one of the administrative people did a similar search to what Miriam had done the night before in Salt Lake. They came up with the same results: two wrecked cars had been supposedly totaled out in accidents and then used to create identification for a car being driven by a refugee student in Salt Lake City. And, depending on which license plate they used, the ownership would appear to be in Pennsylvania or Salt Lake but would not show Cas or Sam as being connected to the vehicle. The vehicle would not appear on any stolen or hot sheet in a cursory traffic stop.

Russ and Wayne placed a call to Miriam and she confirmed what they had found. They knew now that one or both of the boys were probably knowingly involved in the conspiracy since they had observed the plates on the car had been switched while the boys were driving the car.

Russ says, "This is a big conspiracy and must involve someone at the insurance company. Someone knew that two similar cars had been totaled, or at least written off as totaled and checks paid to the previous owners. Then, someone takes one or both of the cars and repairs it and sells it on the black market and the buyer has a vehicle that appears legal and registered but actually does not exist on paper."

"For this to work to the maximum effectiveness, the boys would need fake Id's to match the tag being used on a given day. That way they could travel under the radar. The next question is why are they doing it?"

"We can turn the info over to the FBI as this appears to be interstate crime," said Wayne. "We can't afford to get bogged down in the theft and insurance fraud involving cars in another state, if that is what it is. We can call Salt Lake and the Utah DMV and probably get the boys detained but we don't yet know why and if this is in any way connected to Barry. They may just say someone sold them the car and they too are victims. The fact that they changed the license plates, though, does seem to say that they are fully aware that the car is not legally registered. But, we need to link the car to the actual shooting and we have nothing that does that yet."

"What should the next step be, Wayne?" Miriam asked.

"Let me talk to a couple of people and to the Chief of Police there in Salt Lake and see how we can proceed. I don't want to have any technicalities that let a bunch of crooks get away. It may be that they will allow Russ to come out and they'll bring in the two guys for questioning, at least. I think they would go along with that. If nothing else, we can eliminate them from our investigation. Utah can decide who prosecutes them, if at all, for the car ownership problem," said Wayne.

"Russ can call you back as soon as we know and you can talk to whomever you need to there if you want to be part of the investigation. Obviously, that is a decision for your folks or the City of Salt Lake, or the State."

Miriam hung up and was shaken by the call. Her daughters were associated with some young men who were possibly involved in a criminal activity! Could these guys be involved in any way with the shooting of Barry Steinbrenner? Or, for that matter, illegal car sales?

Miriam called Lisa who was still in bed at her house. "Hi, Mom." She said with a big yawn and rubbing the sleep out of her eyes.

"Is anyone there with you, Lisa?"

"Just Laura. Did you think we'd sneaked some boys in or something?"

"Not really, but I need to tell you something very confidential and you must promise to keep quiet until we get some answers. Understood?"

"Sure, Mom. What is going on?"

When the girls started working at the refugee assistance group, Miriam had thought it a grand gesture that her daughters would want to help the students coming in from the war ravaged areas of the Middle East. In fact, she had encouraged it. But when they had become personally involved with two of them, she had expressed misgivings and they quickly branded her as being prejudiced and anti-everything.

But over time, the boys had become to seem very nice and they treated her and the girls very respectfully.

Her fears had subsided as she got to know them and the girls were seriously infatuated with the handsome men that they knew to be from Iraq. But this was now being seriously tested. She had the safety and the welfare of her daughters to think about.

"Confidential means that you cannot discuss with Cas and Sam, either. Understood?"

"*Yes, Mom!*" she said with a sound of exasperation in her voice.

"I want you and Laura to stay away from them the next few days until we can get some questions answered. Especially do not get in the car with them."

"Mom, what are you saying?! These are our best friends. We like them and they like us. I thought you had come to like them too. But you never have liked them because of them being from Iraq and the fact that they are Muslim and their skin is darker! You are just a raciest Islamophobe!"

"Now listen, Lisa, we can talk about this more when I get home but you have to do this for right now!"

Miriam knew that she was losing it. She and Lisa were about to get very angry with each other so she said softly, "I need you and Laura to do what I'm asking. This is possibly a very serious situation. Very serious!"

"Mother, not if you don't tell me what this is all about. We have enough Islamophobic people to deal with as it is. I don't want to have my mother one of them. I am not going to stop associating with them for no reason. I think I'll get Laura and we will just go back to the dorm and you can spend Christmas by yourself."

That was a jab to Miriam's heart. "Look, Lisa, there is some problem with where their car came from. They changed the license plates when we went to Montana and changed them back when they got back here and their car doesn't exist on the State's Motor Vehicle Department registry."

"You've been investigating Cas and Sam!? Mother, how could you do that?"

"Because the issue of their car registration came up in the investigation of the shooting in Montana. Russell Baker and the Sheriff are trying to get to the bottom of things and until they do, we are not sure it's safe for you to be around them."

"So that's it Mother? Russell Baker, who everyone knows you have a thing for, has it in for Cas and Sam so they are going to find something wrong with them. You could expect that from someone from Georgia but I did not expect it from you."

"Lisa, I don't ever try to force you and your sister to do anything against your will. You are both adults. But you know I would not be asking this if I did not feel it was terribly important. Yes, I like Russell Baker a lot. Maybe I love him, I don't know for sure. But, I do know one thing: I would not ever put my feelings for him over your happiness. You know that. Please do what I ask. Okay?"

"I guess so, Mom." And she hung up and went to her sister's room to tell her about the call from their mother.

Laura Alexander did not take the news well. "I did not promise Mother anything, Lisa. I guess you can do what you want but I do not plan to stop associating with them. Absolutely not! I will find out about the car. We can just ask them and get that cleared up easily, I know. In fact, they are supposed to be picking us up in a little while, you know? Did you tell mom that?"

"No. I did not think to mention it and she did not give me much time to think."

Laura said, "We need to get ready because they will be here in a few minutes."

There were a number of jurisdictions involved in trying to get someone to follow up on the two young refugee students that were attending school in Salt Lake. The State of Utah was the best place to start Wayne thought and so did Russ.

Wayne and Russ asked the local District attorney to get involved and all the legal hoops they had to jump through made it seem painfully slow. Could they get a warrant to search the boys' property for which the only address they knew of was the school dormitory? Tricky, at best.

"Russ, the DA says what looks to be the best bet will be to get a location on the car and pick them up driving the vehicle which has the suspicious paperwork. If we can get the folks in Salt Lake to agree, then you could go out and sit in on an interview of the boys," said Wayne.

Cas and Sam pulled in at Miriam's house to pick up the girls and go to the Student Center. They liked being with the pretty brunettes. They always attracted envious stares from the other young males and further fed their egos. Cas rang the bell.

Laura was still upset and angry that her mother would tell her that she couldn't associate with these two young men any more. She knew these boys and they were nice and there was a certain mystery about these two Middle Easterners and she had grown to be more than fond of Cas. She opened the door for them and as they came in she called, "Lisa! Cas and Sam are here. It's time to go."

Lisa came into the room and looked at Laura and then the boys: "I'm sorry but something has come up and we won't be able to go today."

But Laura said, "I am not letting mother ruin everything. I'm going."

A shouting match followed and finally Cas wanted to know what was going on but Lisa just said they were having some problems with their mother. But, Laura, in her anger, blurted out, "Our mother is trying to break us up and came up with some story about your car being stolen or having phony license plates or something and that we could not be riding around with you in it."

Cas and Sam were frozen for a minute and quickly recovered. Sam said, "Cas, we need to get that license

117

straightened out. You have been ignoring that problem and now look what that has caused. We should go first thing tomorrow to the license place and see what needs to be done."

Cas quickly picked up on what Sam was saying. "Yes. You are right; I have let that go and should have seen about it. Lisa and Laura, we are sorry we have offended your mother. We will postpone our trip tonight to the student center and go now. We will see about resolving this."

"That would be wonderful, Cas," replied Lisa. "Wouldn't it, Laura?"

"Of course it would. Maybe we can get together tomorrow evening," she said.

"Then we are off," Cas said with a smile and a wave of the hand. "We will see you tomorrow."

"See, Lisa, you and mom make mountains out of ant hills, or whatever. All we had to do was let them know that needed to be cleared up."

"That sounds good, Laura. I guess I'm glad you told them even though mom said not to say anything to them."

Laura replied, "Screw what she said! It's time she learned to trust people and to stop having bad feelings toward them because she doesn't like where they are from. Maybe she will learn a lesson from this."

"I hope you are right. But, she is not going to like it that we said anything to them," said Lisa.

"Who says we have to say anything to her? They can go get the stuff straightened out and that will be the end to it," Laura added. "They can just stay clear of her and not come by here and we can see them someplace else."

Cas and Sam had two vehicles and it would have been a simple matter to just wipe the car clean and dump the Ford had it not been that a lot of people had seen them in it and recognized them in the car. And now, someone in law enforcement had some suspicion about the tag changes. A normal traffic stop would not have revealed anything about the car. It was not on any stolen or hot car lists. A cursory look would show a car that matched the registration. It was when the license plate and the VIN were compared that a problem would show up.

But there was more at stake than the car which had been provided to them by a supporter when they arrived in Salt Lake. The whole idea was that it could not be traced to anyone after the paper work had been created by using numbers and parts from junked and totaled cars.

Their job had been to assimilate and stay below the radar. But they had grown to like the social interaction and the company of the locals, especially the female locals who were much more accessible than back home. Now, some nosey person associated with those pretty local girls was shining unwanted attention on them. Some action was warranted. Luckily, they had been given a heads up by one of the headstrong young women and they could react in time, they hoped.

They needed to contact their sponsor and see what he wanted them to do at this point. Would they stay or disappear? It would not be up to them.

Kasim Rahmani and Samer Mustafa had arrived in the US from a refugee camp in Iraq. They had been vetted thoroughly. They had all their papers and Id's and had been accepted by Homeland Security and every other possible agency. Two nice, although unfortunate, young men whose parents had been killed by insurgents and they had been given a new lease on life to come to America where they would receive help and support to get an education and make something of themselves in spite of the horrors they had been through. And, by all accounts, they were doing well.

But, there was a flaw in the program. Kasim Rahmani and Samer Mustafa never made it to the US. For, like their family members, Kasim and Samer had met the same fate: dead at the hands of insurgents. But all of their background and details that could help in identifying the young boys had been gathered and used to resurrect the two young men.

The two young men in the car were not from Iraq, but were from Syria. Kasim Rahmani was actually named Abdul samad Arazi. Samer Mustafa was actually named Manzur Najafi. They had come to America on a route through Turkey with papers and ID's that had been meticulously manufactured and here they were waiting to bring vengeance and justice to the country that had invaded Iraq and Afghanistan with bombs and drones and soldiers. This was the country that had assisted in the overthrow in Egypt and Libya and was a supporter of their mortal enemies in Israel. This was the country that was launching strikes in Syria at that very moment and was involved in several other places like Somalia and Yemen. America was the very same country that had trusted them and offered them peace, safety, security, education and a future. And it was the same country where they had been accepted and received warmly and offered friendship and love.

But they were here to make sure that America paid a price. They had accepted a call and they were waiting right below the surface to rise and do their duty. They had been training and preparing for the moment they were needed. Now, this was all being threatened. They needed to make a phone call.

The call was brief. Draw no attention to themselves. Park the car in some downtown parking garage and wipe it down clean. There was nothing that could connect it to anyone other than a retired postal worker in Salt Lake City who had been in an accident months before and a school teacher in Harrisburg Pennsylvania that had been rear ended on the way to school one morning.

They were to load up Samer's car and wipe down the dorm room and take everything with them and find a dumpster for stuff they did not need like lamps and their small assortment of household items. Dump everything going out of town.

They were to make their way to the Double Barr Ranch and someone would be there waiting for them near Ennis, Montana and do it before there was a serious effort launched to find them. In other words, do it now!

They would miss their easy life in Salt Lake and the girls that had been their daily companions. They would miss their crowded dorm room that was actually nicer than their home in Syria. But they had answered a higher calling and now they had to leave that behind.

Unknown to them and their support team, while they thought their enemy was in Salt Lake, he actually was in Ennis, Montana. But neither knew it yet! And in a few hours they were gone from Salt Lake and Kasim Rahmani and Samer Mustafa would be gone forever and they would have new ID's and a new address. And Sam's Toyota Camry that people had seen them in in Salt Lake would be driven up the driveway just off State Road 287 in Madison County, Montana and would be pushed into a newly excavated hole and compacted very neatly and the area manicured to look like the surroundings. Life would go on.

Finding the information on the car had set some investigative wheels in motion. Calls to Harrisburg and to Salt Lake had resulted in conversations with very confused citizens who thought their totaled out car was in a large compressed pile of scrap metal for recycling somewhere.

Russ and Wayne were waiting on the folks in Salt Lake to respond to their request to pick up the boys and allow Russ to come out to sit in on the questioning. He had not been able to connect them to the shooting and had no reason to suspect them in the break in at his house. And, there may not been any way to do either. But, if they could get the car, they would have a chance to examine it for evidence. Though that was a small possibility.

The word finally came from Salt Lake.

"Miriam, we have everything in place and I will be coming to Salt Lake tomorrow. The Salt Lake and Unified Salt Lake departments are going to put out a look out for the car and will be watching your house and the school. As soon as they pick them up, we will try to do a thorough forensics exam on the car and see if we can link it to the shooting. They have agreed not to move on them at your house to avoid any embarrassment for you and the girls if we have mud on our face."

"It will be good to see you, Russ. Do you want to have dinner with me here tomorrow night?"

"I would suggest that we keep my presence quiet until we see what happens. I will be at the Hilton Garden Inn downtown on West 600 Street. Maybe you could pick me up and we could have dinner close by there, if that works."

"I do feel badly having to put the boys through this and I hope it is nothing, for their sakes and the girls'. Call me when you get settled, then, tomorrow." She said good night and ended the call.

Nancy had not heard from Russ in several days. Christmas was just a few days away and she wasn't sure how to handle the relationship, if there was one now, with Russ. She called her brother, Chad.

"Have you heard from Russ? I was wondering how the investigation is going into Barry's shooting."

Not prone to beating around the bush, he answered, "Crap, Nancy. What you want to know is what Russ is doing and who he's doing it with and if you are ever going to see him again. Right?"

"If you were not my brother I would call you some really bad names sometimes and this is one of those times! You are just like Russ and you both can be so mean!"

"Well, I have not seen him in several days. He called and asked me to go eat hot dogs and I could not go that day. But what he really wanted was to find out how mad you were and if you were ever going to speak to him again. I told him you never wanted to see him again, to never call you about doing shuttles for him again and that you were going to marry Dr. Carter right after Christmas. You will remember that you told me to let him know not to call you."

"Chad! I do not believe you would do that! Why did you tell him I was marrying Dr. Carter?"

"Well, I did make up the part about getting married. I really did not say that."

"Chad! I hate you! I hate you! I hate you!" Nancy was now screaming into the phone.

"Nancy, I told him that you were mad with him because he said some rough things to you on the phone and I did tell him that you might not get over it. And, I told him you wouldn't do any more shuttles for him because you did tell me to tell him that."

"I got the impression that he was expecting that and is probably ready to move on because he doesn't think that the two of you have a future and that you probably can't just be friends. At least, not now. If you want Russ to ever know anything else about you or you want to know anything else about him, I suggest you call him because I will never have this conversation with you again. And, I can get someone to do my shuttles, too, if I need to. Good night, Nancy." He was gone.

Nancy sat in stunned silence. Her brother had never spoken to her in that fashion and would have always walked through fire for her. Was she going to lose her brother, too?

14

Russ had his small travel carry-on and his laptop as he made it to the airport. He would have liked to have his service weapon but flying made that impossible. Wayne had told him to fly and fly he would. He had made this trip once with Barry Steinbrenner in his Cirrus airplane but that would not happen again for a while.

He left home early and in the light he did not take any notice to the Toyota Camry he met just outside of Ennis as he headed to the airport in Bozeman. Had he been looking closely, it might have saved him a trip.

In a few minutes, while Russ was parking at the Bozeman Airport long term lot, the Toyota Camry was pulling up to the ranch house at Double Barr Ranch. The two occupants unloaded their car into the back of a pickup and a man took the Toyota and drove it away, followed by a large backhoe. They went in to see the Imam. Cas and Sam and the Camry were no more.

Russ rented a car at the Salt Lake City airport and headed to the Salt Lake City Police Department which had jurisdiction since the school is located in the city. Salt Lake Detective Debra Taylor had been given the case and told to assemble a team meeting to review the notes, which were few, on the possible fake car papers and the

Ford Edge. It was about as well received as a slap in the face. A nothing case and a waste of time for the detectives. "This should be handled by the patrol officers," she had told her boss.

"Just appease the guy and get him back to Montana. Apparently his department has a well-connected sheriff from a big family of sheriff's in Montana and we want to look concerned. All about good PR, you know."

"Those weren't the letters I had in mind, sir. BS seems more appropriate. The guy is in a town of 169 people. I thought Virginia City was where the Cartwrights were, or somebody. This must be some really high level guy." Detective Taylor said the last part with the most sarcasm possible in her voice.

When Detective Taylor was told that their appointment was there, she rolled her eyes at the people in the room and said, "Let's get this over with, guys."

She went to the waiting area and was shocked by what she saw. He was a tall, handsome man in a blue blazer and blue button down shirt and nice dress pants that looked more like a person who should be on the cover of GQ magazine standing by a Porsche. "I am Russell Baker from Madison County, Montana Sheriff's Office," he said with an accent that certainly didn't sound like anyone she had met from Montana before.

"Nice to meet you, Mr. Baker. I am Detective Debra Taylor. You don't sound like a man from Montana."

"I'm from Georgia, Detective Taylor. I've been in Montana for a few months."

She took Russ back to join the others.

Russ was experienced enough to know that no one wanted to be involved in this crappy type case. He also knew that she'd been assigned to the case and likely did not take the case as being too serious. After all, to her it was just a possible auto tag fraud.

In the small meeting room there was also a Sergeant from the Patrol Division and Assistant Chief Detective. After introductions, Sergeant Taylor asked Russ to brief them on why he was there asking their help.

Russ gave them a quick overview. "I realize this is a case most people would not want to be snagged on. So I appreciate your cooperation and will try not to waste your time."

"We started out with an investigation into the shooting and attempted murder of the local sheriff in Madison County, Montana. Sheriff Barry Steinbrenner was shot five times and left for dead beside the road while stopping to assist a car that had spun out and hit a snow bank. We have little in the way of clues and no forensics yet. In fact, we have no leads of substance."

Russ had gotten right to the point and had grabbed their attention.

"However, the two students that have been driving the car in your description there were in the area on or about the time of the shooting. In fact, they stayed at my house that I rent from a local Salt Lake resident, Miriam Alexander, who works in the Forensics section at the Unified Police Department here. Her daughters are friends with, and have assisted these young men, who are refugees from Iraq. We have no evidence that they were in any way involved with the shooting but we became suspicious when I noticed their car had a Pennsylvania license plate when it was in Montana which I mentioned to Mrs. Alexander. Upon their return to Salt Lake, she noticed the car had Utah plates so it appeared that the students were trying to someway hide their tracks. She called to advise me of the license switch."

"Further investigation has led us to the conclusion that the car has some registration problems and may be one of two vehicles that were supposedly totaled out and scraped, or a salvage vehicle made from the two which does not seem plausible from where they were. Or, there was a third vehicle involved. All of this is probably in your file there in front of you."

"There may be some conspiracy within the insurance company personnel who had the insurance on both cars. If it turns out there is no issue or that the case is only about the car title and some scam there, we will drop our interest in the case as related to the students and the car and at that point the State of Utah, the State of Pennsylvania, you folks here in Salt lake or maybe the FBI can follow up or drop it. We will have no jurisdiction and no further interest. But, we are hoping we can take a look at the car and see if there is any connection with the shooting of our sheriff."

Sergeant Taylor and the other officers were surprised at the manner and professionalism of a small town sheriff from Montana. They went from being bored and non-interested to seeing the underlying importance of this inquiry: an officer was shot in the line of duty in cold blood. Now it mattered to them, too.

Sergeant Taylor said, "Detective Baker will accompany me to the school and we will try to make contact at the dorm. We are asking the patrol units to be on the lookout for the vehicle and to stop and detain the car and driver on suspicion of fraud related to the license and title of the vehicle. Once we determine if the car is fraudulently titled, we will have authority to examine the car and we can do a forensic examination and the Unified Police Support Team will handle that for us. With probable cause, no warrant will be needed to search the car."

"Sergeant Taylor, excuse me for interrupting, but I would like to ask that we try and secure the warrant for searching the car as that may be the only evidence we have and we do not want any legal cloud over it."

Detective Taylor was offended by the request but when she looked at her boss, he gave a shrug and a nod to say he was in agreement. Chalk one up for the redneck sheriff.

Russ and the Sergeant got into her unmarked car and headed to the school about five miles away. She couldn't help but catch a glimpse of him out the corner of her eye. He was nice to look at and had a strange poise about him. He was not some greenhorn, was her guess.

"You have a family back in Montana, Mr. Baker?"

"No. I have some in-laws in Marietta, Georgia just outside Atlanta. My wife passed away some time back."

"You been in law enforcement long?"

"I was a detective with the Cobb County Police there in Marietta for a little over eight years, until my wife died. I only work some part time now when the sheriff's office needs a little extra help, like now. How about yourself?"

"Five years."

They had acquired a search warrant specific to the dorm room of the two students only and would be accompanied by school security. When they arrived at the dorm, they were greeted by the school's campus security.

The dorm room door was closed when they arrived. They knocked and there was no answer. After announcing themselves several times and knocking repeatedly the security officer tried the door and it was not locked. When they opened the door they all saw it: an empty room. The drawers were empty, the closets were empty and there were no personal items or trash to be seen. The room had been obviously cleaned and sanitized. The floors vacuumed. They had gone to great effort to leave no trace. Why?

Russ looked at Sergeant Taylor. "Sergeant Taylor, I believe they knew we were coming."

"It sure looks that way. But how would they have known? Who knew about this?"

"Not many in Madison County. One person here other than your folks and that is Miriam Alexander and I am certain she did not tell them. But, they were warned, that's for sure."

"I'll get a CSI team here but it looks like they scrubbed this place from top to bottom." Detective Taylor said.

"Yes, it does. I wonder what this is all about, now. There's more here than meets the eye, I'm afraid."

Russ and Detective Taylor checked all the parking garages around the school and interviewed some of the students in the dorm. They learned that Samer (Sam) Mustafa had a Toyota Camry. Since there were thousands of those around, with no tag number they still had nothing. And no one had seen them around today. It was looking like this would be a wasted trip.

Russ and Detective Taylor drove back to police headquarters and decided they would touch base in the morning. "Officer Baker, do you have plans for dinner tonight? If not, I could take you to dinner on my very tiny expense account."

"That is very nice of you Detective but as it stands now, I am already meeting someone for dinner. Maybe we can do something before I leave."

"Sounds good."

Russ got in his rental car and went to the motel. More frustration.

The phone rang just as Russ got out of the shower. Miriam was calling and Russ was looking forward to seeing her though there were some pressures involving her daughters and the boys. "I'll be there in about fifteen minutes, Russ."

"That will be just about perfect. Where are we going?"

"There is a place called The Porch that has great meatloaf. I thought we'd go there. How did the day go?"

"I'll give you the full recap at dinner. I'm starved!"

As usual, Miriam was a standout in the restaurant and they made a handsome couple. Heads turned when Miriam and Russ walked in and were seated. Russ was a little self-conscious for himself but Miriam was radiant and feasting on the attention. She hadn't had a date in months that made her feel the glow she was feeling. Just a simple dinner with Russ was something special. Most of the dinner was small talk.

When the dessert came, Miriam finally said, "I can't wait any longer. What happened today about locating the boys' car?"

"The boys are gone, Miriam. At least that that is how it appears. Their dorm room was cleaned and appeared to be scrubbed. No one has seen them since yesterday. Do you know if Lisa or Laura has spoken to them at all?"

"Not as far as I know, Russ."

"It appears that they got tipped off somehow that we were checking on them. It's just too coincidental and we have not found either car but we really don't know the plates on the other car and can't find any car registered to Sam, either. Of course, it could have been in a relative or some other sponsor's name."

Russ went on to fill her in on Barry's improvement. The news was better for his recovery but he had provided no help from any recollection of the events of the night he was shot. Frustration.

Russ heard a message notification on his phone and saw it was from Sergeant Taylor. *Room scrubbed clean. No prints and no leads found there. No car yet. Call me in the AM. Det. Taylor.*

He showed the message to Miriam. "What's Detective Taylor like? Was he glad to see you?"

"She's a she and she was fine. Not happy to have been hooked into this deal, I'm sure."

"Is she pretty and hitting on you already?"

"Yes to both questions," Russ said and laughed.

Russ wanted to ask Miriam back to the motel but just did not feel good about doing that. Miriam was thinking about that too, but did not push it. Maybe tomorrow when the problem at hand was solved. She drove Russ to the hotel and dropped him off. No good night kiss. No nothing.

When Miriam got home, she walked by Lisa's room and she did not see a light on but she did under Laura's door. Laura was listening to some music on her headphones when Miriam tapped on the door.

"Come in," she said.

"Good evening, Sweetie. Did you have a good day?"

"Just another day, Mom. But you look very nice. Did you have a hot date?"

"Yes, with the hottest and best looking man in Salt Lake. Is Lisa out?"

"Yes, she went out with Wendy to some stupid movie and I did not want to go. Who was the man?"

"Just you never mind. Have you seen Sam and Cas today, Laura?"

"No! Lisa said you did not want us seeing them. So, thank you very much!"

Miriam turned and stepped into the hall. She stopped and looked back and said, "I love you Sweetie." She softly closed the door and leaned against the door facing for a minute.

It was hard being a parent to adult children. It was hard being alone in her room when the one man that meant anything to her was in a motel a few miles away. Very hard!

15

Nancy Freeman was at yet another Christmas party with Dr. Carter. The various department heads and alumni of the school at Montana State University loved parties and Dr. Carter loved them too. Most of all, he loved walking around with Nancy Freeman by his side.

Dr. Carter was used to fine parties in Newport, Rhode Island and used to fine wines and champagne. Fine bourbon was also on his list. More and more Nancy had become uncomfortable with his drinking. While she liked a beer once in a while, especially on a hot day on the river, she never drank a lot and had stayed away from the crowd that did. And, tonight his drinking seemed worse than ever.

"Steve, you have had a lot to drink. Maybe we should think about letting me drive you home."

Dr. Carter was also not used to having anyone question his drinking and did not respond well to being told to stop. So, with the suggestion that he'd had too much, he walked in and ordered another drink from the cash bar. He turned and held it up in Nancy's direction as if to toast her with the drink. That was about all Nancy could take for the evening.

Dr. Carter was normally very nice, charming and witty. He was old money and did not mind letting everyone know it in one way or the other. Most women in town would have done anything to be in Nancy's shoes with such a prize catch chasing her around. But looking at him across the room tonight, just a few days before Christmas, made her sad. She did not feel like someone to be envied.

In spite of everything, she never got the tingle in her neck, the lump in her throat, or the skip in her heart when Steve Carter walked in as she did when Russell Baker came in the room. And yet, Russell Baker could just be so nice that he was totally exasperating! And she had no idea where Russell Baker was tonight.

She walked across the room to where Steve Carter was making some joke to one of his group of colleagues and quietly put her arm around him. "Come on, Steve, I'm ready to go. Give me the keys and I'll drive you to your house."

"I'll drive me to my house when I get ready to go. I am taking you home with me tonight and you might not get home for days!" he said in a booming voice that embarrassed Nancy. He swung his arm around the room as if to show he was talking to everyone and said loudly, "Look at the most beautiful woman in Gallatin County and she is here with me! I love this woman and I am going to marry her!"

Some of the crowd cheered and clapped and Nancy was very embarrassed and angry for being the center of attention in this fashion. Without making a fuss, she walked to the coat room and got her coat and bag and took out her phone. She was shaking she was so angry and hurt. She wanted to call a cab but could not stop shaking long enough to think about how to get one. She'd never called a cab in her life in Bozeman, Montana. She scrolled to Chad's number and hit the call button.

Chad was snuggled up with his wife asleep when the phone rang. "Nancy, do you know what time it is? What do you want?"

"I'm out at Belgrade on Dry Creek Road at Dean Merritt's house. I need you to come get me. Now, please!"

Not since high school had Nancy ever called him to come get her. He knew she must be desperate.

"Is that the place someone just rebuilt out there, Nancy?"

"Yes."

"I know where it is, I have been out that way. I'll be there in about ten to fifteen minutes."

"I'll be on the front porch."

Chad was there in ten minutes and Nancy was on the porch. As she started down the steps, Dr. Carter came out on the porch and grabbed Nancy by the arm and she almost fell down the steps trying to get away. Chad was out of the car and up the steps before Nancy could stop him and before Dr. Carter knew what was happening he was being slammed up against the wall of the house.

"I don't know what is going on here, but it will be a big mistake on your part to try that again!" Chad said firmly.

"I'm sorry. I'm sorry," was all the drunken professor could say.

Nancy was tugging on Chad's arm, "Let's just get out of here Chad before there is a big messy scene."

They made it to the car and left without anyone inside noticing. Chad drove Nancy home and walked her to the front door.

"Are you okay, Nancy? Do you want me to come in and have a cup of coffee with you or let you cry on my shoulder?"

Nancy opened the front door and then she turned and gave her brother the biggest hug he'd ever had and kissed him on the cheek. "You are the best brother anyone ever had. I'm sorry I yelled at you the other day. Thank you for coming to get me."

"That's what I'm here for."

She looked at him and cocked her head and asked somewhat amused, "Here to come get me when my date gets drunk or here to be yelled at?"

"Both I guess," he said with a wave of the hand as he walked to the car. "I have to get home before my spot in the bed gets cold."

Nancy went in and laid down on the bed in her beautiful cocktail dress. "Nothing like this would ever happen with Russell Baker," she thought. And then she went to sleep.

Russell got a call at 7:30 AM and it was Detective Taylor. "My budget will allow a coffee and donut at Dunkin Donuts just down a couple of streets from your motel. Are you game?"

"Well, I am a Krispy Kreme man myself. But tell you what; if you come by here they have a good restaurant downstairs and I have a big budget so I'll buy you breakfast and even throw in the coffee."

"I'm on the way. I'll see you in ten minutes," she said.

As they waited on their breakfast she asked, "What do you want to do today, Officer Baker? Any ideas?"

"I was trying to think last night what I would do if I were these guys and had what might be a hot car or at least one with questionable papers. Would I drive it out of town? Or, would I park it somewhere it would not stand out, at least for a while."

"What did you decide?" she asked as she took a bite of her sausage.

"I did not decide anything. I just asked myself the questions. What would you do?"

"Dump the car at a place easy to get to and get out of town. A hospital parking garage would be good. People often come and stay for several days in one of those. An office building parking deck would be good. People are often in them 24/7. The long term parking at the airport would be excellent. People leave cars there for weeks, sometimes."

"Then, there are farms and barns and sheds and woods," said Russ.

"How long do you have to look, Officer Baker?"

"I have as long as it takes. I am not too concerned about the students and their car, one way of the other. But, if they are involved in the shooting of Sheriff Barry Steinbrenner, I will do my best to find them and bring them in. I've sort of made it my mission."

Detective Debra Taylor was use to macho talking cops and men, in general. She liked men fine. But she had learned to filter out a lot of the BS, as she called it, and not get too immersed in it when she was around them on the job or at a bar. She did not mind a little sweet talk if a free meal and a show or concert or a long weekend at Park City was involved.

Somehow, listening to Russell Baker, she did not detect the usual macho sound. She was glad that she was working with him and was not on his suspect list.

"So you don't work full time as a cop any more, Officer Baker?"

"No. I do some part time work guiding trout fishermen around Bozeman."

'Man, I wish I could get away with that. Are you independently wealthy or something?"

With a smile he said, "I have enough to manage to get by. I wouldn't call it wealthy."

Detective Taylor had risen through the ranks quickly by being able to cut through the gender issues and the BS. She knew that last comment from Russell Baker might have been the first BS she had heard from him. Russell Baker was doing alright, she suspected!

"I went fly fishing a few times. My dad was really into it for a couple of years. He took us to the Green River in some place; I think it was Dutch John, Utah. There is nothing in Dutch John, Utah unless you fish but it was a beautiful river. And we went to the Provo one time. Then, he took up golf."

"Those are both beautiful places and I have been to both," said Russ.

"Let's go check some parking decks," she said.

As the day came and went, they saw a lot of cars and parking decks and a BOLO was in place in and around Salt Lake and all of Utah for the silver Ford Edge with Utah plates. They also had the Pennsylvania plate numbers, just in case. No car. No students. More frustration.

Detective Taylor dropped off Russ at the hotel and left saying she had some paper work to do at the office. They would meet there in the morning to see where they were in the investigation.

When she arrived at the office she sat down at her computer and tried to see what she could find out about the fishing guide/detective she was working with from Marietta, Georgia and Ennis/Virginia City/Bozeman, Montana. She found plenty! She was working with a bona fide hero who had been in shootouts and had brought down some big time crooks. All while working part time! The Bozeman papers had story after story. Fishing guide, indeed!

Miriam got home and had hoped Russ would call but she knew he was busy. Lisa and Laura were in the kitchen making some sandwiches and Laura looked at Miriam with a look of fierce anger.

"I hope you are happy, Mother! Cas and Sam won't return our calls and they aren't coming to see us. They aren't coming to the student center and they are not at the dorm! What did you do to them?"

Miriam was taken back by the verbal barrage. "I have not done anything to them. I have not spoken to them or seen them. Do you know any reason for them to be avoiding you and not returning your calls?"

Lisa looked at Laura with her hands on her hips waiting for Laura to reply. "Are you going to tell her, Laura, or do I have to?" she asked. Laura turned and looked away and could not bring herself to tell her mom what she had done.

"Tell me what? What did you do Laura?"

"I told them the law was after them about the car tags or some such trivial deal. It's not like they are major criminals! You just never liked them!"

"Oh, my God, Laura! How could you do that? I told you that to protect you and you have now aided men, who are possibly involved in the attempted murder of a law officer, to elude being brought in for questioning! This is not a trivial thing, Laura! Now I have betrayed Russ and you have betrayed me! How could you?"

"Attempted Murder! Mother you never said anything about them being wanted for attempted murder!" Lisa chimed in.

"They would never hurt anyone!" screamed Laura.

"They may be fine, but Russ and the Salt Lake police need to talk to them and see if they had anything to do with the shooting of Sheriff Barry Steinbrenner or any knowledge of the events. This is terrible. Now they have sanitized their dorm room and left without a trace."

Laura ran out of the kitchen and went to her room and slammed the door in tears. Lisa stood speechless and

Miriam sat down at the table with her head in her hands. How could she tell Russ?

Russ had taken a shower and turned on the TV in his room. He sat down in the chair, feeling really very tired. A good night's sleep would help. But, he was seriously reconsidering the wisdom of accepting the task of finding the people that had shot Barry. He just might have reached the dead end that everyone talks about. Maybe he should be in Marietta and working for the Cobb County Police Department where he belonged.

But, where did he belong? That was a nagging question that he went to sleep thinking about and was still unanswered every morning when he woke up. He was in Cobb County but did not have that sense of belonging after Sarah died. He had thought Nancy Freeman was the answer for a while and he truly cared for her but not enough to make any sort of long term commitment and neither would she.

Their relationship was like the old pair of jeans that a person always seemed to wear but had to take off to go to the mall or a movie or a restaurant. They just did not seem to be right for all occasions.

Miriam Alexander was steady, pretty and he knew she cared about him. But she had tried to do what she thought was right and moved away. Now she was back in his life. At least, she was out on the edges and she wanted more, he could tell.

The young attractive Sergeant Taylor seemed to be giving off vibes. But maybe he just had too high of an opinion about his sex appeal and charm. Maybe it was his ego all along.

At some point, he had to get on solid ground and let nature take its course. Sarah was gone and not coming back and she would surely approve of him being happy and in love. Not miserable and alone in some motel room in Salt Lake City feeling sorry for himself, again! He thought he had gotten over all that!

Then the phone rang.

"Hi, Miriam. I was about to call you." Another white lie but who would know?

"Russ, can you come to my house? I have to talk to you. Something awful has happened."

"What is it Miriam? Has something happened to the girls?"

"Can you come, Russ?"

"Certainly. I will be there in fifteen minutes."

He had been brought out of his state of remorse and he was now running on adrenaline. He knew something had Miriam upset and she was hard to get upset. She was normally rock steady.

She met him at the door and they went into the kitchen where her daughters were sitting at the table. They would not look at Russ and they had been crying and Russ could feel the tension in the room.

"Russ, we have done something awful. We are all guilty."

Russ sat and waited for her to continue but Laura interrupted: "Mother did not do anything except try to protect Lisa and me. It's all my fault. I told Cas and Sam that you were looking for them and that's why they left. I thought they were being singled out because of where they came from."

Russ felt like he was punched in the stomach. He leaned back in his chair and looked up at the ceiling. This explained why the boys left so suddenly. The people they were closest to had sounded an alarm and those same people were very close and involved with the police. It was like flashing lights and sirens.

"Russ, what should we do at this point? Are the girls in any legal trouble?" asked Miriam.

"Laura, what did they say when you told them?" Russ asked.

141

"They just looked at one another and said they knew there was a problem with the paperwork on the car and they would go and get it straightened out the next day. It was like it was no big deal. I told them mother was afraid we'd get caught up in something if they got pulled over and we had to stop being with them until it was fixed. They left and all seemed fine."

"The next day we could not get them on the phone and they did not come to the student center. We went by the dorm, although mother had told us not to, and they were not there. We could not go up to their room on our own unless we were accompanied by one of them. So we didn't know they had moved out that day."

"Do either of you know where they might have left the car?" Russ asked. He was now back into detective mode.

"No."

"Do you have any idea about what the tag number was on the other car? The Toyota Camry."

"No."

"Do you know anyone they hung out with other than you two and the people at the student center?"

"I never saw them other than when they were with the two of us or there at the Student Center. I never saw them out with anyone else, did you Lisa?"

"No," she answered.

"If you should hear from them, it is critical that you do not let them know there is any problem. They probably already know and if they are in any way involved with what happened in Ennis, they have gone aground. I will meet with Salt Lake Police in the morning and see if they will help get Homeland Security and the FBI involved. I need the numbers for the phones they have been using, also, although they have probably ditched them."

"The phones they used when we were in Ennis were not their regular phones, Russ. They claimed they had phone problems and had to get their phones fixed so they had throwaway phones while they were there." Lisa added.

"That's another sign that they may have been up to something. By itself it would not mean much, but there are too many coincidences popping up now." Russ said.

"Russ, we are so sorry. We know we screwed up. Please don't hold mother accountable."

"What will you do now, Russ?" asked Miriam.

"I don't know but it seems clear they have something to hide. Maybe several somethings. We shook the tree and a lot of stuff started falling out. I will have to regroup in the morning and the Salt Lake Police may want to interview the girls. I will let you know in the morning."

Russ touched Miriam softly on the shoulder and left. There was a heavy cloud in the room over the girls and their mother. It would be a while clearing. There had always been trust and respect in addition to the love although that was sometimes hidden under growing pains. There would have to be some rebuilding.

Miriam walked out of the kitchen and went to her room and closed the door. When someone tapped softly later and called, "Mom," she did not answer, preferring to pretend to be asleep.

14

Russ drove back to the hotel and was in an unusual state of mind. He was angry, hurt, sad and frustrated. Frustrated, again. The one person he had been able to rely on and her daughters had just caused him to lose the only possible lead he had, and it wasn't much. Then, his phone rang and it said *Chad Freeman* on the screen.

"Hello, Chad. What's up?"

"I was just checking in with you, Russ. I thought I would see if you wanted to eat hot dogs with me and my wife tomorrow."

"A Betty's hot dog sounds real good right now, Chad, but I'm in Salt Lake City and may be here another day or two, I don't know."

"Oh, I see. Is this business or pleasure?" Russ knew he was fishing and not with a five weight rod.

"There hasn't been any pleasure so far, Chad. And I just got kicked in the groin, figuratively speaking. I am out doing some follow-up on Barry's shooting. But, you didn't call me about hot dogs, did you?"

"You are a good detective, Russ. You're right. I wanted to tell you, in case you are interested, I had to go and pick up Nancy at a big party she was at with the Dr. Carter. He was drunk and she wanted to go home. He was being an ass and I went out and got her. She would not want me telling you this, of course."

"Did you do anything that might cause you to get arrested when you got there, Chad?"

"Naw. When I grabbed him and slammed him up against the wall of the porch, I think his educated mind told him it was best not try anything. He was too drunk to be too scary."

"Well, when I get back I'll give Nancy a call and see where it goes, Chad. I think you'd make some girl a good big brother," Russ quipped.

"I have one sister and that's enough. I want to marry her off to some real nice guy that will take her somewhere and drive her home sober. If you see anyone, let me know."

"Chad, there aren't many nice guys left." The call ended.

"Man, oh, Man," thought Russ. "If it's not one thing it's another."

Russ was pacing the motel room floor trying to figure out what would be his next move and a few miles from the home he rented in Ennis, Montana two young men he had met and knew as Kasim Rahmani and Samer Mustafa were having their pictures made. They would travel on the dark web to a lab in a shop in Nigeria and in a few days, two new US passports would arrive by US mail. They would be undetectable from the real ones, holograms and all. Then, Abdul samad Arazi and Manzur Najafi, their real names, would be free to travel under the next new names that they would be given. They had sworn allegiance to the group and were committed to bringing the infidels to their knees for the evil that had been done in their world. One sheriff here and there that was sacrificed for that holy and noble purpose was just part of the deal. Theirs was a holy war. One in which they would soon be prepared to carry out anywhere in the world.

Morning rolled around and Detective Debra Taylor had her team assembled in the small interview room she had been assigned. In her hand were some copies of the news articles from Bozeman, Montana telling about how a major crime ring had been brought down, a state agent shot and a murderer killed in a shootout with a Madison County Montana cop outside a motel room.

The pictures showed the guy they had met with in this same room a couple of days before and his name was Russell Baker. And then someone stuck their head in and said, "Someone named Russell Baker is here to see you Detective Taylor." He was right on time.

"I'll come get him," she said.

Russ outlined the situation with the two young ladies, Lisa and Laura Alexander, who had become infatuated with the two handsome and somewhat mysterious Middle Eastern men. He explained their blunder by alerting the men of the interest that Madison County, Montana and Salt Lake City had in them. Russell gave them what he had learned from the girls the night before which was really nothing but the information on the phones seemed to add more intrigue to the situation. Now, finding the men and/or the car was crucial. And still there was nothing linking them to Barry Steinbrenner's attack.

"Where to now, Detective Taylor?" asked Russ.

"I thought we might try the airport lots today, if that works with you," she replied.

"Good as any," he answered.

As they drove she asked, "You said your wife had passed away. I guess that was a very tough time."

"Just about did me in. I quit my job and sold everything and moved to Bozeman. Her parents are great and they are very much family now and they are all I have. My parents are gone."

"No serious girlfriend back there in Bozeman?"

Russ thought she was getting a little too personal, but he let it go. "Not at this time," he answered. The truth was he did not know anymore.

"How about you, Detective, are you married or anything?" Russ asked as he played the twenty questions game with her.

"I can't seem to hold on to a man very long. The work gets in the way and sometimes the hours. And some guys are a little intimidated by a girlfriend with a gun."

Russ nodded in agreement as she drove and he looked at her as the light came through the car window behind her. She was an attractive woman but worked at minimizing her attractiveness. No makeup, no lipstick or eyeshadow. She seemed to be making an effort to insure that she was treated as any other detective and not seen as making it on her female good looks.

They had to enter each airport parking lot and work their way through and they came across a number of the Ford Edge models but they dismissed them as they computer checked the license numbers and Russ and the detective checked the VIN labels against the tags and all checked out. More frustration. Then lunch.

After lunch, as they were walking to the car, Detective Taylor got a call to a hostage situation. "I have to go on this call to assist in hostage negotiations. Do you want to ride along or get your own way home? It may be a while."

"I'll get a cab from here to the hotel. I don't want to be in your way. Why don't we meet in the morning and regroup?" he said as he turned to leave her at the car.

"Sounds fine," she said. She was gone with lights flashing and sirens blaring.

Miriam was at her office when Russ called. "How are you and the girls today, Miriam?"

"The girls are scared and mad and hurt. Hurt because they feel let down by the boys. Let down by me. They are scared because they got a call from the police and they are coming out to the house at 3:00 to question them."

"Well, that is a courtesy doing it at your house. They could have requested the interviews at their office. They don't have to allow you to be present, you know. The girls are not minors," Russ stated.

"I know. And Russ, I am so sorry that we let you and Barry down. I was only trying to keep the girls safe and keep them out of harm's way." She was sobbing into the phone. "You don't think they will charge the girls with anything, do you?"

"They don't have anyone charged and we don't know what crimes have been committed by the boys, yet. Just a lot of suspicions. Their cooperation today will probably get them off the hook. But, you can't let this cause a big rift in your family. They probably won't be too hard on them. I think its best I'm not there."

"I agree, Russ. I want to spend some time with them tonight, if they will agree, and see if we can put this behind us as a family. Would you like to come over later?"

"Let's wait until tomorrow and see how things go tonight. No need in me adding any stress. Okay, Miriam?"

"I'll see you tomorrow, Russ. Good night." Miriam really wanted to grab Russ and hold him and be with him but she knew she had another role to play tonight. Mother.

Russ turned on his laptop in his room and went to Google Earth and looked at satellite shots of the Salt Lake area. Where would you park a car in a hurry in Salt Lake City, Utah to hide it and get out of town unnoticed? A place where a car could be in plain view and no one would think it out of place?

There was the possibility it was stashed somewhere. Someone's garage, for example. There was no way to search every house in the area. A warehouse maybe? A garage? A barn somewhere nearby? Many possibilities. Much frustration.

He needed to call Deputy Wayne Dunkin and give him an update and check on Barry's progress. Hopefully there had been some.

"Hello, Russ. Barry has made some improvement. He is able to sit up in bed and he is talking better but he still hasn't shed any light on the people who shot him. He does believe that the shot came from the left rear window of the car."

Russ filled him in on what he had found so far. "Wayne, if the shot came from the left rear window that would seem to suggest that there were other people in the car. Maybe a person or persons in the back seat in addition to whoever was in the front seat. Do you agree?"

"Not likely that a person is riding in the back seat if there are only two people but he or she could have been sleeping. That would seem unlikely under the severe driving conditions," he said to Russ.

"I'll meet with the folks here in the morning and see where we are. It may be that I should just come on back. If they feel we are at a dead end at the moment, I'll be on a plane day after tomorrow."

Since Russ was in the calling mode, he scrolled to Nancy Freeman's number and touched the call button. It hadn't been too long since they had their blow up on the phone but Chad's call seemed to suggest there were changes in the wind regarding her dating Dr. Carter.

"Hello, Russ." Nancy's greeting when she answered the call was cool and business like. But, at least she answered.

"Hello, Nancy. I hope all is well with you. I didn't want to leave things the way they were after our last conversation. I was out of line and I want to apologize. I want us to be friends."

Nancy hesitated before answering. "He wants to be friends," she thought. "Friends!"

"I think we can be *friends*," Russ. "Would you like to grab a coffee somewhere or maybe lunch tomorrow?"

"I am in Salt Lake right now, Nancy. I won't be back until day after tomorrow at the earliest. I'll call you then."

"Okay, Russ. *You do that.*" Again her voice sounded cold and business like. "*Good bye.*"

A thought was racing through Nancy's head: "He's in Salt Lake with that woman Miriam and calling me wanting to be friends. That's just super!"

Then she called her brother.

Chad answered, "Hi, Nancy."

"Your friend Russ just called me."

She could not see Chad giving a fist pump and mouthing to his wife who was nearby a big All *Right*!

"He called and wants to be friends and he's out in Salt Lake City visiting that woman Miriam. Can you believe that?"

"Sounds good to me, Nancy. He may be visiting that woman Miriam, I don't know, but I did hear he is in Salt Lake working with the Salt Lake police on trying to solve the Barry Steinbrenner case. That's why he is in Salt Lake."

"Who told you he was in Salt Lake? Did he tell you? Have you talked to him?"

Chad did not want to lie and hesitated a moment before answering. That was all Nancy needed.

"You called him and told him about having to come get me, didn't you! I hate you! Again!" and she shut the call off.

Chad looked at his wife, shrugged, and said, "Nancy hates me again." They both burst out laughing.

A few miles away there was no laughing. There were prayers five times a day in the gym and training on the gun range with hand guns and AK-47's. There was video training on how to fabricate homemade bombs from household products being streamed from the dark web in places known as .onion domains and using search engines like Tor, Shodan, Wired and other not widely known names.

There was the I2P2 area, also in the dark web and places called .i2p. These systems use random paths to the server they are looking for and utilize many individual computers along the way, hop scotching from place to place and making tracing the user and the source almost impossible. And if someone happens upon them the encryption further protects them from interpretation and discovery.

Some experts have said the typical internet users see only about ten percent of what is on the overall internet when using the World Wide Web interface. The Russians and the Middle Easterners and the drug cartels and the child porn participants are all crawling around in that space. And, more. Planning, plotting, and executing their destructive plans and sending out their messages of death.

The two young men from Salt Lake were good students and would serve the cause well.

Nabil Mussan, the gunman who had actually shot Barry and Mahdi Shamah, were the two men who had been brought to the ranch by Cas and Sam and were still somewhere on the ranch waiting for their forged passports and other papers so they could be relocated to a city somewhere in the eastern US. Cas and Sam had not been told where that was. They believed that the two men were from Egypt but that may not have been their country of birth.

They had arrived in Panama on a container ship and eventually crossed under the Mexico/US border, through a tunnel 2756 miles to the north of Panama, for a fee, blindfolded and at the mercy of drug dealers who picked up extra money by smuggling anyone from anywhere into the US. Terrorists were just paying customers to them.

But the two young men who were students at a fine school in Salt Lake City just a few days back knew the two men they had brought with them were capable of just about anything. They had seen how calmly that Mussan had shot the sheriff out on the highway. They hoped they could become just like him.

Russ was thinking about going down to the hotel's restaurant or maybe ordering room service. Between Miriam and her daughters and Nancy and her cool reaction to his call, he was feeling a little forgotten. He and Sarah had been a perfect match and there was never any drama in their relationship. Why couldn't life be that way again? Maybe it just couldn't.

Then, his phone rang and he hoped it was Miriam or Nancy. Anyone with a smile in their voice would be welcome right about now. And he heard it on the other end but it was not Miriam and it was not Nancy.

"Russell, this is Debra Taylor. Detective Taylor. I hope I'm not calling at a bad time but I still have that small expense account and I have not had dinner and lunch was a long time ago. I think we should have dinner, if you haven't already, and discuss the case with a nice glass of wine. What do you say?"

Russ started to say no but then, "Sure. Sounds great and I have not eaten. I was about to call down for room service. I guess you got the hostage out safely?"

"Yeah. It was a domestic deal. Wife and husband getting a divorce kinda thing. I'll pick you up in the lobby in fifteen minutes."

Russ felt somewhat awkward about accepting the invite but it would have been awkward to have declined when he would be working with her the next day. Besides, no one had made any commitments to anyone and right now he did not know who that would be if he did.

Russ stood inside the lobby door waiting for the police car that he had been in earlier in the day to pull up. As he was waiting a BMW pulled up and tooted the horn and as he looked he could see Detective Debra Taylor waving for him to come and get in.

He opened the door and greeted Debra, "Good evening. Nice wheels you have."

There was a hesitation as he tried to speak because the woman driving the car did not look much like the dressed down cop he had been with the past couple of days. She was in a nice cocktail dress with her hair down and a look like she had just had a professional makeover at a spa. Gorgeous, was the word that came to mind.

"Well, I have to have a little fun out of life, you know. That police car, I've found, kinda turns men off."

"I know about that. Well, not turning the men off, but I know what you mean."

She tossed her head back with a little laugh and gunned the BMW out into the street. The Six Series Coupe was an expensive car in the high 70's and was nice inside. Not what you would expect for a cop's salary.

"And, no Russell, before you ask, I can't afford this car but my dad can and he gave it to me for my birthday this year. I started to give it back and after thinking about it for about five seconds I decided to keep it." Debra did the little move again with throwing her hair back and doing the little laugh.

They drove to the Salt Lake City Country Club where Debra pulled up and a valet took the car. Russ thought it odd but the valet said, "Good evening, Ms. Taylor."

"Good evening, Billy."

Debra Taylor was on a first name basis with the valet at the oldest country club in Salt Lake City. This was turning out to be one strange evening.

As they entered the restaurant, the hostess met them. "We have your table ready, Ms. Taylor. By the way, your father is here with some clients, I believe."

"Please don't put us close to them, Michele."

"I have you in a nice place by the window and the best golf course view in the world. Well, maybe next to Pebble Beach."

"So, Debra, when you said your dad took up golf, this is where he came to play, I take it," Russ inquired.

"Well, he grew up here and his father and grandfather played here. A family tradition, I guess you would say."

"I guess you know what my next question is, Debra?"

"Sure. Everyone asks it. Why in the world am I a cop? Right?" she asked.

"You *are* a good detective, Debra."

"It's simple. When you can afford to do anything in the world you want to do, why not do what you really want to do?" Debra said.

Russ looked out across the golf course and into space as he pondered that question. And he realized that was exactly what he was doing in his life right now.

And she seemed to read his mind as she asked, "Maybe that's what you are doing, too, Russell. Am I right?" What did she know about him, he wondered?

He looked at the beautiful lady with the beautiful smile sitting across from him and nodded, "Could be."

A slender and handsome gray haired man walked over in a very expensive suit and Debra said, "Hello, Dad. This is Detective Russell Baker from Marietta, Georgia who currently resides in Ennis, Montana."

Russell stood and exchanged greetings with her father and then Debra said, "Say good night, Dad."

Her father smiled and gave a wave and turned and as he walked off he said, "Good Night."

"I have to be nice to him. I'm putting our dinner on his member number." She laughed again. "Let's order a wine and we'll order our meal and step out on the patio while we are waiting. I love it out at the pool but it's closed for the season."

Detective Debra Taylor was use to the finer things and finer places in life and it showed. Russ found himself very comfortable in her presence.

After dinner, she drove Russ back to the hotel and pulled under the canopy.

"I'll see you in the morning, Russell. I had a nice evening and I'm glad you went to dinner with me."

"I enjoyed it, too, Debra. What a nice place and you were nice to ask me. Next time, I pay."

"Next time?" she asked. "You think there will be a next time?"

"Well, it seemed like the right thing to say. A next time would be fine with me. I guess we'll have to see, won't we? Good Night, Debra. I'll be there at 8:00."

He stood as she accelerated the big Beemer out of the hotel drive and on to the street and in a few seconds she was gone. He stood for another minute and for just a while that evening he had forgotten about Miriam, Nancy, Barry and, perhaps, Sarah. It was a strange feeling that way when the lady he was with he had only known for a couple of days. Strange, indeed. But, then, in another day he would be gone and back to the real world that did not include include the Salt Lake City Country Club and $78,000 BMW's.

The real world reality started at 8:00 AM and Russ was walking in to the room where the group was gathered. The two detectives that had interviewed Miriam's daughters, as well as Miriam, the night before were also there. As was the chief detective.

Russ took quick notice of Detective Debra Taylor, the beautiful socialite that he was out with for dinner the night before. She had her hair pinned back up and had her dress down thing going. No one would recognize her as the same person.

They said good morning and neither gave any indication they had been together the evening before. But, by any standard, their *date* was very benign and non-threatening, It could have been viewed as a romantic evening by the casual observer but it could just as easily been seen as a business meeting. Russ enjoyed being with her but there had been nothing beyond casual in their time together.

Russ had wondered if she had expected him to be more forward but she came and went and left him standing under the hotel passage way just where she found him. Not even a handshake.

The interview of the Alexander girls had not turned up anything new and the detectives came away feeling the girls were naïve and idealistic but had no malice when they told the boys about the investigation into their car registration. Miriam had a stellar reputation with the Sheriff's office and now the Unified Police Department.

Conclusion: nothing learned and they were no further in the investigation.

The chief detective spoke up: "Detective Baker, as badly as I hate to say it, I think we have spent all the time on this we can with no more than we have to go on. We will give you our full assistance today and we will keep the BOLO out on the car and the two men, but I suspect if you find them, they will be in Los Angeles or New York or some big place where they won't be noticed at all."

"I understand and we appreciate your help in this. We were asking a lot with no real case and no real suspects but we thought it was worth a shot. Maybe someone will come forward that knows something, but I am not counting on that."

"I will be returning to Montana in the morning. If we turn up any new leads, I will contact you if there is any way that you can help. The car and the title are only part of a much bigger situation in my view and there may be a real case here yet. Thank you all," Russ concluded.

"Detective, please contact Detective Taylor as she is the lead investigator assigned to the case. We'll treat it as an open case. Maybe you will turn up something today." He smiled and shook Russ's hand and left.

Russ knew from experience this case was over in Salt Lake and they were not likely to be doing anything else on it but the little speech sounded politically correct. It was not seen as a case that would make anyone a hero or further their careers.

Detective Taylor picked up her stack of papers and put them in her briefcase, looked at Russ with a smile and said, "Detective Baker, shall we go and beat this dead horse one more time?"

"Sure, Detective Taylor, and, lunch will be on me today but not at the Salt Lake Country Club. I seem to have misplaced my member number."

"I always have Daddy's number, Officer Baker, and we can go out there anytime. Daddy can put your name in for membership if you move here."

Russ liked the way she said *anytime* but wasn't sure there was any special connotation in the manner in which she said it. Then she repeated, *"Anytime at all."*

They got into her unmarked police cruiser and she said, "Where to, Officer?"

Russ said, "I was looking at Google Earth satellite views last night and something occurred to me. I would like to go back to school today if you don't mind."

"You want to go back to Westminster, Russ? We covered that pretty well, I believe."

"No. I want to go to the University of Utah. There are an awful lot of cars there with over 30,000 students coming and going. No one would notice one car sitting there unless it was in someone else's spot. If they got a visitor spot somewhere, they might have been able to dump it and be gone in a few minutes. I think it's worth a shot. You may know your way around out there."

"As a matter of fact, I do. I went to school there. We are on our way," she said,

Debra Taylor did know her way around and taking out the city street guide book she showed Russ where some lots were and they could work them in succession, "It will be difficult to get to all of them but I will get the patrol officers to come and we can get school security involved. Maybe we can catch a break."

So far there had been no further mention of the dinner at the Club and their discussion was all business. Russ assumed there probably would not be any more. Detective Taylor had been a good host to an out of town, small town, cop and that was it.

A patrol car called Detective Taylor's Unit number. She acknowledged.

"Detective, we are at the Union Building parking lot on Central Campus Drive. This is across from the pharmacy. We have your vehicle of interest here in the visitor parking lot."

She gave a thumbs-up to Russ and they headed in that direction.

"Great job, officer. Please tape that off and we'll be there in a couple of minutes to decide how to proceed with processing." She then called her boss. They were back in business, at least for the moment.

"Russ, do you think there is any chance this car is booby trapped?"

"It would not hurt to have a check on it before we start trying to open it up, assuming it's locked. Probably overkill, but who knows."

She called the patrol officer and said, "Be advised. We will treat this as a possible booby trapped car to be on the safe side. Secure the area and we will get the bomb squad out here and the dogs."

"Well, Russ. It wasn't such a wild goose chase after all."

"Debra, it sounds like we found the goose. Let's hope it lays a golden egg!"

The rich girl turned detective, Debra Taylor, was beginning to like the trout fisherman detective Russell Baker more and more.

When they pulled in the campus police and two squad cars were on the scene and the bomb squad was on the way. One of the campus police was asking a lot of questions about jurisdiction and who had authorized the blocking off of the parking lot and putting up tape limiting access. He was trying to convince the patrol officer he was in charge.

Debra Taylor and Russell Baker approached them and the patrol officer said that the school security officer was saying the city did not have jurisdiction. He sounded like he knew what he was talking about.

Debra Taylor looked at him and said, "*I am* the officer in charge here. I have a possible homicide investigation, a possible terrorist and a possible car bomb. This is a crime scene as of now. We have the bomb squad on the way. I would suggest that you go and reroute the traffic so we blow up as few civilians as possible. If you want to observe, feel free. But, if you interfere with me and the other officers on scene, you will be arrested. Understood?"

"Yes, ma'am," was the reply as he hurried off to direct traffic.

"I do not like BS," she said. Russ was beginning to like the rich girl turned cop more and more.

"I think he probably figured that out," said Russ.

It wasn't but a few minutes before there were crime scene investigators, bomb sniffing dogs and men who looked like they were wearing space suits or a Pillsbury doughboy outfit. Over eighty five pounds of armor plates and aramid based materials all designed to provide a bomb disposal team member with some manner of protection in the event of a bomb blast while removing and disarming an explosive device. With all the technology and Kevlar combined, a large bomb would still likely kill the wearer.

A special truck showed up with a round explosion containment vessel with two inch thick walls and weighing about five thousand pounds.

It would allow safe detonation of a bomb, if found, by remote control. And, it also carried a bomb disposal robot to move a bomb around and safely put it in the containment vessel.

After about an hour, the bomb squad decided that the vehicle was not booby trapped. Then there was a meeting to decide whether to try and process the car there are to move it to an inside facility and that became the conclusion. A rollback wrecker was used to carry the truck to a police garage facility and the work would begin first thing in the morning. First, the team would meet to see what they were looking for specifically and to be sure that in looking for one bit of evidence they did not corrupt or lose something else of importance.

Russ walked over to the side of the parking lot away from the crowd of officers and called Wayne Dunkin. "We found the car, Wayne. They plan to start processing it early in the morning."

"That's good news, Russ. I guess we'll know in a day or so if there are any leads to be had. There is nothing happening here and the State DCI has about put this case on ice. We are really on our own, now."

"I'll call you tomorrow and it looks like I may be here at least another day." Russ disconnected and called Miriam.

"Miriam, we found the boys' car."

"That's wonderful Russ. On the one hand I hope you get a lot of evidence from it and it helps you find Barry's shooter. For the girls and maybe me, too, down deep I hope it doesn't connect the boys to the crime. It will always be a big disappointment for the girls knowing that you can be so wrong about people."

"Would you like to get together tonight, Miriam? Maybe we could get a bite to eat somewhere simple and maybe a movie."

"Russ, what I would like, since the girls are here, is to come over to see you and order room service and maybe we could just watch a movie on television. Would that be alright with you?"

"It sounds fine to me, Miriam. Better than fine."

As Russ was hanging up, he walked back to where Detective Taylor was wrapping up with the crime scene leader. "We will get started in the morning at about 7:00 on the car, Russ. They will have someone in to get the doors open and then we will start going through everything. I would accept a dinner invitation, if someone were to invite me."

"I'm not available tonight, Debra. I already have plans. But that is nice of you."

"Is she pretty?" Debra asked as she playfully punched Russ on the arm.

"Very pretty." answered Russ. Debra was surprised by the answer and did not know if he was joking but decided not to ask.

It was a struggle to get going and be at the office by 7:00. Miriam kept tugging Russ back under the sheet every time he started to head to the shower. "If you don't let me go, Miriam, I will have to arrest you for interfering with an officer," as he kissed her on the forehead.

She thrust both arms out and remarked, "Go ahead and put the cuffs on me officer. I surrender."

15

When Russ got to the garage, the team was getting set up and got their first surprise: in an effort to preserve the integrity of the crime scene, which was the car, no one had tried to open the door at the school parking lot. To everyone's surprise it was not locked so no locksmith was need to get entry.

The team would first do a methodical search of the car by hand and visual means. Latex gloves, tweezers, little vials and zip lock type evidence bags would be used to keep hair samples, soils, trash of any kind, and every effort would be made to avoid any contamination of the scene.

A HEPA vacuum cleaner with extremely high filtration capability would be used to vacuum out the car, under the seats, consoles and floorboards, rear storage area and carpets in an effort to find anything that could be analyzed that might point them to people or places. Old fashion fingerprint detection and recording to associate suspects to the car would be used before any chemical tests were conducted which might interfere with other steps. High tech microscopes and spectrum analysis could be used on items found. But Russ was hoping for at least two things: some gunshot residue in the car (GSR) and one or more .40 cal. S&W cartridge hulls.

For many years GSR testing was a way that shooters could be identified and even small traces of the gun-powder residue were enough to get a confession and even a conviction. But time has shown that GSR is almost everywhere and easily transported from place to place.

Cops going to a shooting range may take some along and actually contaminate a crime scene accidently with his/her own GSR which cannot be determined as different from any other GSR. They all have traces of antimony, lead, barium, titanium, and zinc. Using nitric acid these traces could be identified using Atomic Absorption Analysis and todays electron microscopes.

But just having traces of the GSR is not enough, alone, to get convictions because the stuff is literally almost everywhere. Large concentrations in the order of 2000 particles of the key ingredients would be necessary to prove direct contact with a gun being fired. Small amounts, like 20 particles, can easily be attributed to contamination. These particles are not gun specific and do not point to a single gun or cartridge.

A spent cartridge hull, or shell, is gun specific. The gun has to be the same caliber as the shell and vice versa. The chamber of each gun usually has some unique structural features that can mark the shell and then be matched up to a certain weapon at a later date. So in Barry's case, they had three bullets taken from him during surgery that could be matched to a specific gun through ballistics if they could find the gun and the shells could also be matched to the gun. All of these together could build a case against a person who could then be con-nected with the car and who might be in possession of the gun or whose fingerprints might be on the gun. Jig saw pieces that could be fit together by trained forensics investigators and detectives: if all the pieces could be found.

As soon as the team opened the door they knew they had a problem. The musty smell and the still damp carpets told them.

"Detective Taylor," one of the investigators said, "it appears the car has been thoroughly scrubbed."

Not a speck of anything was left and there wasn't anything obvious to be found at the garage. The boys, or someone, had wiped the inside with Armor All. There was the unmistakable feel of the cleaner and lubricant.

The forensics team went over the car from top to bottom. When they finished their work and knocked off for the day, the lab personnel would run various tests overnight and they could meet the next morning to compare notes and decide the next steps. So far, there was nothing to go on.

This would probably be the last chance for Debra to have dinner with Russ before he went back to Montana and Russ was hoping that Debra would drop the subject. He had spent the night with Miriam last night and going out with Debra might be awkward. He had never been one to bar hop and take a different girl to bed every night. He did not want to hurt Miriam by careless behavior, especially with someone she might have to work with some day.

As if she sensed how Russ was feeling Debra said, "Russ there is a Subway a few blocks down by I-15. I was going to stop in there and get a quick sandwich and go home. I am tired out. If you want to join me, you'd be welcome."

"Debra, if you don't mind I want to get to the motel and prop my feet up for the rest of the evening. I'll see you here in the morning and I will probably catch a flight out tomorrow evening unless there is some startling discovery." There it was again: frustration.

Debra Taylor was not accustomed to men turning down any offer she might make. But here was Russell Baker driving off and leaving her at her car to go home and prop his feet up. He might be a one of a kind.

On the way to the hotel, Miriam called. "I am in the neighborhood. Want to grab a burger somewhere close?" Russ was glad he had said no to Debra. This could have been awkward!

"I would really like a good hot dog. Is there a place we can get a good hot dog this side of the Varsity in Atlanta or Brandi's in Marietta? And don't tell me Pink's in LA."

"Well there is Red Hots but I believe the one close by closes in the evening. We can go to Wienershnitzel. That's a good place. Lots of onions, if you want them."

"Maybe I'll leave off the onions. You gonna pick me up at the hotel?"

"Pulling in now," she said.

Miriam was in a better mood and looked as great as she ever had. Far better than a dinner at the hot dog place, but that was Miriam. She was always easy to get along with.

The hot dog place reminded Russ of the old IHop that was once in Buckhead in Atlanta. It was not too elaborate and showing some wear and tear. But what they lacked in décor, they made up for in food! They said they were the biggest hot dog chain in the world.

Maybe so, Russ thought, but the Varsity would give them a race in the number of hotdogs sold in a year, he would bet on that. Brandi's in Marietta was small but they did all the business their place could get in and out every day. Get there early if you wanted a seat!

Russ woke up early and looked at the sleeping Miriam who had spent the last night they would probably have together for a while. He would be going back to Bozeman on a plane in the early afternoon. And, it looked like he'd be going back with egg on his face. He'd taken a long shot, against really long odds and came up short. So far, there was nothing other than suspicion as far as the shooting of Barry Steinbrenner.

Miriam was a beautiful as ever and theirs was a warm and caring relationship but one that seemed to keep the other at arm's length. No commitments. No strings. Nobody tied down. How much longer could he keep up two relationships like that? One with Miriam and there had been one, for a while at least, with Nancy.

He slipped into the bathroom and got a shower and got his stuff together. Miriam was propped up on her elbows as he sat down on the edge of the bed and kissed her goodbye. "I have to go and wrap up things with the Salt Lake folks. I will be out on the afternoon plane but I will call you on the way to the airport. Okay?"

"I will miss you. I sent you a nice Christmas present. Hopefully it will arrive before Christmas day. Come back as soon as you can."

"The same for you, Miriam. My house is your house, you know?"

"My, what a sense of humor so early in the morning."

"I'll put the Do Not Disturb sign on the door and you stay as long as you like. I'll come back and throw my clothes in the suitcase on the way out and I'll get a late checkout for the room."

"Bye, Russ," she whispered as she rolled over toward the opposite wall so he would not see the tears.

Russ arrived at the garage where the forensics team had been going over the car. Three special trained officers had gone over the car thoroughly and had found nothing except that the VIN plate on the car was apparently from the wrecked car in Pennsylvania and the rest of the car was the wrecked vehicle from Utah.

The conclusion was that the two men had taken the car somewhere to have it detailed, or did it themselves, and there were only a couple of hairs that were long and brunette and Russ believed that they would turn out to belong to the Alexander girls.

The car's carpets and floor mats had been thoroughly cleaned and shampooed. Expertly, it seemed. Russ believed that they must have used a detail service. If they were trying to get out of town, he could not see them doing that themselves. Everything was spotless and had been wiped down. No finger prints to be found. Almost unbelievable.

Russ and Wayne Dunkin had hoped to get enough evidence to show the car was in and around the crime scene but so far: frustration and disappointment. Days were passing and nothing was coming together.

Russ sat in the car and opened his iPhone and put in a search for auto detailers in Salt Lake. He was particularly interested in any close to the University of Utah parking lot where they found the car parked. One popped up that caught his eye: Diamond Executive Detailing and it was right around the corner from his hotel where he had been staying those past few nights.

When the three techs arrived and Debra Taylor, they had a quick gathering at the car. The lead crime tech said, "We're done with the car at this point. You folks can have it to do with as you see fit. We have checked it, vacuumed it and taken plenty of pictures for our purposes. Nothing other than the physical changes like the replacement of the VIN plate have been found. Nothing to suggest the car was involved in any shooting and the cleaning was extensive so if there was any evidence it is long gone. About as clean a vehicle as you would ever see. I'd like to know who cleaned it. I would like them to clean mine up."

Russell said, "I believe I might know where to look. I believe it is likely to have been Diamond Executive Detailing on 235 West 500 South, right around the corner from the Hilton Garden. They advertise spotless cleaning by experts. I think we are seeing an example of their work."

Debra Taylor said, "I know that place. I've used them on my personal car! They do a wonderful job and that would explain what we have here."

Russ said, "I had hoped we would find some GSR in the car or a shell casing or something. No GSR, huh?"

"We did find a trace of GSR on a seat belt but nothing that could not have been contamination by someone just getting in and out of the car. The amount of particles was very small. Would these guys have been around any shooting otherwise?"

"Yes, the ranch they went to has a lot of sporting clays and skeet shooting. They would certainly be exposed to a lot there. So you went over the entire interior and found nothing?"

Almost as if he felt Russ was questioning the quality of their work, the tech snapped back, "I said we went over every inch!"

Debra Taylor said, "Let's not get into a row over this. We're just all frustrated."

Russ stood looking at the car and asked, "Is it okay if I get in the car?"

"Sure," the tech said. "I told you we were through with what we can do."

Russ opened the left rear door of the car and sat down on the passenger seat of what was once a very nice, deluxe interior. He tried to picture himself as the shooter in the car and as he sat there he looked at the headliner of the car which was the normal tricot fabric that feels like closely knitted felt and is applied on a molded poly-urethane foam board like structure and is seldom given a second thought in a car other than color and some offer sound absorption.

Russ put one foot out the door on the ground and was about to exit when he asked, "You checked the headliner for GSR, too, I guess?"

The lead tech was about ready to explode! He was now feeling that his work was being questioned, but he managed a controlled but not reassuring response, "I 'm pretty sure we did the headliner." But then he looked questioningly at the other two techs, "We did check the headliner, right?"

A quick discussion revealed that no one had actually checked the headliner. The seats and doors and carpets had been swabbed but no one had actually swabbed the headliner. Another method was to use a spray of sodium hypochlorite to cause a chemical reaction to show GSR patterns.

GSR kits used in the field consisted of two parts: one for a presumptive test of a suspect who might have fired a gun using swabs in a vial wet with the liquid test material and the hands were swabbed. Then there are tests to be sent to a lab for more detailed electron microscopic analysis. If they tested the upholstery and floors, it would seem they would have detected the residue there.

"We'll try a swab from one of the GSR kits and then we'll spray a small area of the headliner just to put the matter to rest," said Detective Taylor. "If we get a positive, then we may have to do more tests on the headliner."

One of the techs got a kit from the van and did a few quick swabs on the headliner over the rear door area and put the swab in the test vial. She applied the test liquid. If there was GSR it would take about five minutes for little blue or brown specks to show under the magnifier in the vial. They waited.

She held the vial up to her eye and said, "We have a positive result."

Russ's heart raced! Maybe! Just maybe!

The lead tech said, "This is not conclusive but we'll spray a small area with the sodium hypochlorite and see what happens." He got inside and sprayed a small area over the door frame and in a matter of minutes the area showed a heavy concentration of GSR.

"For there to be this much there must have been several rounds fired," the tech said.

"Barry was hit five times. We don't know how many shots there were but at least five." Russ was so excited he was almost hyperventilating.

"I don't know why we did not get any off the floor and seats and carpet," the tech said.

"They cleaned everything but I have never seen any car detailer clean the headliner unless there was some specific reason," said Russ.

Detective Taylor agreed. "And, the shooter may have been shooting over someone else who took the entire spray pattern on them self."

"We'll do some more tests, Detective Taylor and we'll rip out the headliner and send it to the lab," he said.

Detective Taylor went around to the passenger side of the car and opened the rear door and sat on the seat. She sat there a moment and asked, "While we are asking, did anyone check these seat back pockets?"

One of the techs said, "I checked them. I found a piece of a Kleenex type paper in there. Everything else was probably removed when they cleaned the car."

"Russell, do you have what you need? That GSR is something more than you had." As she was talking, she pulled the seat pocket open as wide as it would go and ran her hand down inside, running her fingers in every corner. She stopped and looked at Russ who was watching her. She said to the tech, "Give me a latex glove."

Detective Taylor put on the glove and reached back into the pocket on the seat and very gently lifted out something that she almost missed with her bare finger and almost could not find with the glove on: an empty .40 Cal S&W shell! She held it up to Russ Baker and smiled, "I believe you have been looking for this!"

Hidden down in the crease where the pocket was attached to the seat cover was a crucial piece of evidence that was missed by the men who had been in the car, the car detailers, the forensic techs and was almost missed by Debra Taylor. But there it was! The young men had found four shells while they were at Russ's house but did not know how many shots were fired. They should have looked more.

Detective Taylor said to one of the techs, "Get me an evidence bag to put this in."

Russ stepped back and sat in a folding chair. He could not believe what had just happened. And neither could the three techs who were saying nothing.

The two detectives had accomplished more by accident than they had in two and a half days going over the car and this was not going to look good in the final report.

Detective Taylor came around the car with the evidence bag and handed it to the lead tech and gave Russ a high five and turned to do the same to the three tech but they had all huddled in front of the car and were talking very animatedly to each other and it was clear that they were trying to decide who was at fault for not finding the two important clues themselves. They were looking for someone to blame.

"Knock this shit off, and now!" barked Detective Debra Taylor. She got their attention and Russ's. "Your standing here arguing and blaming each other is not getting us anywhere. Detective Baker is headed back to Montana this afternoon and he and I have a few notes to go over at the office. You guys need to get the tests done on the headliner and the shell casing and see if there is anything else and get a report on my desk by noon tomorrow so we can see how to proceed. We have our case to pursue here regarding the car title and possible conspiracy and flight to avoid prosecution here and Detective Baker needs to try and resolve the shooting of their sheriff. You guys have your work to do so get it done!"

The lead tech started stammering out an apology and she cut him off, "I will not speak for Detective Baker but we got what we were looking for. We'd like more, but we weren't looking for miracles. As far as I'm concerned the only report from this garage will be the one that you guys write. I am not going to be bad mouthing anyone as long as we get an accurate, prosecution worthy report. How about you, Detective Baker?"

"That's how I see it, Detective Taylor. I want to thank all of you for your hard work. If I can get that analysis back in the next twenty four hours, I will be a happy man." Russ extended his hand to the three techs and turned and walked to the exit and his car with Detective Taylor following.

Debra Taylor closed the secure door to the garage as she walked through and let out a yell.

"Hot damn, Russell Baker, we make a helluva team!" With that, she grabbed Russell in a hug and held him for a minute. "Can you believe we just pulled off a frigging miracle in there?"

"I'm pretty excited, Debra. You sure kept me from looking like an idiot for coming out here. And, what you did for those techs by not writing them up and reaming them all new butt holes is the stuff you read about! That was a class move on your part."

"Well, to tell you the truth, I'd begun to think we were wasting our time but your pushing all of us to do one last test for the GSR lit a fire under me. This little nothing case has become quite an experience."

"Debra, you said something about going by the office for some follow up before I leave. So we'd better do that so I can get out to the airport."

"I don't really have anything for us to do there; I was just using that as an excuse to get away from here. I don't suppose I could interest you in staying one more night? We could have a real boy girl date and leave the detective badges at home."

"I thought we did that at the country club. I would like to stay but I told my boss I would be back in the morning. You are making it very hard to leave," Russ replied. "But you sure made it nice when I was here and made my return home a lot better."

"Russell Baker, here is my card with my personal phone number, my personal email and my personal address. If there is anything else you would like, just ask. I would really like to see you again. I can be in Bozeman on a moment's notice and we could go to Big Sky and ski. Maybe even get in your boat and go fishing. My Dad has a Pilatus airplane and if I talk sweetly, he has been known to let them take me on little junkets. Or, I can get them to go pick you up and bring you out here. Just let me know."

"It sounds good to me, Debra. I will call you. Thanks for the contact info and thanks for everything."

"Russell, you know my pet peeve is people who try to BS me. Don't you be BS'ing me!"

"I would not want you mad with me, Debra. I'll be in touch. Soon." With that he gave her a hug and went to the car and was about to drive off when she ran over and motioned for him to stop and let down his window.

She leaned in the car and kissed Russ and as she stepped back away from the car she said, "If you don't call, I'm coming after you! And, Merry Christmas!"

Russ drove away and looked at her in the rear view mirror. The little rich girl from Salt Lake who was a Detective Sergeant had just put him on notice.

His life was already complicated with Nancy and Miriam and now, was he going to have to deal with Debra, too. "Well, things could be a whole lot worse," he supposed, "than having three lovely ladies interested."

When this case was over he might have to take his 8 weight fly rod to the Bahamas and Green Turtle Cay for some bone fishing to clear his head. He wondered if the Pilatus could make it there without having to refuel. Well, that wouldn't be his problem, would it? He had always wondered how the one-percenters lived. Maybe he was getting a glimpse. But right now he would settle for a glimpse of his RO boat and home.

When the plane landed in Bozeman, getting to his car was a little simpler than in Atlanta. His practically new black Silverado was waiting right where he left it. He could have used the police car but thought someone might need it when he was gone so he had left it at the courthouse in Virginia City.

With only less than a week until Christmas, he would be trying to cram a lot in the next few days. Those days between Christmas and New Years were tough with so many people taking time off. He needed to get a little something for Nancy although she might throw it in the trash, or, at him.

A quick call to Wayne set up a meeting at the courthouse for the next morning. He was about half way to Ennis when his OnStar phone rang in the truck. He seldom used that feature and never used the one in his old Tahoe but once in a while but he did like the satellite radio. The satellite phone was nice because there were few places it would not work, unlike cell phones.

But the sound of it startled him and he had to remember to push the button on the steering wheel cluster to accept. He did not know who would have the truck's number, now that he thought about it.

Russ pushed the button. "This is Russ Baker."

"Hi Russ. I was wondering if you were back in town and how things went. Are you tired out from driving?" It was Chad Freeman.

"I flew out and back Chad. But I'm just getting in to town and have not made it home yet. Things turned out okay and we have some stuff to work on. Just waiting on some lab results to get back tomorrow. How are you?"

"We are having a late supper and Nancy is coming over. Would you like to join us?"

"Chad, I am just not up to that right now. Thank you anyway. Can I take a raincheck?"

"Sure. Catch you later."

Russ hit the end button and then pulled over to the side of the road and stopped. His Chevy had OnStar and he did not pretend to know how it all worked, but he knew they could find his truck and he had GPS that could tell him, or OnStar, exactly where he was. What about the car in Salt Lake they had been going through? Had anyone checked on that?"

He scrolled to Debra Taylor's number and touched the call button.

"Well, that did not take long, Detective Baker. You just had to talk to me, right?" Debra Taylor answered with that little lilt in her voice.

"That's right. I just landed and thought of something that has probably already been followed up on but wanted to ask anyway. Does that car have a GPS system or a satellite phone and can we tell where it was on the night in question?"

"I'll find out in the morning and let you know. I'll call you as soon as I know anything. Goodnight, Russ. Sweet dreams."

Russ was very glad to pull in the long driveway up to his house. He drove around back to one of the three sections of the garage he used to keep his truck. There was a riding lawn mower in one side and he had a table set up in the last section to rig up fly rods, clean and lube reels, and tinker with tying flies. The garage was heated and usually comfortable if you kept the doors closed.

The drive circled by the shed where he kept the boat and it looked like all was well with it sitting there with the boat cover over it as well as being under the shelter. The place was nice. Nice and lonely, most of the time.

Maybe after they put the guys in jail that shot Barry he could hook up his boat and go down to Ellijay or Blue Ridge and do floats on the Toccoa, the Hiawassee, or even the Holston. Just maybe. And never come back. Just maybe.

16

The next morning was catch up day with Wayne Dunkin and a quick trip the hospital in Bozeman to see Barry. The bad news was Barry could not shed any new light on the case but was very happy with what Russ and the team were doing to try and find the shooter. He would be home before Christmas, the doctors said. Maybe even tomorrow.

"Barry, we are almost certain that the people who shot you were driving the car that was at my house with the two young students who were here from Salt Lake visiting Miriam and her daughters. We have a shell casing and we have GSR. No one can say yet that they are absolutely sure but I would bet a Stetson hat on it. We have pictures from their student information and that the girls had on cell phones and we will be putting out a lookout for them in all the usual channels plus social media. We are trying to put the vehicle at the scene using satellites phones or GPS in the car. Don't know on that yet."

"You will probably have to get a Federal Judge to get that info. I have a couple of friends that are federal judges since they left the Air Force JA service. Let me know if I can help," Barry said as he was trying to get the energy to get back to work.

"If I can put that car at the scene, we will try to get a warrant to search that ranch, too. I'm keeping my fingers crossed," Russ said as he stood to leave.

"How is Miriam doing with all this? I hope she knows that I don't feel she and her daughters are involved."

"She is embarrassed, mad and about everything else. Hurt, too, that the boys might have been using them."

"I'll call her this evening and talk to her. You take care Russ. These guys might take a shot at you, too."

Tomorrow is another day. Today he wanted a call from Debra Taylor with some news on the car's GPS and satellite phone.

The call came as Russ sat down for dinner at the Bear Trap Grill. "Hello, Debra."

"Hello, Russ. I hope I am interrupting something," she said in that lilting and smiling voice. "I received some info on the satellite phone and GPS question."

"Great. Tell me about it."

"The car does have the Ford Sync. The phone system uses your existing phone on Bluetooth and works where ever your phone has service. It does not incorporate a satellite phone, like your OnStar. So if they had their phones on and there was no signal then we will be out of luck."

"However, the car does have GPS tracking and navigation and you can request a report on where they were within a certain time period and you should be able to get that with a court order. Ford is tracking their cars, as well and under what's known the third party doctrine, there is no expectation of privacy using the GPS. The user knows that they are being tracked and agrees to it when they set up the service. So, at the very least, you should know where the car was at the time of the shooting."

"That is great news, Debra. I will see about getting the sheriff and district attorney working on this tomorrow," said Russ.

"You will have a fax and an email in the morning that shows the lab analysis on the headliner. The headliner had a high concentration of GSR. It was on the order of 2500 per twenty square inches. It is a certainty that the shooter, or shooters, fired a gun from inside the vehicle and likely several rounds."

"As to the cartridge, there are no distinguishing fingerprints on the small hull. However, the firing pin on the weapon used seems to have a small burr that is causing an unusual appearance on the impact area where it hits the primer cap. The lab thinks an exact match can be determined if you find a weapon. We went back and did another check of the interior and found no other shells."

"That's some great information, Debra. Thank you and thank your people for me," said Russ.

"We are here to protect and serve, Sir. Call me anytime. You got that part, right? Anytime."

"Loud and clear, Ma'am. Loud and clear."

Dinner would be a lot better tonight. One more piece of the puzzle could get them focused.

Salt Lake City Police and the State of Utah had already put out a BOLO and Fugitive Arrest Warrants had been issued in the matter of the car salvage operation on the students known to everyone as Kasim Rahmani and Samer Mustafa.

Their pictures had been put on the police computer system and could be checked in the National Crime Information Center Data Base. Any police department in the US could pull up the information on these two men.

The head of security at the Double Barr Ranch had been sent the information by a person they had in place to advise them of such matters and he went to the Imam with the information. "Do the authorities have any reason to suspect the men are here?" the Imam asked.

"Not that we can see at this time."

"I believe that tomorrow we need to practice having all the people here go into the bunkers to make sure everyone knows the drill. We need to be prepared in case they try to come in here," he said. "Do you have any suggestions as to what we should do about this possible threat?"

The French speaking manager, who was actually an Algerian national said, "Everyone here who is safe to move should be sent away now. Let them return to their base cities and once we know that there is no more danger we can resume our operations and training. To have a large group here makes it hard to conceal. It is winter and we can clean up everything and if someone should show up here, they will find empty buildings and some horses and cattle. Nothing else, Imam. That will leave only a few who can use the bunkers for now."

The ranch had hired a company to build underground bunkers for concealment purposes using combinations of concrete and large corrugated drain pipes. The bunkers could hide a large number of people for several days with food and water stocked in each one. They had electricity but also had solar and wind turbines for back up and had storage batteries.

For the most severe situations they had hand powered ventilation systems. One was in a feed lot and another under a hay storage shed. Both were a considerable distance from the main compound. None were visible by satellite and were not detectable in a casual drive by. Anyone in fear of imminent arrest could be placed in the bunker for extended periods and people coming and going from the ranch would never see them.

They were going to be shipping out the two men who had come to the ranch with the boys and they had been in the bunkers a good part of the time. Kasim and Samer may have to go to one of the bunkers until they could be relocated. None of the other people there had any warrants or histories that would alert anyone and their papers and passports with their new names would pass most any routine inspection. The people that made them had their lives and the lives of their family members at stake if they failed to deliver perfect forgeries. On a 7500 acre ranch it was easy to be out of sight.

By daylight the next morning, most of the *guests* at the ranch had left by a church bus or a van or by private car to blend into the background in Philadelphia, Atlanta, San Diego, New York, and several other cities across the country.

All that could still move freely would be gone by noon leaving two men who were valuable assets but who were on every list at Interpol, MI6, Homeland Security, and the FBI and on and on. And the two students who were now on a fugitive list in Utah would still be there. And, they were wanted by the Madison County Montana Sheriff's office and Detective Russell Baker. At the Double Barr Ranch the big fish were below the surface, for now.

It would be up to Wayne Dunkin and the Sheriff to work with the District Attorney, and maybe state and federal authorities, to try and acquire the GPS information from the car for the night that Barry was shot. Several cases have revolved around this information in the country and some have ended up in the Federal Courts. Tom Tom and other GPS manufacturers had resisted providing the information for privacy reasons but courts had sided with the police saying there is no reasonable expectation of privacy with the GPS units under the third party doctrine but the companies all made it tough to get.

Once he got a location of the car for that evening, if it was in a snowbank on State 287 near the Double Barr Ranch, he would have a reasonable chance of getting a search warrant.

He needed to find out if the people at the ranch were involved and try to get a lead on the whereabouts of the two students from Salt Lake. The only records they had found so far were from the time they came from Iraq and it ended at the school. No connections anywhere could be found. There was no explanation as to how they got the salvaged car. All Russ could do was wait.

The early blizzard and wintry blast had subsided and the days were nice and it looked like it was going to be a nice Christmas. At least, weather-wise.

An average Bozeman and Ennis day in November would get up to the low forties and for some this was fishable. In December, thirty three degrees was average high and it could be an average of twelve degrees at night. This was, for Russ, just too darn cold to fish and about everything else. He would leave any fishing to the hardier souls. He would fish elsewhere, if he went. If a really warm day showed up, he could hook up and go in just a few minutes. But, look for him maybe in March.

Nancy Freeman stood in her store with a far way look in her eye and she was interrupted by her mother, "You have been moping around for days, now. It's Christmas and business has been good. You need to be having some fun. Why not call Dr. Carter and give him a chance to apologize?"

"I can let you listen to my voice mails, Mother, and you can listen to about twenty five apologies from Dr. Carter. I don't like being embarrassed like that and the problem is I don't think that will be the last time if I continue to go out with him, or, for Goodness sakes, marry him. He likes the parties and the attention he gets at them. And, he likes the drinking."

"Well, there is that nice Russell Baker. I know you are really crazy about him, or at least, you were. He has never embarrassed you, has he?"

"No, he hasn't. But he hurt my feelings by blasting me when I was trying to apologize to him. I really know how to pick 'em."

"Nancy, you could do a lot worse than Russell Baker and maybe not much better. He would be someone you could always count on."

"Well, Mother. You think so much of him; maybe you should ask him out! As long as he is still married to his dead wife, I don't think I will get anywhere with him. I tried."

Nancy's mother embraced her and said, "As long as you are still engaged to a dead fiancé, he might be able to say the same about you." Nancy was about to respond when a customer walked in.

"I have to help my customer, Mother. Maybe you should go find something to do and stop giving me advice on my love life."

Nancy's mother turned and started to walk away and stopped. She said softly, "What love life, Nancy?"

Miriam's present was by the front door when Russ got home. It was a nice pullover fishing sweater that she had ordered online. A note said *Merry Christmas Russ* and had Miriam's name signed to it by a computer in Vermont or some place.

He walked in to the empty house and felt a longing to be in Marietta with Sarah. He missed her, especially at Christmas. She loved getting a tree, decorating the house and buying presents. And, she loved getting presents. She loved to get several and they did not have to be expensive as long as she could open them on Christmas morning. She would have made a great mother. She was a great wife.

He sent a text to Miriam:

Could not wait,
Opened my present.
Thanks so much!
If I knew how to take a selfie, I'd send one.
Take my word.
Looks great on me.
Russ

He was standing there with the sweater in his hand.

Russ walked to the window and gazed off across the empty ranchland that spread out for miles from the house. He wished that Nancy or Miriam or Sarah, or someone was there with him at that moment but he was a million miles from them all. Merry Christmas, indeed. He was not the kind of person to be alone at Christmas.

He placed a call to Dan and Doris in Marietta and wished them a Merry Christmas and asked them about the move to the new place on Lake Lanier. "We're still putting up stuff and organizing. It's pretty every morning with the sun coming up over the lake. There are ducks and geese galore!" said Dan.

"You may have to come down here and help me keep Dan busy, Russ. He's been retired about three weeks and he's already starting to drive me crazy! Can he come out there and go fishing with you?" asked Doris.

"Sure, Doris, but I suggest he waits until it gets warm. Now, if he wants to fly us to the Bahamas, I'll be down as soon as we are able to catch a few bad guys."

"Russ, I'll pay for you to fly first class!" she said with a laugh but somehow Russ thought she just might be serious.

The next morning all the paperwork, phone calls and strategy to get the GPS locations on the car were set in motion. "They say it may take a week or more to get the report, especially since its Christmas," said Wayne after talking to the District Attorney. He is hoping to get a judge to write the letter today and get it out overnight FedEx. Barry's brother is making some calls and so is Charlie Neilson.

"Wayne, do you think it's possible that the Double Barr Ranch is somehow involved in this?"

"I've lived in and around here a long time, Russ, and I have never had any dealings with anyone except one of the grandchildren of the Barr family who went to school here. The family moved to the East coast when all the old ranch family died out and the rest became Wall Street tycoons. The family had owned a lot of those open pit mines over behind the current ranch and sold them. They soon lost interest in this place and split it up. They still have some land left but as far as I know they do nothing with it. I've had no dealings with the ranch and have had no reason to go out there. Most people around here would say they are a model neighbor and that just means they mind their own business and have not bothered anyone."

"Maybe it's all coincidence. But there seem to be a lot of those. Then, there is the break-in at my house. The more I think about it, if those two students are involved in the shooting of Barry, and the salvaged car ring, if it is a ring, then maybe they broke in to my house for some reason. We need to get in to that ranch and see what's going on. The students may be hiding out there, for all we know. Who knows what else?"

"We'll try to get a search warrant if we find the car was out there at the wreck scene. Maybe it made it to the house. But, from what I saw out there, I do not believe a car had traveled past where we found Barry's car that night," said Deputy Dunkin.

"What if we can't get the judge to give us a warrant?"

Russ was surprised and curious about how Wayne answered: "Then we'll have to find out what's going on another way, won't we?"

Somehow, Russ decided it was best to leave that question for another day. So, they would wait and hope that their criminals did not fly the coop; if they ever were at the coop in the first place.

The phone screen said *Nancy* and Russ had to look twice. Was she really calling him? He took a deep breath and tried to sound nonchalant, "Hello, Nancy."

"Was that nonchalant enough?" he wondered.

"Would you like to accompany me over to the Rivers Run Fly Shop Christmas party tomorrow afternoon? They are closing early and have invited the guides and their families. I imagine you got an invite, anyway. You probably know the next day is Christmas Eve?"

"That would be very nice, and I did get an invite but I never RSVP'd. They are not expecting me. Will that be a problem?"

"I am sure that John would like for you to be there, Russ."

In fact, she had accepted for two originally. It was going to be her and Dr. Carter. But, Dr. Carter would not be attending, as it turned out, so Russ would simply take his place. Russ did not know that. John would simply change the place card and the name tag and no one would be the wiser.

"Nancy, when should I pick you up?"

"Cocktails are 6:30 to 7:30 and then the meal and we will probably get out of there by 10:00 or so."

"I'll pick you up at 6:15."

"Goodnight, Russ."

So! He had a date with Nancy! At least she was speaking to him again. Maybe he was not her first choice, he wasn't sure, but he would not quibble!

Christmas Eve, eve was here and he was whistling as he got dressed to go pick up Nancy.

The Rivers Run had rented the large meeting space at the Hilton Garden and had encouraged anyone who might be tempted to drink too much to get a room there to avoid any possible drunk driving incidents and wrecks.

Nancy was a knock out when she opened the door. As usual, she would be the prettiest lady there and Russ would be the envy of all the guys there having Nancy as his date for the evening.

In addition, she would be one of the people there that was admired because of her success at the store and the guides who used her shuttle services would admire her for the nice job she did for them. They all regretted that she was so stunning in front of their wives and girlfriends who felt threatened by her.

But when she met anyone for the first time she would always make them feel good about her.

The room was done up right and there was a big tree with tons of presents. The shop had gone all out for the guests and children. There was a new Sage rod and a new set of Simms Waders as door prizes among other things. A lot of the suppliers had been asked to help out and Rivers Run would, in return, support them on their very successful on-line site.

Just outside the door they met her brother Chad and his family and while Nancy was greeting the nieces and nephews, Russ picked through the name tags that were on a table beside the door. He spotted Nancy's right off but could not find one with his name on it.

There were a few blank ones and a Sharpie pen so he wrote his name on one and as he put the pen down he saw a tag with Dr. Stephen Carter's name written on it. He put on his tag and went and handed Nancy hers. She noticed that his was different but did not say anything about it.

After they got inside and Russ went to get a drink from the open bar, she slipped out and looked at the table and saw the name tag for Dr. Carter. "Damn it! They did not change the names!"

She took the name tag and threw it in the trash can. Then she thought about the place cards at the tables! She hurried in to the room hoping she would beat Russ to the table but Russ was already standing there with their drinks. She saw her name on a place card but there was no card in front of Russ. He handed her the glass of wine and she could see in his other hand what looked like a crumpled up place card. She knew what it said: *Dr. Stephen Carter!*

Russ picked up his glass of wine and held it up in a toast toward her, "To a nice evening," he said.

"And the same to you, Russ. Thank you for coming tonight." But for Nancy, she felt her evening had just turned to crap!

It was a fun night and well done by all accounts. Everyone was on their best behavior and the kids got entertained by Santa Claus and all attending got a small gift.

Russ and Nancy expressed their best wishes and Merry Christmas greetings and said goodnight. No mention had been made of the name tags and the place cards.

In the truck, Nancy put her hand on Russ's arm and said softly, "I'm sorry about the name tags and the place cards. They were supposed to have been changed."

Russ replied, "No problem, Nancy. I understand. The good news is that I was here without a name tag and a place card but Dr. Carter was not here at all. I think I came out ahead on the deal."

Nancy did not respond. She thought it was best to leave it. Russ had already dealt with the matter in his mind.

Russ drove straight to her house. She found herself wanting him to drive to Ennis and to his house but he did not suggest it and she was too embarrassed to say anything. He walked her to her door, gave her a hug and said, "I had a nice time tonight Nancy. Thank you for inviting me."

She slowly closed the door as he walked to his truck and drove off. She remembered she did not thank him for the Christmas present she had received at the store from him. "Nancy you are just a loser!" she thought. "You can foul up anything!"

She went into the kitchen and was aimlessly looking through the refrigerator and her mother came in. "I'm sorry, Nancy, I did not hear you come in. You are home early. Is Russell here?"

"Russell is not here and I think you should go back to bed. That's where I'm going! Alone! As usual!" And she almost ran from the kitchen.

Her mother put her hands on the table as she leaned over, shaking her head. "I just don't believe you sometimes, Nancy," she said mainly to herself.

17

Christmas Eve morning and Russ was at the office early. There was no word on the request for the GPS info. And likely there wouldn't be if they did not get it by midmorning as most places would be winding down until after Christmas. He would just have to wait. But would the bad guys wait? Were they still around or were they back in Iraq or wherever they came from? There was that word again: Frustration.

His phone rang and it showed *Debra Taylor*. "Hello, Debra."

"Good morning, Russ. I just wanted to know if you were able to get the information you wanted on the GPS."

"Not yet. We haven't heard any more. The letters went to them."

"I'm just checking. What are you doing tomorrow? Big plans?"

"No, Debra. I think it will be me and football on TV. How about you?"

"I'll do Christmas with Mom and Dad at their house and then my sister and brother and their families will join us at the Club. Then we'll all be back over for the evening watching old Jimmy Stewart movies here and listening to Dad tell the same old corny jokes and do s'mores in the fireplace."

"That sounds so nice, Debra. I hope you have fun."

"It would be funner if you were here Russ. Want me to send the plane for you?"

"I guess not this time. But it is a nice thought."

"Oh, pooh. Well another time then. Merry Christmas. Call me if you get lonely."

Russ looked at the phone as he ended the call. Then he realized that she was probably not joking about sending the plane! The one-percenters did stuff like that!

Then his phone rang again and it was a number he did not recognize. "Hello, this is Russell Baker."

"Russell, this is Janet Steinbrenner. I am probably way too late in calling you but Barry and I would like for you to come to our house tomorrow for Christmas lunch, if you can. We couldn't make plans too much until we knew Barry would be home. Bring someone with you if you want. Barry's brother is coming as well as Sheriff Neilson and Wayne Dunkin. Their wives will be coming and maybe a kid or two. Will you be able to make it tomorrow about 1:00?"

"I will be there, Janet. How nice of you to invite me."

Russ would not have to spend Christmas alone, after all.

Nancy Freeman and her mother were preparing lunch to take over to Chad's. The kids wanted to be home with all their junk, so one more Christmas would come and go and Nancy would be on her own. No Dr. Carter and no Russell Baker. Things were back to her normal, too: spending time with her mother and her brother.

She couldn't help but wonder what Russell was doing and that thought made her sad. And, mad with herself.

Christmas is a time that makes people lonely and the experts all talk about how blue people can get at what is supposed to be a happy time. In Salt Lake City, Debra Baker had everything a girl could want by a lot of standards. She had a doting and rich father who did not want her to be a cop but kept saying, "Whatever makes you happy." A lie he told her to avoid confrontation.

She liked her job doing what was a *man's job* and she did it well. And she had all the guys that went to the private Waterford School at $17,000 per year where she had attended with a lot of other rich kids for 12 years and at the Country Club and college, and at just about every place she ever went, wanting to ask her out and a lot did. But for this Christmas, she would have liked to have spent it with Russell Baker who seemed not too impressed with her social status and was comfortable working with a female. That made him alright in her book.

Miriam would have liked to have been with Russ but things were a little awkward. She would spend most of Christmas with her daughters and some with her family and some: alone. But, she'd had a few days with Russ. That would have to do for now.

The day was bright and beautiful. There would be no snow today and the people gathered at Barry Steinbrenner's house were hoping that it would be a quiet day. It was Christmas and Janet Steinbrenner had gotten a present a few days early: her husband and the father of her children and the Madison County Sheriff had managed, with the help of a walker and with her helping hold him up, to walk in from the car to his chair in the den.

For a while, she did not know if that would ever happen again. It was a good Christmas for her!

Barry waited until all the eating and toasting was over to ask Russ and Wayne to go into the study where he closed the door. "I appreciate all the work you are doing on my case. Thank you, Wayne, for sending the reports by every day. I have gotten caught up. I think we will get the information from the GPS on the car that you need. A little bird told me we would have it in two days." He could tell by their look of surprise they wanted to know who the little bird was and where the bird was located, but he held up his hand and said, "Its best we leave it at that."

Russ and Wayne Dunkin could tell there was some leverage somewhere and pressure being applied. Then he said, "Montana buys a lot of Ford products and so do several sheriff departments in the State."

"I hope to be back to work soon and be where I can be some help. What do you think our chances of catching these guys are, Wayne?"

"We will get them Barry. One way of the other," was Wayne's response. Russ saw the nod that Barry gave Wayne and wondered exactly what the exchange meant. He also knew it was best not to ask.

"How about you, Russ? You feel okay with how things are going?"

"Better now that I know we will get that car tracking report. If we can place it at the scene, I hope we can build enough probable cause to get a warrant to search that ranch. I just can't imagine them being out there and it not being connected somehow although they did leave Utah with that as a destination."

"Russ, how many people came to your house?"

Miriam, her two daughters and the two students were there at my house. Why do you ask?"

"The girls were not with them that night. Correct?"

"Miriam and the girls came in by plane earlier, before the weather was so bad. They were at my house all night. The men came in later after calling and saying they had gotten delayed and the road was impassable and asked to stay at the house."

"I feel sure there were more than two people in the car. I could make out people in the front seat and I feel certain the shooter was in the back left passenger side," Barry added.

"That would be consistent with the GSR patterns on the headliner," Russ concluded.

"Damned fine work on getting that detail and the cartridge shell."

"I had some real good help in Salt Lake."

"Pretty, too, right?"

Russ started to ask how he knew that and again, Barry held up his hand and smiled, "I have my sources and I know the forensics team failed to get the evidence and that you and Sergeant Taylor pulled it out in the bottom of the ninth! I also know that the report does not state that and that you and the pretty Sergeant covered their asses. You can bet that lady will get whatever she needs from that crew on a priority basis in the future. That was a class thing to do."

Russ leaned back in his chair. "I'll be damned," he thought. Barry Steinbrenner was connected to the Salt Lake City police. Somehow. Or, he was connected to Debra Taylor. Somehow. It was unlikely that any of the three techs had gone in and confessed.

The picture was coming more into focus now. The two student refugees were into some clandestine operation that was serious enough to kill people over. They had met up with a person or persons and came to Ennis to a dude ranch, apparently willingly, and the weather and snow and a minor accident had caused them to attract the attention of the local sheriff who was trying to do the protect and serve thing and help out some people in distress. Instead, he came within inches and minutes of dying as a result. Was this all about a ring putting together wrecked cars with phony titles? Not likely.

They had somehow gotten the car out of a snowbank and come back to Ennis and ended up at his house. He had not figured that out for sure yet how they did that with the road conditions.

They then probably were involved in staging the break in at his house and he sure as hell did not understand that. What did they expect to find?

They then went back to Salt Lake and business as usual. What about the person or persons in the car? The only thing that made sense was either they panicked about being found out with the car title, or that the person or persons in the car were wanted. There were no known warrants on the students at the time, Or, they had something in the car they did not want the law officer to see.

Maybe it was some of all of it. Did the person or persons return to Salt Lake with them? If not where were they?

The answers, Russ believed, were at the Double Barr Ranch. But when they went out there the French guy seemed business-like and willing to help and everything looked normal. When they ran him through a background check he was clean and all his immigration stuff looked fine.

The Hispanic man that ran the ranch operations had all of his ID and was actually born in Texas and had come up from around San Antonio after working for a cattle ranch down near there. Something was wrong somewhere, but what?

Russ thanked Janet and Barry and headed back to his place to get out his legal pad and pencil and see if there was any way to put this down in a way that made sense. He wanted to call Nancy. He wanted to call Miriam. He wanted to talk to somebody but settled for calling Dan and Doris in Marietta. Actually now, Cumming, as they had moved. He told them he'd had a nice visit and lunch with some friends and was headed home. It was a nice call between family.

The next day was a little overcast but the TV was predicting temperatures in the high forties. Russ was miserable sitting around the house so he rounded up a 6 weight fly rod, a pair of waders and put on his *wading in cold weather clothes.* He headed to a spot in Bozeman that he had been to a few times that nobody seemed to ever be in. He had managed to catch a few nice rainbow trout there and he would go kill a couple of hours in his secret place.

Fishing in cold weather to Russ is like skiing: you dress for it in layers and try to not fall in. Water inside the waders was to be avoided!

He put on a pair of thermal underwear and then he put on a pair of ski pants. Thick socks and a warm shirt with a nice and warm pullover would round out the outfit with waders covering everything.

He could add another jacket if needed and he had a pair of neoprene gloves with no fingertips. He also had a pair that had a fold over to cover the finger tips like mittens if his hands started getting cold. As long as he could keep the fingers warm and the guides on the fly rod weren't freezing, he could fish.

Russ's solution to the fly rod guides freezing was a simple one: stay home when it's that cold. But for the more hardy souls, there was Loon Ice Off paste, Pam Spray, WD-40, and Vaseline. Some even try Chapstick. Apply one of these products to the rod tips. Or, some just wash the ice off by sticking the rod in the water every few minutes.

An overstuffed vest would be added before going in the water and a good pair of polarized sunglasses. He'd been putting stuff in that vest for several years but never seemed to take anything out. He also had a folding wading staff that had saved his butt more than once. He was off to the river.

When Russ had first arrived in Bozeman he took a room at the Super 8 Motel and his comings and goings had taken him out by the Hampton Inn on Baxter Lane. He drove to the end of Baxter one day and saw that the farms there backed up to the Gallatin River. He had driven around and came across a spot where the river was more into two channels and there was a house that had a sign saying *no trespassing*. Russ had driven up to the door and got out and asked if he could go fishing.

The owner was absolutely startled and had first asked him if he could read. Russ replied that he wasn't best reader but he managed to get by in a half joking sorta way and added, "I read a lot better when it's written in Southern English."

That led to a *where are you from* question and after a few minutes the gentleman had told Russ he could come go through behind his house but he could not bring anyone with him or it would be all over.

Russ found out that fellow liked key lime pies so Russ would stop at the Sweet Pea Bakery and get about four of their Key Lime Torts and drop them off for the guy. The bakery was out of his way on the far end of Main but he felt it was worth it. Today the Sweet Pea was closed for Christmas. He'd have to make it up next time.

Russ waded into the cold water and it was if he had been morphed into some other place and time. The door to the real world closed behind him for a moment and there was nothing expected of him. He would not have to worry about doing or saying the wrong thing. There was no one to please. There was just him and the Gallatin and some wary fish that may or may not cooperate.

He may not catch a fish today, but he was fishing. He was not having to row a drift boat, tie on flies for some know it all jerk and listen to him tell about all the fish he'd caught and all the women he'd gone out with while throwing his Chernobyl or stone fly pattern into the only bush on the bank of the river within a hundred feet.

And it was throwing for a lot of the guys who seldom fished but talked like they went every day. Casting was an unknown art to them. And there were the ones that could cast and would keep on casting so everyone could see how well they cast rather than dropping the fly where Russ was telling them the fish might be. Today there was no one else to please.

Russ had tied on his favorite combination: a big black bead head wooly bugger and a smaller green bead head wooly bugger dropper on the nine foot 3X leader.

He might add a little weight because he wanted it to bounce on the bottom in the current as it drifted and swung around downstream but he would cast a couple of times to see if it was working. There were a number of deep pools and if the fish were lying there as the rig came through, watch out!

The most fun fly fishing for trout, probably bass fishing too, Russ thought, is to have that big giant fish come up and pound a fly on the top of the water. The sight and feel of that is something every fly fisherman lives for.

The dry fly floating on the surface being taken by a big rainbow or a big brown is incredible. The fish just *blows up* on the fly sometimes, as some like to say, and other times they seem to sip it in. But the experts say that eighty percent of the fish feeding is done under water on some subsurface lifecycle of an insect or sculpin, or worm, or another small fish.

Subsurface fishing. It was just like looking for the bad guys. They were never just sitting on top of the water in plain sight for the taking. They were submerged into a world of blackness and safety and where they, like the rainbow or the brown or the cutthroat or brookie could lie motionless and not be seen until they were ready to pounce on an unsuspecting life form passing by. Like the people who shot Barry. Hiding. Waiting. But what were they waiting for and what hole were they in? What log were they hiding under or what rock were they behind?

Russ made his first cast and the big streamers swung around in the current and he could feel the small ticks on the line as the flies bumped along the bottom. He could feel the line stretch out and stop at the top of the hole and he let it sit for a moment and then: strip-strip-strip-strip until it was back in front of him and he cast it out again. Strip-strip-strip-strip. Nothing.

The next cast he let out a little more line. Maybe the fish was a little further down. Tick-tick-tick-tick as the flies found their way over the sand and rocks of the Gallatin. The line finished its swing around and stopped. Then strip-strip-bam! A hard hit by a big fish! That's what he was looking for! The fish pulled off line and ran and he coaxed him back only to have him run again. The Sage rod vibrated with the energy of the big rainbow.

Just when Russ almost had him, he had some more fight in him. Coax and reel and not too hard. Then the fish tired and he finally got him close and Russ could lift up the rod tip and put his hand gently under the twenty inch rainbow.

Russ lifted the fish up and removed the barbless hook. He looked for a second and put the fish back in the water and in another second the mad rainbow swam away to be caught another day. Russ had gone fishing. And Russ had caught fish.

After about an hour and a half he had landed about four more nice fish and missed a couple. The wind was coming up and a chill coming on. It was time to go and get some coffee and sit by a fire and reflect on the day and look at old pictures of Sarah.

One day he might be able to put those pictures away in a closet. But not yet. One day he might be able to have pictures of Nancy or Miriam or, who knows, Debra Taylor, or some yet to be met young lady on the nightstand and on the mantle. But not yet. Today he was still thinking about Sarah. And there did not seem to be room for anyone else. The living were all around him and beckoning him but he was holding on tight to a memory of a dead woman.

Russ tapped on the door of the house where the gentleman lived who had given him permission to fish but there was no answer. Probably off with family and friends enjoying the holiday. Russ went home.

Tomorrow would be Sunday so there would be no word coming in about the investigation. Hopefully Monday.

Then there would be New Year's Eve and New Year's Day and more down time and the bad guys would have more time to slide deeper below the surface and further downstream out of Russ's range. He knew time was running out! He sat down with his coffee and moved his chair close to the fire. Russell Baker fell asleep with his coffee still in the cup on the coffee table and Sarah's picture in his lap. Her memory fresh in his mind. Sometime during the night Russ had made it to his bed and it was barely light when he woke up.

Sunday morning in Montana and no Waffle House. He liked to stop at the Waffle house when he was on patrol back in Cobb County, before he became a detective. They gave the cops their first cup of coffee free. And, most of the time, the second one too.

The waitresses and cooks liked having the cops there in the wee hours when the druggies were coming in trying to get straight and the drinkers came in to sober up and sometimes there were people trying to steal a hundred bucks from the cash register or just looking for trouble. Having a Cobb County Police car in the parking lot was better than a nice billboard and it said *No Trouble Allowed Here*. It was worth a free cup of coffee, any day.

On weekends Russ and Sarah would often end up at a Waffle House and have breakfast and listen to the orders being called in to the cook.

How they got the right stuff to the right person remained a mystery to Russ. Boy, he'd give anything for a

Waffle House right now. Another reason to think about moving home to Marietta. Maybe. But there was a Perkins in Bozeman and that was pretty good, too.

18

It was 8:00 when Russ finally got a shower and some clothes on. Still early for most on a Sunday. Then a notion struck him.

Russ picked up his phone and scrolled to Nancy's number. He knew she was probably headed for church later but was probably still asleep at 8:00. He touched the call button and it rang and rang then went to voice mail. No luck.

As he was getting in the truck, his phone rang and it was Nancy. "Russ, did you call. What's wrong? Why are you calling me at 8:00 on Sunday morning?"

"I'm taking you to breakfast at Perkins. Get some clothes on and I'll be there is a few minutes."

"What if I don't want to go to Perkins for breakfast with you?"

"Well, you are awake now and you can enjoy a good breakfast free at Perkins so it really doesn't matter who you are with. And we won't need a name tag there."

"If you are going to be a smart ass, I'm really not going."

"I'm just like Popeye, Nancy, I yam what I yam. I'll be there in a few."

"Russ, wait."

"What, Nancy?"

"Who is Popeye?"

Russ laughed and hung up the phone. She probably did not know who Popeye was.

It was crowded at Perkins as it always is but would get worse as people started stirring around and looking for brunch. Russ and Nancy finally got a booth and a newspaper and looked like a young married couple. There were several familiar faces in the place but Russ just acknowledged them and kept going. Just about every woman in town knew Nancy, at least by sight, because of her ladies clothing store. It was a little awkward at first being with Nancy but Russ did not have in mind starting any serious conversations at Perkins on Sunday morning.

After a lot of small talk and catching up on her shuttle business and the holiday shopping season, Nancy finally asked Russ about the case involving Barry's shooting. He told her as much as he thought he could. He wasn't worried about Nancy talking to the bad guys but it was best to keep some things from being made public, even if accidently. He tried to leave out the part about Miriam coming to stay with him and him seeing her in Salt Lake, just to avoid rubbing salt in old wounds.

They were about through with their meal and had avoided any thing to argue about after an hour of being there. Just a nice Sunday morning in Bozeman. Then she hit him with something unexpected.

"Russ, these are dangerous people. They have already shot Barry in cold blood and who knows what else they are involved in and what they are capable of. Why don't you just let the sheriff's department and whoever else is involved handle this? Why do you have to put yourself in such danger? You came close to being killed on the Warren Cason murder case. Can't you let this be someone else's problem?"

As she spoke, Russ saw the tears starting to roll down her face. Nancy put her face in her hands and said, "Russ, I think we need to go."

Neither Russ nor Nancy spoke walking to the truck and nothing was said until Russ pulled up in front of

Nancy's house. He was at a loss for words and Nancy was in no frame of mind to have a serious conversation with him. He felt the less he said the better.

Nancy opened the door and stepped out of the truck and turned to Russ and softly said, "Russ, I was engaged once as you know and that person saw it his duty to go to fight in Iraq. He was killed there. Now, I'm supposed to love a man who is volunteering to put his life in danger and possibly get killed *doing his duty* as everyone likes to say." Russ said nothing.

"Do you know why I was dating Dr. Steve Carter? Because he was safe. I would not get a call that someone had shot him out beside some rural road and left him to die. I don't think I can go through that again. You don't make much money doing it and you don't need the money. Why do you do it?"

Before he could answer she softly closed the door and walked away. She was not angry. She was not yelling. She was hurting inside. And Russ knew it.

Russ started to go after her, but stopped himself. What she wanted him to say, he could not say right now. He had made a commitment to find the people who shot Barry Steinbrenner. He hoped he would not get killed or have to kill anyone else. But, he would not quit on the job now.

But, at least he had seen the elephant in the room that was keeping Nancy from being able to let him in her life in a major way. The trout bum in him she liked. The cop, she didn't.

Why was he doing it? He wasn't sure. Maybe because he was a cop through and through, no matter how many trout he caught and no matter how much he loved it. No matter how much money he had. He thought for a second that he was not unlike Debra Taylor in Salt Lake who had all the money in the world but it was her badge, at least at this point in her life, that made her happy.

He wondered if Sarah had those same fears that Nancy had just voiced and she had just chosen not to express them. He would never know that answer. And, he may never be able to solve Nancy's struggle with it.

Maybe it was time to move on. Let Nancy be happy with someone else and he would try to do the same. Marietta was looking better all the time. He probably would not call Nancy again, at least until this case was over. Well, the breakfast thing had *sounded* like a good idea.

Monday morning and Russ was at the Sheriff's office at 7:30 drinking coffee and waiting for a phone call, a fax, an email or any damned thing that said where that car was on the night Barry was shot! Wayne Dunkin had arrived just after Russ and was pacing around in his office.

Dunkin was anxious and looked like a cage animal. Russ looked at him for a moment and he saw something in him he had not recognized before but had been told about by Barry Steinbrenner: determination and anger. There was fierceness in his expression.

Barry had told Russ this was the man you wanted by your side when the going was rough and Russ was beginning to see that part of Dunkin. He thought about what Dunkin had said to Barry on Christmas day at Barry's house. "We will get them Barry. One way or the other."

Russ went back into the jury room where his maps and investigation notes were and stood looking at the map on the makeshift corkboard he had set up. Wayne Dunkin walked in. "What are you thinking about Russ? Did you get an idea?"

"I am going to call Miriam and see if she or the girls can recall what time the boys got to my house. It seems to me it was about 8:30 but as you know I was in Atlanta. You left patrol out there at Alder at what time?"

"It was not quite totally dark when I left out there but it was about 5:00 I would say. Sunset was about 4:58 that day because I looked."

"So the car you saw headed out in the snow storm would have been in Alder about 5:00. That is one time we can put on our time line for the car. If they got to my house about 8:30, that gave them three and a half hours to go out, get stuck, shoot Barry, and then come back to my house."

"That would be about right. I fixed a cup of coffee in the Market and they were about to close. I was probably there five, maybe ten minutes. I went out and sat in the car for another five minutes, maybe, when Barry called me to come switch cars. It probably took me fifteen minutes to drive the nine miles back here and I had four wheel drive and chains on all four tires. Barry and I did not take long to switch cars but probably no more than ten minutes," said Dunkin.

"There is no way we can say how long it would have taken them to get to the ranch under the conditions. It had been a while since the snow plows had been out that way. I saw no signs that anyone had been that way in a while. It was getting pretty thick on the road. You could not really see the road to drive," Dunkin continued.

"I would guess it took them longer to go their seven miles than it took me to go to Virginia City. Probably couldn't go over twenty miles an hour, tops. But I would bet it would have taken twenty five or thirty minutes."

"So we are looking for the car to show us it was in Alder at about 5:00 and the scene of the shooting about 5:30 and it would be dark."

"For Barry to get there would be another forty five minutes to an hour and we can confirm that time with the dispatch call records. Putting that about 6:15 to 6:30. Then, how did they get out of the snow bank and what happened to the other person or persons that were in the car? Where did you miss them coming back if there was nowhere to pull off in the snow and this was made even worse when your snow plow piled even more snow up going out there?" asked Russ.

"Coming back from out there, Russ, they would have made some ruts going out and then Barry would have probably gone in their same ruts. Snow was piling up on the road to Virginia City again. I do not believe they went any past Alder coming back."

Wayne continued, "I believe they stopped where you and I looked beside the bar at the RV park. The folks there had cleared a path for the camping trailer and they were probably sitting there when I went back out looking for Barry. With the plow, the Army truck, me and the ambulance we had left a pretty clear path back to Virginia City. They could have made it there fairly easily. We made it possible for them to escape!"

"I agree, Wayne. They had a least an hour to come back to the RV park and hide there and then they came on to my place with that story about being held up and Miriam took them in with no reason not to and no reason to suspect anything was up."

"Why did they shoot Barry, Russ?" Wayne asked but was not really expecting an answer. He was asking Russ, himself and no one in particular.

"The students were not fugitives at that time, at least not under the names they were using. The car was a problem but there is not much chance Barry would have been checking that sort of thing too closely. But, there was someone in that car, apparently a dangerous someone, who did not want to be seen. That person or persons may have had warrants on them. Maybe they had drugs in the car. Maybe they had guns or explosives. Maybe a combination," concluded Russ.

Dunkin agreed.

"Since the students showed up at the house alone, the person or persons had to be dropped off somewhere. In Alder, would be one possibility, and at the scene where Barry was shot the other. We interviewed everyone in Alder and no one saw anything, according to the folks there but most were hunkered down inside," Russ continued.

"Not likely it was in Virginia City as no one was moving when I was there," Dunkin added.

Dunkin's phone rang. "Madison County Sheriff's office. Dunkin speaking." He listened and said, "I guess we don't have any choice, then."

He looked at Russ and said, "We won't have the report until tomorrow. Their legal department has to sign off."

The Double Barr Ranch was quiet. Most of the *guests* had slipped out under cover of darkness over the past few nights.

Some had simply driven over to I-15, a few miles away and headed south to Idaho Falls, on to Salt Lake City and Las Vegas and Los Angeles.

Some would go north to Seattle. Others would go north to Butte or Bozeman and jump on I-94 to Minneapolis and all points east. What had been a full scale training camp that taught bomb making and

internet cybercrimes and weapons usage and served as a
safe haven for men whose faces were known to international law enforcement was now back to raising Angus
cattle. It was undergoing remodeling and getting ready for
the spring and summer season as a dude ranch if anyone
asked or came inquiring.

The Imam and the four remaining guests would be
gone soon but for now they would be out of sight in the
two underground bunkers. The security manager moved
like a shadow around the property making sure that the
security had not been compromised.

The Frenchman had contacted a painting contractor in
Butte who was a second generation Jordanian and he had
sent a crew of painters. They were painting all the rooms.
Covering all traces of who had been there.

The carpets were cleaned and some replaced. Every
scrap of paper and trash and garbage had been burned.

Let them come, those infidels, they would find nothing
here. The news had reached the Imam and the ranch
manager and the security agent that the two students
were being sought and warrants were out.

Two students named Kasim Rahmani and Samer
Mustafa now had new names and new passports and new
photo ID's. They were the finest money could buy. The
two of them would evaporate like a fog on the Madison
when the time was right. No hic cop from a hic town was
smart enough for them.

They had survived F-16's, drones, US Special Forces
and attacks from their own countrymen. This was no big
deal. No Waco, Texas standoff would happen here. But
there were enough booby traps on the ranch to deter
anyone from trying to breach the security in the darkness
of the night. These people were experts in death and
destruction.

Finally, the sheriff and the district attorney got the
word that the car location data was being sent! A meeting
was convened at the Madison County Sheriff's office and

there was an FBI agent, a State DCI agent and some guy that no one was real sure who he was but he said he was with Homeland Security.

The FBI was there, Russ supposed, due to the possible interstate conspiracy on the salvaged car. Maybe interstate flight to avoid prosecution. As far as the Homeland Security man, he wasn't sure but wondered if they knew more than they were letting on about these students.

The digital file showing the car's movements the night Barry had been shot arrived and was downloaded. They took the thumb drive to the jury room and put it up on a big screen TV.

The first file showed the local map overlay and there was a timeline bar at the bottom for the day that Barry was shot. He sat in the room staring at it from a chair. The data covered from 1:00 PM until 9:30 and there were several gaps due to satellite coverage and poor signals. The weather at the time did not help.

The students had told the Alexander girls that they had gotten lost and that was likely since they apparently had no signal on the GPS around Dillion when they came up from Salt Lake. If the GPS had been working it would have likely routed them on to State Route 41 to Twin Bridges and then to State Road 287. But, 41 was closed to traffic anyway that afternoon due to the heavy accumulation of snow, forcing them to go on north on I-15.

The interstates were being kept open and the students ended up traveling all the way to Butte and then east on I-90. Again the State 41 was closed from that direction and they had to continue on to Three Forks where they got on US 287 and went south to Ennis. This made the distance they had to drive from Dillion about 180 miles to the ranch rather than about forty if they could have gotten off at Dillon. So it added at least two and one half hours to their trip, throwing them into arriving at sundown in the middle of an historic snowfall.

The car's GPS data showed the car at Alder at 4:58 PM. This was exactly the time that deputy Dunkin said he saw it. No new information there, but it was verification that the car he saw belonged to the students. Then the car traveled about nine miles in twenty minutes and ended up at the location where Barry was shot at about 5:18 and stayed in that location for an hour and twenty two minutes. The signal came and went during that time.

This was at the place where Barry was shot and left for dead just down the road from Double Barr Ranch. There was no question now! The students and whoever was in the car with them had been involved in the shooting of Sheriff Barry Steinbrenner! They had the probable cause they needed to arrest the students. If they could find them.

Then, Russ, Barry, and Wayne Dunkin got an answer to a question: how did Wayne miss seeing the car? The car traveled for thirty minutes and came back the nine miles to Alder, an indication of how bad the road conditions were. At Alder they pulled in at the parking lot by the bar. The snow had been cleared off to allow the stranded camping trailer to be towed to the RV park. They sat there for an hour and ten minutes. When Wayne Dunkin and his search and rescue team had plowed through and cleared the road to Virginia City, they had seized the moment to drive to where Miriam and her daughters were at Russ's house. They had lucked out several times that night. But their luck may have just run out!

Now, the car with the high concentration of GSR and a .40 Cal S&W cartridge shell known to have been driven by the two students could be positively put at the crime scene! It could be verified by witnesses that they were driving that vehicle on the night in question.

Where were the other occupants that were in the car? That was the question. Russ put a big circle around the satellite view of the ranch. "They had to end up there," he said as he pointed to it. Who did the actual shooting they did not know but they could all be sentenced in the shooting if they could be found. Russ wondered if they were still in the country.

Now, what? Should they watch the ranch and see what was going on? Should they get a search warrant and find the students and the other passengers in the car?

A decision would be made by morning in conjunction with the State and the FBI. They would likely get a search warrant and do a joint raid on the place! It was about time.

Anyone looking at the ranch this morning would see normal ranch activities. Hay and silage was being delivered to the feed lots and automatic feeders and waterers were sending those items out in special feed troughs. The feeder calves were bought at auctions and brought to the ranch and fed with the hopes that the feeders would put on lots of weight and could be sold at a profit to slaughter houses for T-Bones, Sirloins, Big Macs and Porterhouse steaks.

There were mixed breeds of steers and heifers and no breeding went on in this section. Each cow was numbered and tracked and the system was all computerized. This scene played out every day throughout the region.

In another section there was a barn where cows could be treated and artificially bred if necessary in their pure bred operation where they bred cows and bulls for use by other ranchers to add new strains to their herds and prevent inbreeding.

The Spa operation was officially closed. Remodeling was in full swing. Places were being painted, new carpet, and curtains and linens were stacked up waiting. The old materials were replaced to be sure there was no trace of who had been there. The old things were burned.

Underground in two secure and well-hidden bunkers, one underneath the feed lot, men were having breakfast and doing their morning prayers and waiting for the right time to fade into the outside world and never be seen around here again. New names and new addresses. It would not be long now.

Down the road a few miles, on the 30th of December, a team was assembling under the direction of the FBI Special Agent that Russ had met in a previous case involving corruption, conspiracy and crime by a high placed state official. There were several FBI agents and several tactical agents with full SWAT team looking attire. Wearing bullet proof vests and carrying automatic weapons in case the fugitives put up a fight. The DCI agents and Madison County also had their vests and everyone was briefed. The Montana Highway patrol helicopter was on hand to provide aerial coverage and try to prevent anyone slipping away. But with 7500 acres to cover, it would be a challenge.

The task force would show up at the gate and announce themselves and if they were delayed too long at the gate they would press on without waiting for the manager to come and be served the warrant. They essentially had a no knock warrant. But they did not have a smoking gun, yet. They hoped they would find it at the ranch and maybe the man holding it.

The FBI agent said he was in charge and no one was to do anything unless he gave the order. Russ and Wayne Dunkin listened and did a slow burn. The FBI had done nothing so far but was ready to ride in and save the day. But, Russ did like the added firepower they brought because he had no idea how many people were at the compound.

They had decided to do the raid in the daylight because of the massive size of the place and aerial coverage was an essential support. Night time and people and helicopters in a panic can be very dangerous, especially if someone decides to start shooting.

At 7:00 AM the group left with lights flashing but no sirens or audible alarms. They flew out the road through Alder startling people pumping gas and walking across the road.

The small army of law officers arrived at the gate and the FBI agent pulled up to the lowered lift arm blocking the way. A startled security guard walked out to the car and the federal agent announced himself and the attendant did not hesitate as he walked to the entrance to the guard house and pushed the button for the arm to raise and the agent and the entourage sped up the drive.

The attendant had two buttons: one for routine arrivals and one to alert the house and the bunkers that something was wrong. In seconds everyone in the compound was on alert and watching as the cars of people and pickups pulling several ATV's arrived and swarmed the main house and started going from building to building.

Chapelle Robichaud was a French citizen with dual citizenship. He was also an Algerian. Both his parents were born in Algeria during a time when it was a French Republic. They had fled during the upheaval in the 1960's.

Robichaud had grown up to be sympathetic to the Algerians and had converted to Islam against his parents' wishes. He was a key man in organizing and serving as a front having worked in the hotel industry in Paris. Now he went where he was needed and had no known illegal activities on his record. He met the agents at the door with a smile and seemed totally unconcerned as Russ looked on.

Robichaud had a quick word with the Agent and gave a sweep of the hand as if to say, "Be my guest."

Robichaud caught Russ's eye and nodded and smiled at Russ.

Russ had interviewed the man shortly after the shooting and was surprised at how relaxed the man was in the face of such massive law enforcement presence. It did not appear that the man was in the least bit concerned about them going through the place.

Wayne Dunkin also noted the casual manner of the Frenchman. "He's way too casual, if you ask me, Russ."

"He knew we were coming and was ready, I suspect."

"You think he was tipped off we were coming today?"

"I would think they have been expecting this and have been ready for some time. I doubt we find anything here. Where are all the people who were here when we were out here last month?" Russ asked.

An FBI agent was keeping an eye on Robichaud just in case he wanted to destroy evidence or run. Russ walked over to him and Wayne Dunkin followed.

"Mr. Robichaud, it appears that business is a little slow. Where are all your customers?"

"We call them clients, Detective, Baker, is it? We are closed for remodeling as you will see. It was time to freshen up the place. New paint and carpets and such. You are free to look at the progress we are making, of course. Our cattle operation is going full speed and we stay busy with that. We will be back open in the Spring for our clients. I hope your Gestapo doesn't destroy what we have just remodeled."

Russ looked at him and surprised the FBI agent and Wayne Dunkin with his question: "What was the name of the man who shot Sheriff Steinbrenner and where is he and the two students that brought the shooter here from Salt Lake City? Or, do they just come out after dark?"

The Frenchman was caught off guard by the question but quickly recovered.

"You are very impertinent and rude to suggest such a thing. You will *find* no such people here, Detective."
"Such people would probably be hard to catch if they exist, and they would likely be way too smart to be seen standing around here. They would be especially hard to catch for a small town operation such as yours."

"But, maybe you will find them somewhere else. Here you will find empty buildings and cows. Lots of cows. And there is lots of cow manure, of which you know a lot about. And that is what this infringement on our rights is today is compared to: cow manure. Perhaps fishing is a better pastime for you."

Russ had to hand it to the man. With local, state, and federal lawmen going through the place inch by inch he was cool and defiant. But two things jumped out at Russ from what the man had said. Two things that set Russ to thinking. He walked over to the side and motioned for Wayne Dunkin to come over out of earshot of the FBI agent and Robichaud.

"Wayne, did you hear how he said that we would not *find* anyone here? It was as if he was saying they are here but we will not be able to find them. And, he mentioned about me fishing. I never said anything about fishing. He got that information somewhere else."

"What do you think, Russ, are we going to find anything here?"

"I believe they have sent all the folks home and sanitized the place. But, I wouldn't be surprised if there weren't some of them still left here somewhere in all this space. But, we aren't likely to find them here today," Russ said.

The search went on for over two hours and men on ATV's rode across pasture and hay fields and looked behind and under and through every crack and crevice and room. Finally the Agent in charge sent out a message on the radio, "We are wrapping this up and leaving. There is nothing here. This was a wild goose chase."

He made sure that Wayne Dunkin and Russell Baker heard the last comment as it was directed at them. As far as he was concerned the Madison County Sheriff's Department had led them on a wild goose chase. Whoever shot the Madison County Sheriff and whatever the two students were up to, they were now long gone. They could not be found at the Double Barr Ranch.

The agent walked up on the porch and said to Robichaud, "Thank you for your cooperation." With that the agents started piling in their cars and left about as fast as they had come. Nothing accomplished.

Russell and Wayne Dunkin had come in separate cars and were among the last to leave. Russ followed Wayne back to Alder where Wayne pulled into the Alder Market and went in and got a coffee. Russ pulled in and did the same.

"I guess we looked like fools out there today, Wayne."

"Russ, you and I know that the only place those guys could have gone was there. The fact that we did not find them today doesn't mean they were never there, and as you said, they may still be there."

"The phrase *gone underground* comes to mind, Wayne. I wish we had a way to do surveillance on them but with that place so far back off the road we'd have to have a drone and they would spot that for sure. I don't know of any other way."

Wayne Dunkin stood there looking back in the direction of the ranch. Russ could see he was in deep thought. "We may have to use plan B." He walked to his car and drove off. Russ wondered what plan B was.

Russ drove in to the Bear Trap for lunch. He had just ordered when his phone rang and he saw that it was

Detective Sergeant Debra Taylor from Salt Lake City.
"Hello Debra," he answered.

"Hello, Detective Baker. How is it going on your hunt
for the bad guys?"

Russ wondered why she would be calling at this
particular time and it crossed his mind that she knew all
about the search of the ranch already.

"Sergeant Taylor, why do I get the feeling you already
know what happened? Somehow, I think you are pretty
well connected out there."

"Well, we do have an interest in the case since the
students are, or were, from here and the car salvage
conspiracy seems to have some local ties." She did not
answer his question, exactly.

"That is a sly way to answer. You do know what
happened, don't you?"

"My boss knows the FBI special agent. He used to be
assigned here in Salt Lake and since there is that
legitimate interest, they talked after the search warrant
was executed and he said that there was nothing to see at
the ranch. I was sure hoping you'd come away with
something."

"I would say you are making what he said sound a lot
better than what he actually said. I imagine he was saying
we were a bunch of idiots that made him look foolish,"
replied Russ.

Debra Taylor laughed. "Now you are making it sound
better, too. He was really bent out of shape! But you have
to keep my name out of it!"

"By the way Debra, while we are on the subject of
secrets, how did Sheriff Barry Steinbrenner know about
you covering for the techs who worked on the car?"

There was a moment of stunned silence.

"Russell, I have no idea! I have not mentioned it to a
soul......oh my." Her voice tailed off as she was speaking.

"What, Debra? Who did you tell that would have spilled the beans?"

"Russell, I can only say this: it was a very close family member. I had no idea he knew the Sheriff."

"Was this family member in the Air Force, by any chance?" asked Russell.

"No, he wasn't. But, he used to go over to his mother's parents a lot in Missoula in the summers when he was a kid. That grandfather was a judge in Missoula and they knew everybody there and they went to the sheriff's house a lot. I have seen old photos of him playing there with the sheriff's sons in the sheriff's car. He took us kids by there once on one of his nostalgia trips. Do you know if your sheriff came from there?

"He came from there and his father was sheriff for many years there and his brother is the current sheriff."

"You can't trust anybody, can you Russell?"

"I think I trust you, Debra. At least until I have a reason to feel otherwise."

"That is about the nicest thing you've said to me, Russell."

"Well, I'm sorry that the leads did not pan out. I was hoping we could clean up the mystery of the cars, the missing students and the shooting. You may need to come back to Salt Lake and let's do some more investigating. I am sure there are some areas we could look at. If you know what I mean."

"I may just have to do that. I'll let you know if I can get out that way."

"Take care of yourself, Russell. And, Happy New Year. Do you have a big New Year's Eve planned?"

"To tell you the truth, I haven't even thought about it. How about you?"

"There is a New Year's Eve party at the club but I hate going. I end up being the only one there without a date since I am always afraid I will get called out and don't ask anyone or accept any invitations. It drives my dad crazy. But I would have thought you would have a date and a party to go to."

"No date. No party."

"That offer still stands. Come to see me anytime. And, Russ, do me a favor, please. Please try to avoid getting shot out there in the boonies somewhere. I would hate to lose a friend in Bozeman that I am just starting to get to know. And, by the way, if I were to be invited, I could come to Madison County and do some investigating, myself. I might could do some undercover work there. Bye."

Russell looked at the phone as the waitress put down his food on the table. Miriam was keeping herself at arm's length and Nancy was pushing him away and here was a beautiful and rich young lady almost begging him to invite her out. "Life takes funny turns, sometimes," he thought.

The next morning, New Year's Eve, Russ and Wayne Dunkin were asked by Barry to come by his house. It seemed odd to Russ that he would ask them out to his house because he had been coming in the office for a few minutes a day to sign papers and catch up on mail and his wife Janet was doing the driving. He was looking better and better but still slow.

When Janet let them in the cinnamon rolls and hot coffee were waiting and Barry was seated at the kitchen table. He invited them to join him.

"I'll leave you guys to it. I am going up and pay bills," said Janet.

Barry briefed them on a call he had received from an angry FBI agent over the failure to turn up anything with the search warrant at the ranch. He had also been called by the Frenchman complaining that the agents had messed up some new carpet and new paint work and demanding that the county pay for it.

"Our new friend Mr. Robichaud doesn't have too high an opinion of us," said Barry with a smile on his face.

"Barry, that guy was way too smug yesterday. He was well prepared for us and they had that place picked clean from one end to the other. Not even a cigarette butt on the ground," commented Wayne Dunkin.

"There is more to that guy than meets the eye. He has been around the block a time or two if you ask me," said Russ. "And before I forget it, Mr. Taylor from Salt Lake sends his regards."

"So, you found me out, did you? Did he call you?"

"His daughter did."

"I see," said Barry with a shake of the head. "Now, what are we going to do about this case and the missing students and the shooter?"

Russ looked at Wayne, waiting for him to take the lead in the conversation, but Wayne just nodded for Russ to answer Barry's question.

"Right now, Barry, if there is an answer that we can find, it is at the ranch. If the students have fled, which is possible, we are nowhere. We have no direction to look and maybe we have every direction."

"I won't try to speak for Wayne, but I believe he and I agree that the Frenchman was almost rubbing it in our face that we would not find the men on the property and that they were there to be found." Wayne nodded in agreement.

Wayne commented further, "We missed them somehow. There are over 7000 acres out there. We need a closer look."

"Well, we are not getting another search warrant anytime soon after the display of manpower yesterday. And if we did, we'd be on our own," said Barry.

Wayne Dunkin stood up and walked to the window for a second and came and sat back down. "It may be necessary to use Plan B."

222

There it was again. The reference to Plan B. Russ waited for an explanation and so did Barry.

"I'll go out there and do a little snooping on my own. A little night recon work," said Dunkin.

Barry said, "That would be illegal and dangerous. And, if you were out there without a warrant, we would not be able to use the info in court. I can't authorize that."

"Of course you can't, Boss," was Wayne's reply. "But if we were able to be *sure* those guys are there, then we figure out how to smoke them out."

"That's Wayne's Plan B," Russ thought. "Night recon work!"

"In the meantime, Barry, I think we post a car out there and do driver's license checks and DUI checks and watch the comings and goings on the road. Maybe we can make them nervous," said Dunkin.

Barry nodded and Russ and Dunkin stood up to leave. Barry said, "I want these people caught but I do not want any of you hurt, Let them go if you have to and don't get hurt."

"Someone may get hurt, Barry, but it won't be us," said Wayne Dunkin and Russ knew he was serious. Dead serious.

But, Russ knew they were dealing with something sinister and very deadly. He sure hoped Dunkin was right!

New Year's Eve and Russ was by himself. He called Miriam but she had gone to some church program and he wished her Happy New Year and ended the call without a long conversation.

He thought about calling Nancy but he was out of things to say.

Nancy's mother was talking through Nancy's closed bedroom door, "I can't believe you are home on New Year's Eve. Get out and have some fun."

Nancy was not accepting calls from Dr. Carter.

Four fugitives were in a bunker under a cow feeding lot at the Double Barr Ranch.

Debra Taylor was dancing with her brother at the Salt Lake Country Club.

Happy New Year? Right!

But, Barry Steinbrenner held up a glass of champagne and toasted being alive and kissed his wife. Some were having a Happier New Year, than others, after all. It had not been that many days past that it looked doubtful he would see a New Year.

19

The New Year had arrived and over a month had gone by since Barry Steinbrenner was almost killed. The two students had disappeared. It was back to school for Miriam Alexander's daughters. They and their mother had begun to get over the shock of having been used by the two refugees but they continued to help at the Student Center with other refugee students. No other students had gone missing so the identity or identities of the other people in the car the night of the shooting were still unknown.

Russ and Wayne Dunkin were convinced their only chance of catching the shooter was to stake out the Ranch but there was also the possibility that he had left with all the other *guests* before the search was conducted. A team of agents and law enforcement had found nothing and there were no records or files that indicated otherwise. They did not have the manpower to stake the place out around the clock and the state DCI and the Feds had decided that was a waste of time.

"Wayne, if you had to guess who those students picked up and where, what would be your guess?" asked Russ.

"Muslim terrorist guys and they picked them up in Salt Lake," answered Wayne.

"The folks in Salt Lake have checked and all the students that have been hanging out at that Student Center and the refugee group are back from Christmas break except the two the girls knew as Cas and Sam. So, it must have been someone that was not affiliated with the refugee student program."

"What are you getting at, Russ. What does that tell us?" asked Wayne.

"We may have asked the Alexander the girls the wrong question. I was focused on the students and that's all I was focused on. I'm going to call Miriam," Russ said as he found his phone.

"Hi, Russ. Happy New Year. Do you have some good news?"

"Happy New Year, Miriam. No news yet but I have a question for Lisa and Laura. Are they around?"

"I'm sorry Russ. They went back to the dorm when school started. Do you want to call them or should I have them call you?"

"Well, you could ask them the question and see what answer we get and then I will have to decide how to follow up."

Before he could ask the question, Miriam interrupted, "Russ you are scaring me! Are the girls in some kind of trouble?"

"No. Not that I know of, Miriam. I was wondering if in the times they were around Sam and Cas if they may have met anyone that looked suspicious or out of place. Maybe someone who was not a student. A relative or a person the boys may have called a friend or someone they knew from wherever they came from. Iraq, I believe they said."

"I can ask them that. Do you need to know back tonight?"

"The sooner the better. Wayne and I feel we are running out of time and may have run out already. Anything they can remember. Anything at all."

"As far as I know, they did not have any relatives here. They were orphans. But I will try and find the girls and see what they remember. It may take a while. They don't always have their phones on. I suppose you have tried tracking the boys with their cell phones?"

"Their cells have not been turned on since they disappeared. My guess is they were disabled and trashed. Don't alarm the girls, Miriam. I may have us barking up the wrong tree again."

Miriam texted both daughters and asked that they call. It was late when Lisa finally did.

"Mom, what's wrong? We have been at the center and then the library so we had our phone off. They get their noses out of joint over people using phones in the library."

"Russell Baker called and wanted to know if either of you had been with Sam and Cas when they might have been around someone that looked out of place or odd. Maybe a relative of someone. No matter how small this may seem, it may be helpful. Maybe they went out with you guys or had dinner with you. Anything like that."

"Not that I recall. Laura is in the shower. I'll ask her when she gets out and she can call you back. I have to get a shower too."

It was a few minutes before Laura called, "Hi, Mom. We can't think of any one. Sorry."

"Well it was worth a shot. Good night." She found Russ's number and touched the call button.

"Hi Miriam. Any news?"

"Yes, there is one thing: I really miss you Russ. I'm sorry. I should not have said that."

"I miss you too, Miriam. A lot."

Well, at least you've got Nancy to call. I don't have anyone. But, I don't want to get off on that! The girls said they could not remember anyone like you asked about. Sorry."

"Thank you for checking, anyway. We'll keep trying until there is nothing else to try, I suppose."

"And by the way; Nancy is not taking my calls. It seems that I am too likely to get killed to suit her. I think she and I are moving on but just not together, it seems. And as for you, you can have any man you want in Salt Lake County."

"I thought you might have enjoyed New Year's Eve with her. I can't believe you are sitting around there by yourself. "

"I was here by myself and watched the ball drop in Time's Square and went to bed. Good night."

Russ had begun to understand why some people kept a lot of Scotch in the house. It was a good thing he didn't because he might guzzle a whole bottle tonight if he had one. There was a first time for everything.

It was about midnight when Miriam's phone rang and she was sound asleep. In the haze of waking up and the darkness in the room she managed to knock the phone on the floor, the lamp off the nightstand and finally answered the phone sounding like a very confused person.

"Hello. What's the matter, Lisa? What's happened? What time is it?"

"Calm down, Mom! Everything is alright. But you made it sound so important that we thought we should call you."

"Laura and I got to talking and there was one time that we were with Sam and Cas at a restaurant and they got a call. It seemed to shake them up and they left us at the table to talk to whomever it was. Then they got very animated at each other. They came back and said an uncle needed some papers they had and that we needed to go pick them up at the dorm and hurry them out to him. Mom, we did not know they had an uncle and thought that they were orphans but we did not say anything about it at the time. Later we just forgot about it."

"Okay, Lisa. What happened? Did you go with them to take the papers?"

"Yes. And the peculiar thing was what they said to us. They told us not to let ourselves be seen because their uncle did not approve of western girls."

"Were you seen by the man and did you see him, Lisa?"

"There were two men in the car, we think. One of the men came over to us and took the box. A shoe box, it looked like. He looked in and saw us and asked who we were. Cas told him that we were taking them to dinner and we worked at the refugee program at school. We left in a big hurry. It was like they were afraid of the uncle."

"Did you get a good enough look at the man that you could recognize him if you saw him again, Lisa?"

"It was only for a second but he was a scary looking guy. Hard looking, if you know what I mean. Maybe we could if we saw him."

"This is probably not anything but, listen, and listen carefully: do not talk to anyone about this until I get back to you. Is that clear?"

"That won't ever happen again, Mom, you can count on that. Goodnight."

Miriam looked at the clock and it was 12:45 AM. She found Russ's number and touched the call button.

"Russell Baker," he answered. "Miriam? What 's the matter?"

"I guess I woke you up, Russ?"

"You did. Is everything alright?"

"My daughters just called and woke me, too, so we're even. They got to talking and remembered seeing some man one night that the boys delivered a shoe box to in a Walmart parking lot. It was done somewhat like it was an emergency. The man looked at Lisa and Laura and questioned who they were and the boys made up some story and got out in a hurry. They say he was a scary looking man and they might, just might, recognize him if they saw him again. They can't be sure but he made an impression on them at the time."

"Miriam, I don't want to alarm anyone, but they should keep this to themselves."

"I made sure that they understood that on the phone. Do you think they are in any danger?"

"I don't know but we don't want to put any spotlight on them, Miriam. Nor you, for that matter. Not until we sort this out."

"What next, Russ? Where do we go from here?"

"I'm going to do some checking in the morning. Let me think this through. I may ask the detective there, her name is Sergeant Debra Taylor, to look into this and help out on that end. And the girls feel sure there were two men in the car at Walmart?"

"That's how they described it."

"Stands to reason that they are the same two men they brought here. These men must be important to whatever group that they and the boys are associated with. The boys have been keeping their noses clean and running errands. They probably chauffeured the men to the Double Barr Ranch. I'll bet you my next paycheck that shoe box was full of cash. And, I'll bet, the folks at Double Barr are up to their necks in this whole thing. Those men must be on a fugitive list, a Homeland Security list, something. I'll call you in the morning, Miriam. Thank you and please thank the girls."

"Russ."

"Yes, Miriam."

"Please be careful. Goodnight."

Russ was now wide awake and his mind was racing. He looked at the phone as he scrolled to Sergeant Debra Taylor's number in Salt Lake. It was now 1:15 AM.

"Hello. This is Debra Taylor. This better be damned important! Is that you Russell Baker?" she asked looking at the phone half asleep. "Did you wake up dreaming about me or something?"

"Were you *asleep*, Debra?" he asked her in a voice trying to sound funny.

"Unless you are standing outside my door wanting to come in, there is nothing you say that's going to sound cute. What's up Russell?"

She had not yet started to call him Russ as most people did. She liked the name Russell, anyway.

Russ explained the new information he had received from the Alexander girls.

"And what do you want me to do on my end Russell?"

"Maybe you could get them in to look at any mug shots or online stuff you have there from FRS Homeland Security, DEA Fugitives List, Immigration Service and maybe Interpol. It's a long shot but if they both came in they might be able to spot a face like the one they saw. It is likely they might see more than one that looks close to the face they saw but that would give us some names to work on and maybe the FBI or Homeland could help narrow it down. We need a name and an MO to help know what we are into. Drugs, guns, smuggling, terrorism, or whatever."

"How many days do you have to get this done, Mr. Baker? I was beginning to like you. Now, you are a pain in.....well, you know."

"We needed it November 25th. So we are a little behind, Debra. I don't know if there is any more sand left in the hourglass, either."

"I'll see what I can do. And, you will owe me a favor sometimes, too, when we get through."

"What, Debra?"

"Mark that *To Be Determined*. Goodnight, Mr. Baker."

Nabil Mussan and Mahdi Shamah were used to being in hiding. It was what enabled them to stay true to their calling and available when needed to make a statement somewhere in the world. They had left a trail of bombings and shootings across the Middle East and in North Africa. They had left their mark in the Sudan, Yemen, and Indonesia. But they were growing weary hiding out at the Double Barr Ranch with the cows and cow manure they had to walk through when they emerged from their bunker under the feed lot.

To prevent someone seeing them with binoculars from some hidden vantage point they were staying in the bunkers during the day. They came out at night and went to one of the cabins with shades drawn and drank tea, beer and liquor and watched porno movies and satellite TV. They could surf the dark web and talk to the Imam and Chapelle Robichaud and the mysterious security man that always stood back and watched and listened.

They wanted to get to the big cities where they could meld into the night life and dance and take ladies to a hotel or go home with them. Get good food and live the good life. Hiding here had to stop and soon. They were growing very restless. So were Kasim and Samer. Cas and Sam as they were known at Westminster College and now called Abdul Samad and Manzur Najafi.

They liked the pretty girls and safety of the school, an occasional errand for the cause. They liked moving people through town and money switched at dark cheap hotels and parking lots. But the living in isolation at the ranch was more than they had bargained for.

When they were doing the training and shooting the AK-47's and practicing with homemade explosives, that was fun. Now, the lying low and out of sight was getting to them. Prayers five times a day was a little much. They had been able to do with much less prayer at school and seemed to do fine and maybe the prayer thing was overrated. What would it hurt to get some chips and a Snicker Bar somewhere? But one of their cars was in a police impound lot in Salt Lake City and the other one was in a deep hole, covered with tons of dirt somewhere on the ranch. A long cold walk back to that little town seemed a little too much for a Snicker Bar.

The shooting of Barry Steinbrenner was not even classified as old news now. It wasn't in the news at all. Life was at its normal routine in Ennis, Virginia City and Bozeman. Over in Alder at the Alder Market people were buying gas and milk and Red Man Tobacco and some cigarettes and once in a while a twelve pack of beer. There were about three people even working on the case now: Russ, Wayne, and Barry. Maybe, Debra Taylor.

No one remembered the cops sniffing around and looking for the bad guys. When Deputy Dunkin was out that way and stopped for a cup of coffee, they gave him a nod and a "Hello, Deputy" and that was about it. Their lives had not changed much.

Many of the ranch hands spoke with a Spanish accent if they spoke English at all and so it was not unusual for a man to come in off a ranch truck and pay for gas and a few items off the shelf and a cold drink and leave with no one ever saying a word. There were always new faces coming and going so that was the norm, too.

With a cowboy hat and boots and Levi's they all looked about the same. That had always been a little extra business at the market and not having those clients around was a drag on their business.

When Russ and Wayne were finally able to put the students' car at the crime scene, they had sent a deputy to Alder with pictures of them from the school and no one had seen them. So, when the Hispanic ranch manager came to the market and had two cowboys with cowboy hats and boots and Levis riding in the back that was nothing new.

They paid cash for the Snicker Bars and potato chips and Coca Colas and a bag of other goodies and never said a word. To the manager at the Alder Market they looked a lot like the people who had often stopped in on their way to and from the Double Barr Ranch. They looked like people wanting to look like cowboys but weren't. The ranch manager had been paid one hundred dollars to take them in on the truck and not to say anything to Chapelle Robichaud or the Imam about it. Why shouldn't they go if they wanted to? No one would see them and apparently, no one did. No one would be the wiser.

Russ updated Wayne on the new developments regarding the men in the car with the students. They were at a standstill for leads. "Wayne, I am thinking about going in for lunch to Bozeman and maybe stop in the River's Run and say hello to everyone. Would you like to go up with me and have lunch? I am pooped out with no sleep last night but I want to be ready if we get a call."

"Just what are you going to do, Russ, if they identify these guys? We don't know they are at the ranch," said Wayne.

"I have no idea, Wayne. What do you think?"

"I think it's time for Plan B."

"Well. What is Plan B, Wayne?"

Wayne walked to the door, picked his hat off the rack and walked out and turned to Russ, "May be best you don't know." He went out the door to his car.

Russ started toward Bozeman. He did not know why he wanted to go there so badly. There would be no fishing in the Gallatin today. No floating on the Madison. No romantic evening with Nancy. There was only one thing now: find the people who shot Barry before it was too late. What in the hell was he doing here, anyway?

Then, it really hit him: he had no place to be, really. No kids to take to little league, no wife to come home to and not even a dog. Maybe that's what he needed: a nice yellow lab. They didn't really need him at River's Run. The only place he was needed in the slightest was the Madison County Sheriff's Department and he was not contributing much there, either.

A buzz on the phone and a text message: "Girls coming in at 2:00 with their mother." It was from Debra Taylor in Salt Lake. "Did you get any sleep last night? I surely didn't."

His reply was short. "No."

He looked at the phone as he stopped at a light in Ennis, and scrolled to Nancy's number.

He had said he was not going to call her any more, but what did he have to lose?"

"Hello, Russ."

"Hello, Nancy. Wanna grab some lunch around 12:30. I will buy. Betty's, Maybe?"

"I would like to go to finish our brunch at Perkins, if that's sounds good to you," she said in a soft voice.

"Perkins it is. I'll pick you up at 12:15."

"You don't need to do that; I'll meet you there at 12:30. See ya then," and she ended the call.

"Nice," he thought.

The parking lot at Perkins at 12:15 was crowded and Russ had to park in the church lot at Faith Baptist Church and run across the road. Nancy was standing inside waiting on a table. As Russ walked in, Nancy walked up and gave him a little hug. Russ was shocked but pleased that it was off to a good start.

"Russ, first, let me apologize for being such a bitch the other day. I don't know what has happened lately. I was out of line talking about your job. I do not have the right to do that."

"Thanks Nancy. That's nice to hear. I appreciate you saying that," he continued.

"I think that we have both been through some things that are part of who we are and may always be. I have to somehow stop being married to a dead woman and I have not done a very good job of it. I know that she has continued to stand in the shadows and I keep seeing her. I have to let her go sometime. She would want that and her mother and father have tried to make me see it too. I care about you but I have to be there 100%. I have not been able to cross the line and not look back."

"You said you wanted us to be friends, Russ. I want that too. If I'm honest with you and myself, I've wanted a lot more out of our relationship than that. But, if we have that, we will want the best for the other and we will see how it goes. I will not try to force anything on you and if you can overlook my weaknesses, I promise I won't be pouring water on any fire that's there anymore."

"Will you still do my shuttles, Nancy?" Russ said with a half joking way with a smile.

"Oh, I guess so."

"Well, there you go," said Russ. We can agree on some things."

"How is the investigation going? Are you any closer to finding the people?"

"We have some new tracks we are following but nothing we can say will solve the case by themselves. We don't know where the people are and until we do, we can't arrest them. Our search warrant got us nowhere. They may be in Iraq for all we know right now."

"What are you going to do?"

"Wayne says we are going to have to go to Plan B, but he won't tell me what Plan B is," Russ said with a chuckle.

"I hope that it does not involve someone shooting at you. But, if it does, I hope you are prepared."

When lunch was over they walked out to her car. She opened the door and then tuned and took Russ in her arms and kissed him. Long and hard. Then with a smile she said, "That was just among friends."

"I'll see you later, Friend." Russ walked with a little skip in his gait as he crossed to the church parking lot.

Main Street in Bozeman becomes Huffine and heads to Four Corners and State Route 84 winds through vacant lands and irrigated fields and by the Madison River for miles. Fifty miles later, after intersecting with US 287 you can be in Ennis.

The bridge across the Madison and the boat ramp there always slowed Russ down just looking at the magnificent view. He always slowed near Norris where a State DCI agent was almost killed by an attempt on her life and left for dead in a field.

Fifty miles to someone from New York seems like going on a long journey but in Montana, that is a trip to the grocery store. If you get caught behind some farm equipment you can get slowed down but speed limit signs are few and far between and in a sheriff's car, you can make good time.

Two lane speed limits of seventy coupled with the universal fudge factor of about ten miles per hour, and you can go the fifty miles in a hurry.

Russ was waiting for that call from Salt Lake. They should be looking at pictures right about now.

"Madison County Unit 8 calling Madison County Unit 2," Russ spoke into his mic.

"Go ahead Unit 8," said Wayne Dunkin.

"I'll be 10-7 for a while. If anyone needs me call me on my cell. 10-4?"

"10-4, Unit 8. Out."

Russ made it to his house and collapsed on his bed. The late nights had caught up with him and he was sleeping soundly when his phone rang about 6:00 and it was Debra Taylor in Salt Lake.

"Were you asleep, Mr. Baker? You sound like it," said Detective Taylor in a very professional sounding voice.

"Yes, ma'am, I was. I did not get any sleep last night and it caught up with me. What can I do for you ma'am?" Russ said in *his* own very professional sounding voice. He was glad he chose to do that.

"Mr. Baker, I am here with the Alexanders; Lisa and Laura and Mrs. Alexander. I have you on speaker phone."

"Great. Good evening all. How has it been going?"

Detective Taylor answered, "We've looked at lots of pictures with nothing yet. Some pictures look a lot alike and that makes for a slow go. We have set aside a few for reconsideration. We plan to get back together tomorrow again at 2:00. Both the ladies are done with class by 2:00 and we will try again with some other sources. Just wanted you to know."

"Thank you, Detective Taylor. I will listen out for your call."

So they had not struck out yet and still had a few at bats left. But, the game would soon be over and Russ knew it. They needed a big rally or, to use a fishing metaphor, they were down to their last cast.

Russ went back to sleep. In Salt Lake, Miriam and her daughters stood up to leave and Debra Taylor said, "That guy is very impressive."

"We think so too, Detective Taylor," said Miriam.

As the Alexanders walked out, Detective Taylor wondered if there was more to the Russell Baker and Miriam Alexander relationship than met the eye. She detected something in the way Miriam responded.

The Double Barr Ranch was going about its daily routine. It grew alfalfa, millet, and other forages to feed their cattle. Silage bins were on the property and hay sheds where hay could be stored out of direct weather. There were farm equipment sheds and maintenance barns. Many of the facilities served dual roles. There were tractors and combines. It was an impressive and modern looking ranch and it hid ancient cultures and beliefs very well.

There was a large feed lot in plain view where heavy rail fences kept the feeder cows corralled up for feeding. There was food, water, and shade available for the animals.

One of the watering troughs had no water in it. It was there to serve a specific purpose not involving the cattle. By stepping on a release pedal concealed under one corner and lifting up on the end where there were handholds, the trough raised with the aid of pressure cylinders similar to those on the rear liftgates of an SUV. When the trough is raised up, it reveals a set of aluminum stairs leading down into an underground bunker.

The bunker had been designed and built by a company that makes shelters for tornado affected areas, for survivalists preparing for the end of the law abiding community and for those who still feared an atomic attack. Thousands of these types of structures exist throughout the US.

The large bunker was made onsite to avoid attracting attention. Some are manufactured offsite and hauled to the place they are being installed by truck. The prefabs are easier and faster to install but attract a lot of attention being hauled around. This unit at Double Barr is 10 X 40 and it cost $91,000, not including solar and wind generators for temporary power. Solar and wind generation was in use in all of the buildings, barns and cabins so the presence of those units looked normal on the ranch to run pumps and lights, etc.

It could easily sleep 6 people and had water, hot shower, closets, bathroom and TV and microwave. In an emergency, like an FBI raid, it could hold 40 people or more huddled together.

On the surface, cows walked around and did their thing and traces of anyone coming and going were quickly erased.

The Imam, the security man and the two men that had arrived with the two students were in this safer and more spacious unit. They could come and go at night to one of the cabins and quickly go back to the bunker during the day or if there was a threat. An air filtration system rounded out the unit's livability. The air intakes were built into the infrastructure of the fences, gates and drain pipes and attracted no attention. With dry rations and bottled water, people could stay there indefinitely.

A smaller unit was concealed under a covered hay feeder area. It was 10 X 20 and could sleep four comfortably and a couple more if needed. It, too, was accessed through a water trough. There were wind turbines that produce 380 Volts of DC electricity in as little as 7 MPH wind and inverters were used to convert the DC power to AC for electrical devices. Storage batteries helped in the down times. The smaller unit could accommodate 25 to 30 people on a temporary basis.

The two students were being housed there and they, too, could use one of the cabins at night. These two bunkers were designed to keep and protect people for a long time and were doing their job well. So far. Each bunker contained weapons and ammunition.

But the confinement was hard to deal with, especially for the two students. The use of the cabins helped.

A surveillance team could be there for days and never see the *guests*. This ranch location had been chosen because it was close enough to interstate highways and isolated enough not to ever be bothered. Men on the run could stay here safely.

Russ, Barry, Wayne Dunkin and Deputy Smisson met with the Montana DCI agent the next morning. The agent said, "I'm sorry to report we have no new leads on your case, Sheriff Steinbrenner. At the moment we are at a standstill. Have you guys got anything new at this point?" He tapped notes into his iPad and looked around the room for a reply.

"Nothing new. We keep looking under rocks but so far, nothing," said Barry.

The agent continued, "We have a task force working with several other states, including Utah and Pennsylvania to try and determine how extensive this salvaged car thing is and what and who is behind it but all we have so far is a possibly dishonest insurance guy who has been selling these fake titles so people can avoid car tags and taxes and travel under the radar. But, he does not seem to care who the buyer is or what they intend to do with the car. Of course, we have considered that some people might want an untraceable car, just like they want an untraceable gun, especially if they planned to use it for a car bomb."

Russ and the others looked at each other with the same conclusion in mind: they had never thought about that.

"After the raid to serve the search warrant failed to produce a shred of evidence, there has been a lot of pressure on us to not be profiling people. Unless we have a smoking gun we won't be able to get another warrant."

A short time later, after the DCI agent left, the four Madison County officers reconvened in the jury room. Russ updated them on the efforts being made in Salt Lake. "We are waiting to see if the Alexander girls can come up with a face and a name today."

"What exactly do we know about that ranch set up?" Barry asked.

Wayne Dunkin was quick to speak: "It is a modern operation as far as technology. They have satellites for TV and internet service. They have solar power and wind turbines in use on a lot, if not all, buildings. Modern farm equipment, modern out building and security that includes infra-red night vision cameras and closed circuit TV."

Russ was very impressed with the assessment that Wayne had made. He had not been aware of the total security system but it was clear that Dunkin had been very observant when he was out there at the ranch.

"They have a number of motion sensitive lights and that makes sense on farm buildings when you are running around out there at night with equipment. The cow operation looks professional and as good as any you will see around here."

"Do we have any idea what is going on out there now?" asked Barry.

Russ commented, "Other than cows and farming, it does not look like anything. They are sprucing the place up and have painters and maintenance teams out there."

They concluded that they would wait on the call from Salt Lake and then determine a course of action as soon as they heard. Another day down the tubes.

20

Russ's phone rang as he was walking out the door. It was Nancy Freeman.

"Hello, Russ. I was wondering if you would like some of my world famous lasagna with all the trimmings for dinner."

Without thinking long he replied, "That sounds really good. What time do you want me there?"

"This will be delivered to your house about 5:30. Does that work with your schedule?"

"Why that will be just great. Is that coming UPS or FedEx?"

"Personal delivery," she said. "See you at 5:30 and I'll bring some wine."

Russ hoped that Miriam and Debra Taylor would call before Nancy showed up. This was getting a little awkward for a man who did not have a steady *girlfriend*! He wasn't sure of Nancy's plans for the evening and he guessed he would play it by ear. He thought they were still at the *friends* level from the conversation at lunch the day before.

Miriam and her daughters showed up at the Salt Lake City Police department at about 2:30 and the women were dreading looking through dozens of pictures of known criminals, terrorists and international fugitives. Many did look the same and picking one face out of all these seemed unlikely.

Miriam had been impressed with the five foot, nine inch tall sergeant the first time that she met her. An athletic build, very pretty face and hardly any makeup and no frills. She wasn't trying to impress the guys with her good looks but Miriam could appreciate the beauty in another woman. She had that same look a few years back and still had not lost it all. With Miriam and her daughters, Sergeant Taylor was all business and very professional.

"Ladies, I know this is a needle in the haystack and your eyes tend to glaze over after a while, but I thought we would look at the Interpol Fugitive and Most Wanted List and if we don't see the guy there, then I don't know where to look. We went through so many yesterday."

With that, Sergeant Taylor started scrolling through pages of pictures and names on her large computer monitor. Like the day before, they would flag any of interest and then come back. Eventually, they would try to eliminate pictures and names from the list by checking sources again.

Face after face, country after country, crime after crime came up and then; there was a reaction from both the Alexander women at the same time: "That's him!" said Lisa.

"Yes, that's him!" said Laura.

The name under the picture was Nabil Mussan and he was, according to the listing, an Egyptian who was wanted in Belgium, France, Holland and Germany.

He was also believed to be associated with a bombing in Indonesia. Whereabouts: Unknown. Known associate: Mahdi Shamam, whose whereabouts were also currently unknown but they had numerous aliases and crimes.

"You're sure?" asked Debra.

"You don't need to show us any more pictures," said Lisa. "If that is not the man we saw, we are not likely to find another picture closer to him."

Debra hit a print button and printed out the pictures on the color printer near her desk.

She then called Russell Baker's number. It was about 3:15 in the afternoon.

"Hello, this is Russell Baker." Again, Russ answered in his most professional voice. You never knew who was listening.

"This is Detective Taylor in Salt Lake, Russell. We think we may have found your man! The Alexander girls are here and they have been troopers but there is little doubt in their mind they saw this man meeting with the two students here in Salt Lake. And Russell, this guy is bad news, as is his known associate. They are wanted in a lot of places for a lot of crimes. "I have emailed the information to Madison County and I will email it to you, if you want," she said.

"Great, Debra! Will you also call Wayne Dunkin and Sheriff Steinbrenner? I think it is only proper that you let them know and thank Lisa and Laura for me."

"Will do. I will also notify the Homeland Security agent and the FBI Agent. What are you going to do next?"

"I'm not sure until I meet with Barry and Wayne. Probably in the morning. But I guess we will take those photos and see if anyone has seen them. We need to have surveillance and do some intel but we only have so much manpower and the State and Feds have grown un-interested, it seems. Again, our search warrant deal has cooled them off and made them gun-shy."

"Well, Russell, let me know if you need anything else here. Call me and let me know how it's going, will you?"

"I sure will, Detective. Good night."

Russ had to get ready for lasagna and a special guest. He would be off duty for a while.

The lasagna showed up right on time and the delivery driver was the prettiest lady in Bozeman, Montana and at the moment she was the prettiest lady in Madison County, Montana. They enjoyed the evening and sat by the fire and drank a glass of wine and for a few minutes they were able to leave their ghosts outside and it was just the two of them. No Dr. Carter and no Miriam, either. And, she would spend the night with Russell Baker.

There would be no work on the case tonight. He was her friend, for sure. If she could bring herself to admit it, Russell Baker was a lot more than that to her.

Russ, Barry and Wayne met at the Madison County Sheriff's office early and it seemed this was now a ritual. Meet, discuss, and then hope. Over and over they kept doing this and over and over the days were passing with no solid evidence to make a case and suspects that were nowhere to be seen.

But now they had a name. In fact, they had two names of men with violent histories in Europe and the Middle East and it was hard to believe they may have been the ones who shot a small town sheriff in Madison County Montana. How did they get here and why were they here? More importantly: are they still here?

"I will take the pictures out to Alder and see if anyone remembers seeing these guys. I have serious doubts we will find anyone who has had contact with them but at least we can cross that off the list," said Russ.

Dunkin agreed to take the service stations, restaurants and stores around Ennis and they would try to patrol the highway more out around the ranch in hopes of getting a clue.

"We need to get on that ranch and see what is going on out there. We need to see if these guys are hiding out there or if we can decide once and for all they have left the area. If we had the manpower to watch it for a few days we might get a lead," Russ added.

The sheriff said, "We have to have some probable cause to get on the ranch again and get a search warrant. Otherwise, we could jeopardize the whole case if it gets to court."

"What do you two think: should I take the pictures out and show them to Robichaud at the ranch?" asked Russ.

Barry said, "I believe it would be a waste of time. If they are involved, he would just say he had never seen them in his life."

Russ rounded up his case notes and photos of the two possible suspects. He also had pictures of the two students that he had been carrying around. He headed out to Alder and the Alder Market. If anyone went to Alder they would likely end up there at the market or the bar across the street.

The traffic conditions the night of the shooting had been such that the normal route the students would have driven from Salt Lake was closed. They would have normally gotten off I-15 at Dillon and headed North on State Route 41. Then at Twin Bridges they would have gotten on State 287 and headed toward Sheridan. The ranch address was actually Sheridan and it was only about three miles out of town.

Russ went in to the Alder Market and showed them the pictures of the two wanted men and no one remembered seeing them. Then, just because he had the pictures of the two students, he showed them again. He had showed them the pictures of the students a couple of times before and no one had remembered seeing them.

The manager said, "Officer, you know the people at the ranch do most of their shopping at Sheridan. They have an IGA grocery there where a lot of people get their groceries. They have some car parts stores, drug stores and restaurants. They are a lot bigger place than here."

"And if someone is going to be traveling on I-15, they would not come this way, they would go over to Dillon. If they have business in Ennis or Bozeman, then they come this way most of the time. So we don't get a lot of traffic from the ranch. But some of the people staying out there will come in here from time to time, get gas or buy a few things. I think they are just seeing the area or going to the Ruby Lake. The most of the people we see from out there are these foreign looking folks and most look like they are from an Arab country."

"They always get themselves some cowboy boots and a cowboy hat and try to look like real cowboys. They come in here and either don't speak English or just chose not to say anything. But since the sheriff got shot, we haven't seen many at all. I understand they closed the dude ranch part and are remodeling out there. We did have some painters coming and going out there from Bozeman stopping in here. But just a few days ago, we did have two guys in here and they were the first ones I'd seen since, I guess, November."

This got Russ's attention. "You had two in here a few days ago? But you say they did not look like these two men?" Russ asked as he showed the two older terrorists.

"No. If I had to pick them out of a lineup it would be hard because they had hats on and never really looked up at me but I would say they came closer to looking like the two other guys you showed me."

Now he had Russ's full attention. He put the two students' pictures back on the counter. "You think they could have been these two guys?"

"Could have been. I don't know how they came or went. I wasn't watching. I just try to keep an eye out on the gas pumps. I think they just bought candy and junk and maybe a soda. They could be anywhere, now."

If the store manager was right, the students may still be in the area! And the two other guys as well. He flew to Sheridan to ask around there!

No one in Sheridan had seen anyone from the ranch in a while, either. They made the same observation: not many clients at the ranch right now. And the ones that they usually saw were all Arabic. There never seemed to be any clients that might be thought of as an American from Seattle or St. Paul.

The picture was even more in focus now. The Double Barr Ranch catered to Middle Eastern clients. That in itself was not the alarming factor. What was alarming was that the four *clients* that Russ knew about so far were all criminals or terrorists or both! Just what was the Double Barr Ranch doing?

"Madison County Unit 8 to Madison County Unit 2," Russ said into his car radio.

"Go ahead, Unit 8. I am 10-20 the Office. Over," replied Wayne Dunkin.

"Are you 10-75 with unit 1? I would like to come in and meet with you this afternoon."

"Roger, Unit 2. I will contact Unit 1"

"I am 10-76 your location. ETA twenty minutes. Out." Russ confirmed he was on the way.

"Madison Unit 8 this is Unit 1, I am 10-69 your message. See you in twenty." The sheriff had been monitoring his radio.

The three Madison County lawmen sat with their coffee and photos of the four men on the table. Russ briefed them on the morning results.

"The two students were likely at the Alder Market in the last week or so. The manager thinks it was them in there buying snacks and candy and wearing western ranch outfits: hats, boots, jeans, the works. He says some of the people who are visiting the Double Barr Ranch have stopped in on occasion when passing through or headed to Ruby Lake. He had not seen many since the night of your shooting. That is why he noticed these two. They were low key, kept their heads down as if to avoid cameras and said nothing."

"He suggested that the visitors from the ranch usually went to Sheridan because it was closer, on the way to I-15 and had a big grocery store and some food places. I went over there and that seemed to be the case."

"It is the same story there. Occasional visitors and all of Middle Eastern appearance. No everyday local looking people. The ranch concentrates, it seems, on people from the Middle East as clients. So far, the ones we know about are all criminal types. Maybe that is not true of all of them that come there and so they feel safe in going about in the community."

"We have names and pictures, but we did not see these people out there, Russ, isn't that correct?" asked Barry.

"Correct, Sheriff."

"If we were able to get another search warrant, do you think we will find them there?" asked Wayne.

"Truthfully, Wayne, I don't. I believe they are there somewhere on that 7500 acres but I don't know that we know where to look," answered Russ.

"How do we find out where to look, Russ?" asked Barry.

"Russ looked at Wayne Dunkin and Wayne answered, "We go to plan B."

It was Barry's turn to ask, "Wayne, what is plan B?"

"We first determine once and for all if they are there. Then, we figure out how to get them off that ranch where we can arrest them on the fugitive warrants."

"How do you plan to do the first part, Wayne?" asked Barry.

"I don't know yet, but you may not want to be involved in that part Sheriff. You may need deniability," Wayne replied.

"I don't want to have to be arresting you Wayne," laughed Barry.

"Sheriff, if you think these guys here are hard to find, you ain't seen nothing," said Wayne Dunkin as he motioned toward the photos on the table. "Wait till you have to find me."

Wayne Dunkin did not smile as he said it and Russ sensed there was a lot of truth in what he had said. And, he felt that the sheriff knew it, too.

It was home for Russ. He made a call to Nancy and then a call to Miriam thanking her for the help in getting the pictures and ID's on the two terrorists.

The FBI, US Marshalls, and Homeland Security had been advised about the two terrorists being picked out of a list of wanted fugitives by the Alexander sisters and at 5:00 AM the following morning, with no notification to Madison County or the State DCI, a large contingent of FBI agents, and Marshalls, and Homeland Security personnel swooped in at the Double Barr Ranch and rousted Chapelle Robichaud out of bed and served him with a federal warrant.

The searchers swept the area and after almost three hours, left empty handed. They had found freshly painted rooms, cows and farming equipment. Stepped in a lot of cow manure.

Ranch hands did not live on the property and none were present. Neither, it seemed, were there any terrorists. Once again, the effort had failed.

The FBI agent notified the Madison County Sheriff as he was leaving and Barry was furious.

But not as furious as Wayne Dunkin. "They just went out there to be heroes and probably drove them deeper into hiding. We may never find them now! They wanted a big arrest and a press conference and thought we had handed them one."

He called Russ who was on his way to the office to tell him the news. "Wayne, they couldn't stand the thought that we might find those international fugitives without them. This ticks me off! They had gotten nowhere on this and now they have put the ranch on high alert. If those people don't run now, they never will."

"Why would they run now, Russ, after two attempts no one has found them out there yet? What place could they be that is safer?"

Russ had to agree.

Once again, morning found Russ and Wayne in the jury room in Virginia City looking at photos and maps and mug shots and trying to come up with a strategy to find the person who had shot Barry Steinbrenner. Russ's phone rang and he saw it was Sergeant Debra Taylor from Salt Lake.

"Hello, Sergeant Taylor."

"Russ, my boss just told me that the FBI and God knows who else did another search out at the ranch. Did you find anything out there?"

"We were not included in the search, Debra. We only learned about it after the fact. It seems someone was trying to grab some headlines and get their ticket punched."

"Well, that sucks! We are the only ones doing anything on this and they want to not even let us know about it?" she said.

"That's how it looks, Debra. I am surprised they did not let you know after all you were the one who gave them the lead."

"Russell, you can count on one thing: if they had told me, I would have told you. I hope you have learned that much about me, at least," she said sternly and emphatically.

"Maybe that's exactly why they did not tell you, they did not want us to know. How would it look if a tiny sheriff's department captured a bunch of international terrorists being looked for all over the world?"

"Now, what?" she asked.

"I'm meeting with Deputy Dunkin right now. The sheriff is not yet back to 100% but I think Deputy Dunkin is about to explain to me what *Plan B* is."

"By God, Russell, that sounds intriguing! Can I play?"

"I have a feeling that if Plan B doesn't work, Deputy Dunkin and I may be sharing a cell at Leavenworth. There probably is not room for three unless somebody doubles up and Dunkin snores, I think. They may do coed, I'm not sure."

"Now I like the sound of that! I don't know Deputy Dunkin but I would probably be sharing with you. Nothing personal against Deputy Dunkin. Be careful and let me know if your Plan B needs another team member. Good night, Russell." Russ was sorry he was on speaker phone!

As he hung up, he saw Deputy Wayne Dunkin doing something he did not do often: shaking his head and shaking an accusatory finger at Russell.

"You dog, you," said Dunkin. "I see now why you are so anxious to go to Salt Lake. Is she pretty?"

"Very," said Russ. "And rich, too. Way out of my league."

"I hope Miriam does not find out, Russ. You might get kicked out of your house."

Then Wayne Dunkin did something else he did not do a lot: he laughed. "Come on; let's go talk about Plan B, Russ."

"Where are we going, Wayne?"

"Follow me out to my house."

It was about 15 miles to Wayne's house on Spanish Peaks Drive in Ennis. It was a nice house with beautiful red wood exterior and an immaculate yard. Russ did not know what he was expecting but he was pleased to see such a nice place. It looked to be about an acre and a half on a golf course and a three stall garage. He had a work-shop in the back.

Russ had met Wayne's wife at the hospital, at the courthouse and at Barry's house on a couple of occasions.

She was an attractive lady that taught school at Ennis Elementary. That was about all he knew about her and that they had two kids. Wayne motioned for Russ to follow him out to the shop.

The shop had a small, neatly arranged work area and tools and a well-lighted work bench. There was steel door that went into another section and it was locked with a deadbolt lock.

Wayne turned and looked at Russ: "No one has been in this room but my wife. What you see in here stays in here. Understood?"

"Sure, Wayne, unless you have some dead bodies or hostages, we are good."

Wayne did not respond but opened the heavy secure door and Russ entered a room full of military type equipment.

There were several boxes and a cabinet containing night vison scopes, a variety of clothing and tactical gear.

There were a couple of hunting rifles and a Remington Model 700 Tactical Chassis chambered for the .308 Cal Winchester with a sophisticated night vison scope. This was a serious weapon used in the military by snipers and looked at lot like the Barrett Rifle Russ had seen on TV and once at a gun range. Not many around.

Then, Wayne opened another wide drawer in the cabinet and Russ could not believe what he was looking at. In the drawer was the most intimidating and lethal looking weapon he had ever seen: there was a Barrett .338 Cal Lupua Magnum 90B Fieldcraft. A rifle that was considered accurate at almost a mile. There was a White Phosphorus ATN Night Vision Scope and Infra-Red Lights.

Russ did not know a lot about these guns and equipment but knew enough to know the Barrett with all the attachments probably cost well over $12,000. He looked at Wayne and Wayne said, "In case we need back up. Some people have drift boats, ATV's and motorcycles. I have guns."

In a military locker there were binoculars, a ghillie suit and camouflage wear and a whole list of other items including military grade walkie-talkies and headsets.

"Do you know how to use all this stuff, Wayne?"

"I was trained by the US Government and used it all in Afghanistan and Iraq. Yeah, I know how to use it."

So that was what Barry had meant about Wayne. "A good man to have in a tough situation," or something to that effect was how Barry had described Wayne. Now he knew why.

There was an ATN-PVS14/6015-WPT night vision monocular headset. The new white phosphorus tubes allowed the image to show up in a more natural daylight look: white instead of green. This was capable of viewing at about 300 yards. A perfect surveillance and attack tool. This was another $3000 piece of equipment.

Wayne Dunkin was prepared. For what, Russ wasn't sure.

"Russ, where do you think the guy is that shot Barry?" asked Wayne.

"Wayne, the only place I know to look is at the ranch. I am convinced they went there. If they are truly not there, then I don't know where to start looking. The information we got yesterday is not conclusive but there seems to be a chance the students were still in the area as late as a few days ago. That gave me renewed hope that they might not have left the area. At least, not all of them. If we can get our hands on some of them maybe we can find the others. The Feds did not get anything out of the Robichaud guy, apparently."

Wayne said, "I am willing to go on that property at night and watch it and see if they are there somewhere. Maybe we could get an idea about where some of them are, somehow. I can only stay out there so many hours at a time and not get my wife crazy and get myself worn out but I will try it a few nights."

"And if you get caught? Are you going to shoot your way out?"

"Not unless I have to. But hiding a vehicle out there is almost impossible. It's wide open so I have to figure that out. I think we would have to arrange for you to drop me off and then pick me up."

"That wouldn't be a problem. The problem would be if you had to get the hell out in a hurry and you're stranded waiting on a ride. Then it's your ass," said Russ.

"Well, do you have another plan, Russ?"

"Can I sleep on it and we talk about it in the morning? I would like to look at the satellite pictures and maps again of the ranch. Maybe you could give me some lessons in using this gear and I could take turns watching with you," answered Russ.

"Maybe," was Wayne's reply. "Let me know what you think in the morning."

Russ stopped at the Bear Trap Grill. He did not know what to do now. He wanted the bad guys but not by taking unnecessary chances. Night surveillance out in the middle of ranchland was a little out of his area of expertise. Then, driving on to his house, his phone rang and it was Sergeant Debra Taylor.

"Hello, Debra. Anything new?"

"What a warm and caring greeting. Now that's what I like, Officer Baker. Is that how you greet all your lady friends?"

"Oh, so we are friends now? That is nice to know. I don't have many rich lady friends."

"Cut the crap! I know more about you than you think!" she said half laughing and half serious. I want to know what is plan *B* is. I have been wondering all day."

"Debra, I really think it's best you don't know and then you won't have to ever be involved."

"Now, Russell, that statement just makes me more determined to find out what you are up to. So, go ahead and tell me so I don't have to call you every hour till you do."

"Wayne has certain skills. He has special ops training in the Army and he wants to do night surveillance out on the ranch. Watch the place to see if we can spot what there are doing. Nighttime stuff."

"He isn't the only person ever trained in those techniques. I was in SWAT for a while until I got a chance to be Detective. They sent me to training for three weeks in Georgia. You probably are familiar with the place at Glynco, Georgia. It's near Brunswick."

"Sure. I am familiar with it."

"I took training in night surveillance, night raids and a bunch of stuff. I did not ever get to use any of it here in Salt Lake. SWAT mainly gets called here when a man takes his wife hostage over child custody or some such stuff. Not too many shootouts in Salt Lake, thank Goodness."

"Well, we have to develop some strategy. In and out is not simple in the middle of 7500 acres of fairly flat ground. We are going to talk about it some more in the morning, but you have to keep a lid on it."

"Don't worry about me. I can keep a secret! See ya soon, Russ." With that she was gone.

Russ called Nancy and was greeted warmly. "Can you come over to Bozeman tonight, Russ?"

"Sorry, Nancy. Things are starting up again on the case and I have to be in the office early. I have some preparations to make before tomorrow. I may be tied up for the next few nights with Wayne so I'll call you as soon as I can."

"I understand. Take care of yourself." She hung up as a light snow started to fall in Montana.

Russ got home and got a cup of coffee. Then he got his computer dialed in to Google Earth and ACME Mapper and laid out topo maps of Madison County and went to work trying to figure out how to work with Wayne and Plan B."

Something that Russ had really not considered before was the large number of roads and trails around the mountains to the west of the ranch. A person could easily use them to drive to Dillon and the Dillon airport. Mining roads, hunting roads and ranch roads that were throughout the area and especially roads like Cottonwood Creek, Ruby Lake, and Sweetwater Creek. Roads that had been used by open pit mines to carry out their ore.

On an ATV or a good four wheel drive, a person or persons could leave Double Barr Ranch and never get on a paved road and drive to I-15 to be picked up or to Route 41. Or, even, the Dillon Airport. People could come and go there undetected for years.

Russ now was understanding that the ranch probably only had *guests* that needed and used their services and training. It was set up to house and hide people and no doubt there was some hidden away place or places to do that.

Just find them and see if there was anyone in them, just like Wayne suggested. But after two teams of FBI and other agencies had not found them even with dogs, where are they. And, how could the two of them cover all the possibilities? Then, what bait would you have to use to lure them out? To get them to the surface.

If there was a route out the back of the ranch it probably looked like the dozens of field roads that crisscrossed the area but would have to be visible. But no one may have used it recently. Or, ever.

The more Russ looked, the more that feeling kept creeping back in. *Frustration.* Russ finally went to bed about 1:00 and dreamed about dirt roads and open pit mines.

At 6:30, Russ was up with a cup of coffee pouring over all the files he had just gone over a few hours before. The more he looked the more he knew they were woefully short of people and time.

At 7:00 AM a sleek turbo prop was on final approach to Bozeman airport. Actually the name is Bozeman Yellowstone International Airport but few call it that.

The plane was landing on Runway 12 which was just perfect because when it finished its roll out, the pilot would take a right on a ramp and pull up to the Yellowstone Jetcenter. Bozeman has one runway while Atlanta has five.

The nice looking older man wearing a turtleneck and expensive pants and shoes and his two assistants would exit the plane and walk through the private terminal, get in a rented Ford Taurus and head to a business meeting involving land development and high finance.

The passenger in the back seat would wait until they cleared the area and then exit the plane carrying a bag and wearing an insulated jumpsuit. The pilot would open the baggage compartment door and he and the copilot and the passenger would unload some other baggage and a rifle case. All this would be taken to the one way walk through gate and loaded in a black Jeep Wrangler Unlimited that had been requested. There was little said but the pilot did ask the passenger, "Are you going hunting?" as he loaded the rifle case in the Wrangler.

He got a one word reply: "Yes."

The pilots walked back to the aircraft and up the steps. A touch of a button and the steps retracted and in a matter of minutes the plane was racing down Runway 12 and gained takeoff speed and was gone. So was the black Jeep Wrangler.

Russ went to the courthouse and laid out all his maps and notes and turned on his computer. Wayne Dunkin was coming in and they would try to come up with a strategy. Barry said he would be there even though Wayne was concerned. Barry said he would not let his people take the blame for a mistake in judgement. Whatever they did, they would do as a team. He would be the wingman.

At a little after 8:00 they met in the jury room and Russ laid out his thoughts and about 8:30 Wayne was leaning by the window, looking out, when a black Jeep Wrangler pulled up. A person got out wearing a jumpsuit and a military style cap and walked in the door to the Sheriff's office. In a minute the administrative person came and knocked on the door.

"There is someone here that insists on seeing Russell and says they are here for the meeting. Should I send the person back?"

Barry said, "Sure, send them back." Looking at Wayne and Russ, he said, "Are either of you expecting someone?" Then the person was at the door.

"You must be Sheriff Barry Steinbrenner. I have heard a lot about you from my father. I am Debra Taylor of the Salt Lake City Police Department and I am here to help with Plan B."

For a moment, the three men in the room were left standing there with their mouths open: speechless. Then Barry said, "The last time I saw you we were skiing some place and you and your family were there. You must have been about twelve at the time."

"I was eleven actually, but I remember that," Debra said.

"What are you doing here? Who sent you?" asked Barry. Russ was still standing there in amazement and so was Wayne.

"I have some time off and no one sent me. I hitched a ride with my father this morning and I am here to offer my help in catching the SOB that shot you. I would like to shove this whole thing up the rear ends of the feds who tried to cut us out and take credit."

"I am trained in SWAT and military tactics. I am available to you on my own time and I won't cost you a dime. And, I have most of my own equipment. I may not be as good as Deputy Wayne Dunkin but I will be better than most."

She spoke with an air of confidence and was very convincing.

"I was their token female for the Salt Lake City SWAT team."

Barry spoke up. "Wayne, you and Russ carry on while Ms. Taylor and I have a talk in my office."

Wayne asked Russ as they walked out, "Did you have any idea she was coming?"

"*No* idea, Wayne. *No* idea. She gave me no indication that she was coming here."

On the ranch, the Imam and the Frenchman were on edge. The two older men were pushing to get out of the area at once. Two raids and two searches were causing them much concern. The two students also wanted out but they wanted to go on their own and not with the two older men who were on international fugitive lists. They were not use to the tension, the confinement, and the lack of contact with the outside world. They had managed to sneak out on the farm manager's truck once and get to the Alder Market and no one saw them but that was not enough. Maybe they could sneak out again.....and not come back. But they had no car.

The two older men were true jihadists and willing to die for their cause. At least, that is what they said. The younger men would rather die on their own terms and preferably sometime far off in the future. But they knew jail was not for them. They had been living under similar conditions and not having female companionship was not to their liking.

Chapelle Robichaud had worked his way to America. It wasn't Paris or Brussels or Munich but he could be in other nice places in a short time without too much trouble. A drive over the back roads could get him over to Dillon where he could get a charter on a small plane to take him to Salt Lake City or Seattle. He loved Seattle. Or, he could go to Denver. Or, wherever. He was not on any wanted list or no fly list. He was a free man and intended to stay that way.

He could drive to Bozeman or Butte and go anywhere he wanted and he alternated between the three airports so as not to be seen too often coming and going. New York was a great place to go and blend into the fabric. Los Angeles and San Diego were nice. He would not allow these four men to put him in jeopardy and if that meant leaving them there at the ranch and disappearing, then so be it.

A few minutes after going in to his office with Debra Taylor, Barry came back and reported to Russ and Wayne.

"Debra wants to be of help and is looking for some excitement. However, she does have the training and probably could help in some ways but I don't want her put in too much danger. I don't need a dead cop funeral to go to. I spoke to her father who says she does as she pleases, to his discomfort. But she is an adult. He would rather her be in the business with him and hopes she will get this cop thing out of her system. He pressured her to get out of the SWAT team and she finally did but there were bad feelings for a long time. She quit coming around. He thinks she hung the moon."

"So where are we on that, Barry?" asked Wayne. "We can't let this slow us down."

"I am in agreement with deputizing her for the time she is here. She says she will give us a week, maybe two. But, I will leave the decision up to you. We could use the extra help," answered Barry.

Russ remained silent. He felt it was Barry's and Wayne's call. But Wayne looked at him and asked, "What do you want to do Russ?"

"I go with what you two decide. After all, I'm a temp here myself. When I'm gone this is your department and you guys make the call."

"Then I say we give it a try. If she can't handle the cold and the schedule or if she looks like she is going screw up the deal, I'll cut her loose without a second thought," said Wayne. No emotion in his voice.

Barry called Debra in. "You are hired and you report to Wayne Dunkin. If he gets concerned about your performance, you will be out. Understood?"

"Understood," said Sergeant Taylor.

"Good luck," said the sheriff.

"Thanks, guys. I did not come here to screw up," she said.

"We don't have enough night vision equipment to go round and won't have in time so we can't all work at the same time. We'll get our plans and then we'll see how to divide up the time," said Wayne.

"Deputy Dunkin, I have all that stuff in the car. I love that crap and bought my own military grade. I have a standard Remington 700 and self-illuminated scope, too. I have my personal Glock and left my department issue weapon in Salt Lake."

"I told you, I came to help. Some girls like perfume and jewelry and nice clothes and I do too. But I also like this stuff. Maybe I love it and I'll carry my own weight."

They went to work trying to figure out what they would do next.

Wayne decided he could get inside the fence by the road and make it to the first rise in the field without being detected.

"The only thing I haven't determined is if they have any thermal imaging devices. If they do and they are monitored, we are dead ducks because we can't detect them."

"If they have infrared the night vision will pick it up. If we go in close, we will try to not use our infrared as they can see ours too if they have any night vision equipment. We'll go in stages until we see what is what. And, they may have booby traps but that's a chance we take."

"Wayne, with the number of people they have had coming and going, I don't believe they could have too much in the way of booby traps lying around or some of their guests would be blowing themselves up," said Russ.

"That makes sense. I hope you are right."

"We have a problem with no place to hide a car. Especially a cop car. Debra, is that your personal car you came in?"

"No. I rented it at the Bozeman airport. We can use it but let's try to avoid getting any bullet holes in it."

"In that case, we can get our gear together and Russ and I will give it a go at dark. You will drop us off at the roadside and stay in the area. They may monitor the police frequency so we will use the walkie-talkies I have. They are good for about 5 miles of consistent range. How good a driver are you?"

"Ask Russ. I can drive hard and fast!"

"You may have to," said Russ.

"Debra, maybe you can give me a crash course in how to use the night vision and I will have to round up some camo," said Russ.

"I have some camo coveralls for you Russ," said Dunkin. "I think they will fit."

"I'll use my ghillie suit and you will stay a little behind me in case we get in trouble, you can cover my retreat. We'll see how it goes. I'll meet you at your house, Russ, and I'll leave my vehicle there. That should give you time to familiarize yourself with the night vision gear. See you about 6:00."

Russ and Debra went to lunch at Bear Trap Grille.

"Debra, it's great that you want to help us but you could get hurt here. We all could. These guys are dangerous. If you want to back out, no one would blame you."

"Russ, this is something I want to do. I may never get a chance to be part of anything like this again. I know you will watch my back and I will watch yours the best I can."

"Wayne will be there and everything is going to work out. I wanted to come here and work because of you. I like what I see and know about you. I figured you would not be coming back to Salt Lake unless it was to see Miriam. That wouldn't do me much good."

"I'm not a good bet for anyone, Debra. I seem to get more people mad with me. You just haven't had the opportunity yet."

"Where can I stay close by, Russ? Is there some place you can recommend?"

"Sure. The Reel Me Inn is a nice place and we came by it coming in. We can stop and see about getting you a cabin there. They know me. I stayed there a while back. Hopefully they are not filled up with skiers."

They stopped at the Cabins and rented Debra one and then they went to Russ's house to get ready for the evening. She briefed Russ on the night vision goggles and checked their other gear and flashlights. Russ wanted to go over the maps and layout of the ranch, the buildings and the roads with Debra.

Debra really liked the house and liked being there with Russ. She could sense he was up tight with her presence and knew there might be something going on with Miriam and Russ. She did not yet know about Nancy.

But, Debra wasn't concerned about any competition. She had a lot going for her, too. Once Russ got to know her, she would have a shot.

The Double Barr Ranch encompassed 7500 acres and ran alongside State Route 287 for about five miles. It was about two and a half miles deep and Russ had seen that Ruby River Road ran the length of the back of the property.

The house and barns and most of the sheds were closer to State 287 and trying to go from the back would mean a two mile trek in and out across the Ruby River and make it very hard to beat a retreat if observed. The river did offer cover with some trees. The only logical approach was from Hwy 287 and that meant more possibility of a car coming by.

The only place to hide their car was on the other side of the road at some hay storage lots where round bales were stacked. It made it further to run if escape was necessary. That's where Debra would come in tonight.

The house set back almost a half mile from the road across an alfalfa field. And, the old abandoned roadbed ran across the front the length of the property and would have to be crossed going to the house and returning.

However, Wayne felt that the old road offered some cover. They would soon see.

If they got in trouble and had to go out the back, Middle Road could be used to get around to Ruby River Road and Debra had to memorize the route. There would be no time for map reading in the event they had to withdraw.

It was time. Wayne drove up in his military gear and was carrying the Remington and a 9MM in a tactical holster.

Russ had his borrowed jump suit and Beretta and Debra had her Glock and her Remington 700. She looked all the part of a SWAT team officer and deadly serious.

They would be outgunned in a close fire fight against several men with AK-47's. But at long range and with their concealment, their targets would not live to get that close. Not if Wayne could help it.

But tonight, they wanted no trouble: go in, look, and see if they could spot the fugitives.

Their next move was not figured out, yet.

They drove past the drop off point and made sure the Double Barr Ranch guard house was closed. There was a camera there but did anyone monitor it in the evenings? Maybe after being raided and searched again someone was watching.

And, they were. The main bunker had a CCTV monitor that had a view of the entrance. Anyone in a vehicle almost assuredly would use the drive because of the field.

But, often after dark, the men in the bunkers were going to a nearby cabin and watching TV and doing internet and watching movies. So, no one was watching every second.

Debra stopped and Russ and Wayne were out of the car and over the fence in quick fashion. She drove on to the first hay storage lot and pulled in behind them with all the lights off. She picked up her walkie talkie and keyed the mic. "Radio check."

She received back, "Check one, okay." And then, "Check two, okay." Russ was *one* and Wayne was *two*.

So far so good. Debra took out her Glock and put it on the console beside her.....just in case.

The men moved to the most elevated part of the field and they were still about a quarter mile from the house. The outside had some yard lights and with their night vision they could get a reasonable view of activity but not good enough to identify anyone. Identification would require a closer look if they saw someone to look at.

They could see the main house and some lights were on but they did not believe they would find the fugitives there since two searches had turned up nothing.

Robichaud lived there alone and when they occasionally had women guests, he always invited them to stay in the house with him and some did. A little added perk for the good job he was doing.

A light came on in one of the cabins but they could not see the entrance from their position, so they had not seen the men walk quickly over from the feed lot.

They did not know who or how many were in the cabin. In a few minutes lights came on in another cabin. Maybe a farm worker stayed there. After three hours, the lights in the cabins went out.

Why were the cabins dark when they arrived, they would later ask, and were people already in them with no lights on when Russ and Wayne started observing them? If not, where did they come from?

"Ready to withdraw, Two?" Russ spoke into his headset mic.

"Ready, One," said Wayne.

In their headset they heard, "Three copies. See you in ten minutes."

Debra could see part of the field and saw them moving with the night vision googles. She would drive with no lights on to pick them up. The night vision unit made driving possible even in the dark except that any on-coming vehicle probably could see them.

The men were glad to be in out of the cold and a cup of coffee would hit the spot. Russ invited them in when they arrived at his house. They talked about their first try at finding out what was happening at the ranch.

Russ said, "Wayne, we will have to be observing from more than one vantage point if we are going to pick up what they are doing. I have no idea if the people in the cabins came in while we were there or were already in them."

"Yeah," replied Wayne, "you're right. Maybe tomorrow I can get around to the other side. It's still a lot for two to watch."

"May I make a suggestion?" asked Debra.

"Sure, go ahead," said Wayne.

"Tomorrow, I can put you guys out and one of you can go to the right and the other to the left and go farther in for a better view. I can park the car and beat it back up to where you guys were tonight if that will help."

"Are you sure you are up to being out there by yourself? If there is trouble it could take us a while to get to you," said Russ. "It is cold out there, too."

"I was pumped just being out there in the car. I can take the cold as good as you. Let's do it," she said.

Russ said, "Wayne, I would bet that Gallatin Valley Arms has some night vision gear. If so, I'll go over there tomorrow and get what I need so we all have them."

"I'll ride over there with you when you go. I might see something I need, Russ. If that's no problem," said Debra.

Wayne got up and headed for his car. It was approaching midnight. Debra went out behind him and they both disappeared toward Virginia City and Ennis.

21

Night two had arrived and Russ now was the proud owner of his own ATN night vision goggles. He was $2500 lighter in the checking account, as well.

"I'll park the car down in the hay storage lot where I was last night and there is a spare key in this magnetic holder and I will have it under the trailer hitch receiver in case something happens and I will have my key, too. It will take me about ten minutes to get back up and probably ten more to get in position. Will you guys go all the way or wait for me to get set?"

"Wayne," said Russ, "I think we would go to wherever we are going and we should be in position by the time she gets there to her spot."

Wayne grunted in agreement.

Debra dropped off the two men and drove by the hay storage lot to make sure there was no one there. "This is Unit Three. Location is clear. Proceeding."

Both responded by clicking their mics twice. It was show time.

Chapelle Robichaud was having a difficult time keeping a lid on things. He was sending messages on his Tor browser asking for instructions. "Where do you want me to send Abdul Samad Arazi and Manzur Najafi. They are demanding that they be allowed to leave here. Please advise." His message bounced off one computer and another and became untraceable and he waited for instructions. "Where do you want me to send Nabil Mussan and Mahdi Shamah?"

The two young students, all fire and zeal when they started, wanted to be around young blond and brunette women and eat fine foods and go to movies and they would be great warriors for the cause. Someday.

But today he learned from the Mexican ranch manager that they had slipped off to the store in Alder a few days ago and put everyone in extreme danger. He had confronted them and they said no one saw them and they simply wanted Snicker Bars.

Snicker Bars! For a Snicker Bar they were willing to jeopardize the whole of everything! And, should the Imam or the security man or should Nabil Mussan or Mahdi Shamah find out they would most certainly kill the two younger men and burn them in a barrel of diesel fuel. And they would put him in, too, if they thought he had kept it from them: this breach of security.

Chapelle Robichaud had family: mother and father and sisters and, yes, maybe a wife and child or two here and there. They would kill them too. He needed to be rid of these fools.

All of them! And the FBI kept coming back.

Twice now and he had answered every question to their satisfaction. But how long could he keep these men underground and keep the lid from blowing off? He knew that they could leave anytime they wanted to in reality.

It was night two and Russ and Wayne made a hasty crossing to the spot they had been in the night before. Then Wayne broke off to the right.

He would go another one hundred or one hundred and fifty yards and set up position in his ghillie suit and scan the area below to see what was moving. Russ did the same in the other direction to the left. And they heard: "This is Three. ETA five minutes."

Debra sounded calm but invigorated with adrenaline and from moving quickly up the road, across and over the fence and on to the spot they had chosen. It was a feeling she had never felt before. A mixture of fear, exhilaration, excitement, anticipation and determination. A woman in a *man's job* and she was loving it! Then she advised them, "Three is 10-97." She was at her spot.

Now the three could scan without infrared and wait. See what they could see. See if anyone was watching for them. The cameras around the complex were on and they cycled through on the monitor in the main house security office and in the main bunker and in the unattended guard shack by the road. But no one had seen anything. All looked quiet. The intruders were just out of range of the camera settings. For now.

The three Madison County officers had almost three fourths of the complex under surveillance, even if there were some gaps due to buildings and trees. No one saw any movement.

Then, just as the night before, the lights came on in one cabin and then another shortly after. No one was seen going in because they still did not have an angle on the entry doors to the units.

They faced away from the main house and actually looked down across the feeder lot and the hay storage sheds which sat away from the house and cabins quite a distance. But no one had gone to or from the main house. After another three hours or so, the lights went out and there was no further activity.

Russ spoke into his headset, "Unit One is 10-42." Russ was calling it a night. Wayne and Debra acknowledged, "10-4, Unit One."

By the time Russ and Wayne made it back to the road, Debra had retrieved the car and was ready to pick them up as soon as they got to the road. She was holding up her end. They left the ranch and started to Russ's house. It felt good to be in out of the cold and the heater in the Jeep would soon kick in.

Russ asked Debra, "Would you turn here at Middle Road? That will take us over to Silver Spring Road. That runs into Ruby River Road and goes behind the ranch compound. The road is a mile and a half from the compound so if they are coming in and out from there, they'd likely be using ATV's, horses or some mode of transportation and not walking. I am wondering where the people can be coming from. There is nothing apparent but cows on the other side of the compound."

It was about four miles around to the point on the map that Russ thought they might be accessing the ranch from the back. They drove the length of the ranch and turned and came back.

They saw a number of ranch access roads that someone could use to get into the cultivated areas and to the river. So that seemed a possibility. But there were too many to check tonight and anyone coming from back there would have to cross the river. They headed back to Russ's house, once again.

When they got to Russ's, Wayne came in with Debra. He got a coffee and said, "I am going on home and get some sleep. Let's meet at the office in the morning and see what we do next. Debra, are you fine with driving on by yourself?"

"Sure, Wayne. See you in the morning."

She and Russ sat down at the kitchen table and she asked where the rest room was and Russ instructed her to use Miriam's room that he never used. As she went in, and turned on the light, she was startled to see Miriam's picture along with her daughters on the dresser. A quick look indicated this was a lady's bedroom. But, Miriam Alexander's?

When she went back to the kitchen she hesitated but decided to ask anyway: "Russell, I see pictures of Miriam Alexander and her daughters in the bedroom. Is there something I am missing about your relationship with Miriam?"

"I don't think so. I told you that Miriam was working at the sheriff's office here when I came to Bozeman. I got involved in a case and worked with her then. We were good friends, and still are, but when she moved to Salt Lake she offered to rent me her house. I just left her room and the daughters' rooms like they were and I use the guest room. They used the house when they were here Thanksgiving while I was in Atlanta."

That satisfied Debra's curiosity for the moment. That word *friends* was still in her mind.

They discussed the case and what to do next and Debra started to leave. It was almost 1:00 AM and Russ said, "If you want to crash in Miriam's room or one of the girl's rooms for the night and not have to drive over to town, feel free."

"I guess I'll just go," she said and started for the door. "On second thought, if you think it will be okay, I will take you up on that. I am tired." Russ showed her to Lisa's room and said goodnight.

Russ was sleeping soundly when sometime in the night Debra came into the room and slid under the covers and over next to him. "Russ, is this okay with you?"

Russ turned toward her and pulled her close to him. "Yes," he said.

The next morning Russ was awakened by the phone. It was Debra. "Where are you Detective Baker? We are all here at the Courthouse waiting on you."

Russ looked at the clock and it was 9:15. "Oh man, Debra. I just plain overslept. I'll be there in about forty five minutes. I have to take a shower."

So Debra had gotten up and left him in the bed and now was calling to harass him with Wayne and probably Barry looking on.

"That would certainly help keep anyone from being suspicious of our conduct last night," he thought.

Russ arrived to some ribbing about not being able to take the hard life of surveillance and late hours anymore. He laughed and good naturedly agreed. And now they we looking at night three and snow and cold coming in.

"Russ, somehow we have to get around to the back side of the house and see where those people are coming from. Any ideas?" asked Wayne. He added, "There are several farm roads that lead down to the river but that puts us having to cross the river and get wet or carry something to cross on. I don't know where to cross or how deep we have to deal with."

Russ put Google Earth up on the big monitor.

"I looked at this and I believe there are two possibilities: One, we go down Middle Road and get out just before the creek there and go across the field. That will be about......six tenths of a mile. Trees obscure the house from the field and can provide some cover. Option two is get out on the main road and follow the drainage ditch to the back of the property that runs by the irrigated field. Hopefully it is dry or at least not too deep."

Russ continued, "We can drive over it and see if there is a lot of water coming through the culvert. That would mean going down the ditch a little over a quarter mile and then cutting across another quarter mile to get a spot behind the house. And, I guess, we could do both."

"That poses an extraction problem in case thing blows up," said Debra. "I can't get to the car and both places at the same time."

Barry said, "I'll drive the car. I am up to that. I can't be crawling around out in the cold and wet in the middle of the night yet but driving I can do. If you are still up to helping with the other, Debra, then I can take over the driving."

Wayne said, "Are you sure, Boss?"

"Absolutely sure," said Barry.

"Alright, then," said Wayne. I'll take the field and come in from the Middle Road spot that Russ pointed out. I'll probably need at least ten minutes to get across to position at the edge of the tree line. Russ, do you feel okay coming down that ditch? It may be wet."

"I think I can handle that. I have a pair of cheap waders that I let my clients use and some cheap boots. If the ditch is full of water, I'll slip those on and keep them on till I get to a get out point. I will leave them there and get them coming out. They are not identifiable and if things get crazy, I'll just leave them. It won't matter by then."

Russ looked at Debra. He was suddenly more concerned about her welfare than on the previous nights. Things had gotten more personal. "Are you sure about going out there again Debra? Our luck may run out one of these nights."

"I came to see this through. Yes, I am ready."

It was a strong willed and confident cop talking and not a girlfriend from a one night stand. She looked at him with a look of determination.

Wayne said, "We're good to go. We meet at Russ's at 6:30. I don't see any need in lying in the cold any longer than necessary since they have been turning on the lights about 8:30 every night. Barry, you will be number four on the team number. Sorry but Russ took number one," Wayne said with a smile.

"I will need to go get familiar with your Jeep Debra. It may be better if we have to go across an alfalfa field than my Explorer," said Barry and they left to go do that.

Wayne Dunkin said as they walked out, "I have grown to like that Debra. I think she is a lot tougher than I thought when we started."

"I like her too. I think you are right. I believe she would shoot a bad guy if she had to," said Russ.

It was Plan B, Night Three. Barry turned the Jeep onto Middle Road and stopped for a moment where the car was shielded from the house by a large round hay bale storage area beside the road. It was next to the field Wayne was to cross. It was barely noticeable that Wayne exited the car.

Barry continued on down the road until he came to a driveway to another ranch where he did a quick turnaround and headed back to the main Road. He drove past the guard house and stopped just long enough to be sure no cars were coming and Debra exited and hit the ground in a trot in her camo gear and carrying a tactical bag and her 700 Remington. It looked like a lot for a man in good condition to carry but she handled it well. The thinking was that if one got in trouble, the long range rifles and night vision would enable assistance from a greater and more secure location than trying to storm a fortified compound with men possibly armed with rapid fire weapons.

Then Barry drove to the drainage ditch which to some looked like a creek and it did have water flowing even with the snow and cold. Russ would have to wade in the water. And, he would have no fly rod this time.

He pulled the waders on as best he could in the car and put his combat boots in his tactical bag where he barely had room. It was show time.

Barry turned the car around and Russ exited the car and into the ditch. Barry drove to the same hay storage lot where Debra had parked behind the large plastic wrapped round bales of hay. Now he would wait. In his bag was an AR 15 and he had a thirty shot clip and a spare. He also had a Glock 9 MM. If he encountered anyone tonight they would have to deal with the AR 15. He did not intend to let someone shoot him again.

It took what seemed forever for the radio to start letting the team know that everyone was safe and that they had gotten in position.

Finally Debra had made it to the high part of the field and she spoke into the mic: "Unit Three is okay."

It was about ten more minutes before Wayne checked in: "Two is okay." And finally, Russ called in, "One is okay." Barry acknowledged each with a quick two presses on his send button which made an audible click in the others radios.

There was no way of knowing how many people were actually on the ranch and how many of them might be armed if they were there. There may only be two and one was going to one cabin and one the other. Charging into the compound could be suicide with their small contingent of three. Their simple rules of engagement: don't be seen and don't engage. Fire only if fired upon.

Now, wait.

Debra Taylor could not believe she had gone into Russ's room last night. She had wondered all day if that was a big mistake and they'd had no time to talk today privately.

She came to Montana to help but she knew she came because there was something about Russ that was different than the other cops she had worked with and different from most of the eligible men in Salt Lake who saw her as some career and income enhancement because of her rich father. Russ had not seemed too let that be a big deal although he was impressed with her father when he had met him.

But tonight, in an alfalfa field in Montana, wearing a headset and night vison googles, she would not have been recognized at the Salt Lake City Country Club. And, tonight it was her job to stay focused and stay alive and help keep her team mates alive, too. And, be ready to shoot someone if necessary. Not the usual Friday night goings-on at The Club.

Wayne had a view of most of the cabins and there was a hay storage shed that had a cover over the top. Hay was stored here to be used mainly in the feeder lot which was down on the other end of the compound. The bales were very heavy and moved by a tractor. The entire area was several acres with a checker board of heavy fences and steel and iron gates and water troughs. There were a few lights on and there were others that apparently were manually operated. Motion lights would not be useful with all the cows moving around and would be on all the time. Cows could be isolated when needed; it was a nice operation if you liked a lot of cows and cow manure.

Russ had a view of most of the cabins and was close to the feeder lot which was also large. There were a number of cows milling around. It smelled to high heaven but he guessed if you worked around it every day you could get accustomed to it.

The cows had not paid him any attention other than a few who wanted to see if he had a snack of some kind for them. It, too, had heavy gates and fences crisscrossed the entire space to allow management of the cattle and the feed troughs and automatic watering system with heaters to keep the troughs and water from freezing.

It was approaching 8:15 when something bizarre happened in the feed lot fifty to sixty yards ahead of Russ.

The end of one of the eight foot long water toughs started to rise up like the hood of a car. Light came out of the opening and a man stepped out carrying some sort of assault weapon. Possibly an AK but Russ wasn't sure. The man looked around for a minute and then three more men emerged and two of them had similar weapons. Russ was frozen to avoid being seen although the cows offered enough muffled sound and movement to hide him pretty well.

Without speaking, Russ keyed his mic one time, waited a second, and keyed it four more times. He waited a minute and repeated the process. The others should know that Unit One had made visual contact with four individuals. It did not require him to speak and possibly give away his presence.

Russ watched as they made their way out of the corral area and they stopped at one of the heated water taps and washed their feet after walking through the cattle yard and then they went up to the cabins and went inside and turned on the lights.

In a few minutes, Wayne Dunkin was startled when the water trough about fifty yards ahead of him also rose up on one end and stopped and two individuals carrying some types of weapons stepped out.

Wayne Dunkin looked at the two through his rifle scope. He wondered if one of these men was the one who shot his friend Sheriff Steinbrenner. He'd have no problem putting a round in that guy!

He put the crosshairs on the back of one of them and he knew he could drop both of them easily. He knew because he had done it many times before. But he just watched.

They stretched and walked to one of the cabins and went in and turned on the lights! Wayne keyed his mic twice, waited a second, then two more times. He repeated the process. Now they knew they had six individuals for sure. If there were more inside those places, they did not know, and, they did not know if there were other people in the cabins.

Wayne had never actually seen the two students from Salt Lake, only photos, and the two men he was looking at were wearing scarf's called kufiyas. Since being at the ranch, the Imam had insisted they look less western.

Debra could not see those men from her position but did see a man walk out on the porch with a cigarette and stand and look first down toward the cabins and then, he looked straight at where Debra was hunkered down in the grass.

She looked at him through the night vision and he was illuminated by the porch lights. She assumed him to be the man that Russ and Wayne called the Frenchman.

He walked inside the house and returned in a moment with a pair of binoculars! As he turned them to look her way, Debra felt like she was crawling under the ground she made every effort not to be detected. She could see the infrared illuminator on the night vision binoculars as it lit up the area.

After a moment, he went back inside. Then, she saw what looked like a mule deer walking across between her and the house and she assumed that to be what the man was looking at. She relaxed her grip on the Remington. She then keyed her mic three times waited and then once more. She repeated the process. She received a response of four clicks letting her know that Barry had received. It was really nice to hear the clicks after nearly being spotted!

And then, there were seven. The team knew there were at least seven men at the ranch. Only one plus the ranch manager and some ranch hands that came and went every day had been there when the Feds had showed up. These did not look like ranch hands.

As in the past two nights, about 11:30, the lights in the cabins went out and the men came from the cabins and the motion lights came on as they walked from the cabins across to the cattle feed lot and to the hay shed.

Wayne could see the two men and he could see the side of the house and realized this underground hiding place was positioned so that anyone from the house could be there in a matter of a half minute if they were running. A minute tops.

They two walked to the hay shed and up to the water trough and one took his foot and stepped on something that raised the end of the trough. They walked in down some steps and the trough lowered. They were gone from view in a few seconds.

The other four men came through the cow lot and were wearing something on their feet. They got to the water trough and raised it and as they stepped in they removed their disposable paper booties that were covered in cow manure and mud and entered the bunker and the water trough lowered. There were soon no signs of their coming and going. Some of the cows came over to investigate and no one would ever know they were there.

Russ looked for air vents or some indication of how the system worked. Wayne flicked on his infra-red illuminator for a moment but saw nothing from his vantage point.

Then he heard in his headset, "Unit One is 10-42." Russ was calling it a night and ending his surveillance.

Wayne said, "Unit Two, 10-4."

Debra also acknowledged, "Unit Three, 10-4"

Barry started up the Jeep and watched for some sign of Debra and she crested the rise in the field where she would no longer be seen she moved to a trot to get to the road.

With the soft ground and light snow and all of the gear, it was not like a jog in the park. And, she had to avoid the cameras on the guard shack that covered the drive way. She had about 500 yards to cover to get to the road.

Russ had moved towards the ditch where his waders were and then he would have to go up the ditch back to the road. It would take him several minutes. He had to cover a total of about 1100 yards, part in a ditch filled with water.

Wayne moved back across the field toward the hay storage lot. He had to cover a 1000 yards.

Suddenly the compound lit up! Lights came on and the sound of the big Pistenbully snow cat could be heard by Russ and Wayne. It pulled out of the shed where it was stored and turned on a large array of lights and headed out a gate and toward the area of the hay storage shed where Wayne had been just minutes before.

Wayne was about a hundred yards away when he saw the big machine coming and there was a man with a rifle hanging out the door on one side. They were looking in the area where Wayne had been hiding for the past few hours.

Wayne was tempted to take his Barrett rifle and drop the man with the gun but he held tight. There was enough light snow that it was hard to see where anyone had traveled without getting down on the ground.

Then a high intensity beam of light hit the back of the cab of the snow cat. The bright light startled the two men.

When they turned to see where it came from it was gone but they swung the snow cat around to see and this allowed Wayne to move further away and toward the hay storage lot. They shined the lights in the direction that Russ had gone and saw nothing.

Russ was hunkered down with a cold weather snow camo outfit that did well in the mixture of snow and grass. He had found one for him and Debra at the Gallatin Valley Gun Store.

Debra made it to the road and Barry was waiting and had the hatch open and Debra threw her stuff in and Barry was keying his mic, "Unit One, what's your situation?"

"Stopped for the moment, but in route."

Then Wayne came on: "Almost at Pick up. Use caution."

Wayne had been able to cover a lot of ground when the snow cat had spun to look for the source of the light. They did not actually see where it came from since it hit the cab of the snow cat from the rear and was only on for a second. It had given them the impression that someone was targeting them. They were just guessing where it came from. Russ had taken a risk but it had paid off for Wayne when he had shined his light on the snow cat.

Barry accelerated the Jeep and turned down the road toward the hay storage lot where Wayne had almost arrived. Debra threw open the door and Wayne threw in the equipment and piled in on top of it all.

Then the former fighter pilot, now sheriff, did a strange thing: he turned on the headlights of the Jeep.

Barry pointed the car in the direction of the snow cat and house which was about 700 yards away and headed toward where Russ was.

Debra grabbed the AR-15 that was on propped up beside Barry. The snow cat spun around and headed in the direction of the car.

Wayne Dunkin saw what the Sheriff was doing; drawing fire from the enemy to allow Russ to escape. In this case, it was just diverting their attention. He yelled into his mic, "Unit One, get out! Go!"

Russ saw the snow cat turn around and he was up on his feet and running, he finally made it to where the waders and boots were but he picked them up and kept running. He was now wet wading in twenty degree weather in a Montana ditch and the fish were not biting!

Barry waited as long as he dared and then left out toward the Ruby River Road as fast as he could drive the Jeep. There was no way for the snow cat to overtake them, even cutting across the field, there was a river to cross and probably not too many places to do so in the machine.

Barry made a big loop and came back around on the State Road 287 to where he had hidden in the hay bale storage lot. He turned off the lights and was about to call Russ when they heard, "I'm here. Don't shoot me when I step out."

Debra let out an "Alright!"

Russ stepped out with his flashlight and Barry turned on the car lights. Debra had the door open, "Get in, we have to go!"

Russ was wet and ice was hanging off his clothes and he was shivering from running in the ditch.

Barry turned the lights off and sped past the ranch. A few miles down the road Barry turned the inside lights on and they looked at Russ who was trying to get warm.

Barry said, "You look like hell, Detective Baker. You really need to get cleaned up." The car erupted in laughter.

22

Chapelle Robichaud was already in a state of high stress from having the FBI breathing down his neck. When he had stepped out on the porch he thought that he saw movement in the snow up in the field. Whatever it was, it was silhouetted in the lights from the guard house and it alarmed Robichaud. He had gone in and gotten a high tech pair of binoculars and looked using infra-red and had seen something moving. As he scanned he thought he saw something in the grass. As he continued to look, he saw a deer or some animal walking and trying to graze on what it could find in the field. The hump he saw was probably another animal as they were common in the area.

When he went back inside, he went to a window that overlooks the main yard and toward the hay storage shed. He looked out the blinds and scanned the area. That was when his night optics picked up the infra-red light that Wayne had turned on for a moment and then back off. There was someone there!

He buzzed the security man who was in the bunker under the feed lot. "Get a gun and meet me at the snow cat. Hurry! We have visitors!"

Russ and Wayne had already started their retreat and did not see them until they heard the snow cat.

The ranch security man and Robichaud went back and looked at the area around the hay lot and saw nothing. The car they saw did not look like a police vehicle but those Feds may be using something else. After looking, they all went into the bunker for the night. Even Robichaud.

"Who was out there?" asked the Imam.

Robichaud responded, "We didn't see who it was. Apparently the intruder had a car waiting at the hay lot at the edge of the field and made it to the car and escaped. We think there was another person on the end by the feed lot because a light was used to point in to the cab of the snow cat, but we didn't actually see where it came as it was from behind us. It was one of those intense beam lights and could have been a long way off. We'll look carefully in the morning."

"Do you think it was the FBI again?"

"No. They would have engaged us, I believe," said the security man. "It may have been someone looking to steal something and it could be the local sheriff snooping around."

One of the two fugitives said, "We need to get out of here. We cannot put off leaving any longer."

"Robichaud said, "I will contact our friends in Paris and see what they can do. Maybe we can get you out in the next couple of days. In the meantime, you have to stay out of sight. We will need some money arranged, too. You have your papers and you should be able to go to Canada or Mexico. I must get the two from Salt Lake out too. But do not tell them about what happened last night. They are almost ready to run now."

Sheriff Steinbrenner pulled over at Alder and got on his handheld department radio. "Madison County SO this is Unit One. Please go to Tac Two. All Units, go to Tac Two."

Without waiting for an acknowledgement he switched to the scrambled frequency. Tac channels mean different things to different departments. In the case of Madison County, the sheriff had gotten a grant and installed a sophisticated repeater radio system to be able to reach the entire area and also had two scrambled channels to be able to talk with out scanners and eavesdroppers listening.

"Dispatch, I need cars sent to the following locations at once and do license, registration and BOLO checks."

"I need a license check and tag check on all vehicles going north into Sheridan on Highway 287."

"I need two cars doing the same at the intersection Of Highway 287 and Ruby Road at Laurin."

"I need one car at Ruby River Drive and Duncan District Road."

"Approach all cars with caution. Observe all occupants and report any suspicious persons. We are looking for extremely dangerous individuals who are on our current warrant and BOLO list."

"Do not. I repeat; do not try to apprehend these suspects alone. Observe and report and then stay at a safe distance until we can get help to you."

"Dispatch, acknowledge," said Barry.

The dispatcher repeated the instructions and the Sheriff added: "Notify adjoining departments."

"Russ, I will get you home so you can get warm and get some dry clothes on. I am proud of the way all of you worked together out there."

They arrived at Russ's house and the Sheriff said, "Can we convene here so you can brief me? I want to try and get a local warrant today. No feds. And you all need to get some rest before we do anything else."

From the yard they could see a Madison County sheriff's car moving at high speed with lights strobing and flashing to go to one of the assigned road checks.

"Sure, come on in. Wayne if you could get the fireplace going and Debra, the coffee stuff is on the counter right there. Maybe you can find everybody a cup. Sheriff, there is a phone if you need one. I will step in the shower and be right back."

"Russ," Debra asked, "could I take a shower some-where too?"

"Sure use the bath in the bedroom on the right, Debra." They both had to smile because that was the bedroom she had stayed a while in the night before.

The sheriff was briefed and they drank coffee and tried to tie it all together. The two men that Wayne had seen were two they were looking for, no doubt. From the manner they walked and the brief look Wayne had of them he thought them to be young.

The other men probably included the two men that had come from Salt Lake with the students. They did not know who the other two might be.

"They have a sophisticated bunker or bomb shelter type deal at the feed lot. Imagine under all those cows and cow piles what that might be like. I would think it would be hard for dogs to sniff out anything with all the cow manure there. The cows walking around erase any signs of someone going and coming," said Russ. "I would guess it is just like the one where Wayne was."

Wayne said, "I think the one by me was positioned so the people in the house could run to it if needed. I also think I screwed up when I turned on my infra-red for about twenty seconds. Someone must have seen it."

"That could have been the guy who came out on the porch. He had some serious looking binoculars looking my way. He turned on his infra-red and looked right at me but I think some sort of deer distracted him and he let it go," said Debra.

"But when they came out in the snow cat they went over the area where I was. It's a good thing I had gotten myself out in a hurry," she added.

"Russ, you saved my butt with that flash light trick. That gave me enough time to get to the hay lot," said Wayne. "That guy on the snow cat should thank you too, because I was about to drop a hammer on him."

Russ and Debra looked at one another and then at the sheriff. The sheriff did not react but they looked at each other as if to say, "No doubt he would, too."

The sheriff went to his car and left and so did Wayne. Everyone was dead tired.

Debra got in her Jeep and started down the drive way and Russ went in and got in bed with no hesitation. He was asleep as soon as his head hit the pillow.

A few minutes later, Debra opened the door to Russ's room and quietly snuggled up to the sleeping trout fishing guide and sometimes cop. She was there when Russ woke up.

The sheriff set about trying to get a local arrest warrant on all the men. He wanted to have no mistakes when they went back to the ranch. He wanted to do everything without federal involvement. Once he and his department got the fugitives and, hopefully the man who shot him in custody, he would be glad to rid himself of them. But he had to get them first. For that, he needed the cooperation of the State Judge, the District attorney, and he would need some help from Gallatin County and his friend Sheriff Charlie Neilson. Madison County did not have enough manpower to safely raid the place that had bunkers and AK 47's.

The security man at the ranch was out early on a small ATV, as soon as they had some sunlight, and tried to get a picture on who and how many intruders had been there the night before. There had not been a lot of snow but enough to cover any tracks that might have been there.

Running around in the snow cat had not helped preserve tracks either. There were no signs.

Russ and Debra got breakfast and coffee at his house and she left a few minutes ahead of him. Soon they were at the sheriff's office waiting on Barry to talk to the Fifth Judicial District Judge. His office was on the second floor of a building across the street. The problem was the judge also held court and served two other counties: Beaverhead and Jefferson. Today he was in Boulder which was north of Butte.

The judge had been involved the first time in the searching of the ranch and knew about the federal guys striking out again and would need convincing before ordering a repeat of the two failed attempts. *Fool me once* or something like that. Elected officials do not like to look foolish to the voters. Getting the judge out of court would require some doing.

The two former students had made their plans a few days back but had to wait until the parts fell in place. They would be saying good bye to the Double Barr Ranch today, unaware of the goings on the night before. They'd had enough of being in bunkers and not being able to enjoy the finer pleasures of life that the US had to offer. The people in the US may all be infidels but things were nice here.

Cattle ranches raise cattle and sell cattle and some also breed cattle. The Double Barr Ranch had a respectable cattle operation that did some of all and that helped conceal their other operations. Their mostly Mexican work force did their jobs and went home and knew not to ask questions and to keep their mouths shut about anything they saw.

The ranch used a large International 4400 Crew cab truck to pull several types of trailers. They moved equipment, hay bales, fertilizer, horses and cattle using the various trailers. For moving cattle to auctions and breeders, they used Featherlite 30' gooseneck livestock trailer.

The trailer has a storage compartment built over the neck of the trailer and tapered for less wind drag. In some of their models, there was even a dressing room and a tack room in the forward section of the trailers.

With some slight modifications a space had been created large enough for two people to squeeze in and a false aluminum panel had been installed. After adding a few bales of hay or feed, anyone inspecting the trailer from the inside would never suspect there was a space to hide anyone in and no inspector had yet found it. Other than Agriculture Department Inspectors, few people would want to go inside and inspect a cattle trailer.

The two former students would be there in the compartment when the trailer pulled out to deliver some of the pure bred Angus cows to a buyer this morning. For a few bucks the driver would pull off at a mobile home park just past down town Sheridan on Wisconsin Creek Road and let the men out.

They would stay in one of the mobile homes till someone came to get them and leave the area. For a few bucks more, the driver would not remember having done so and the truck would continue on to Three Forks to deliver the load of cows.

The truck pulled out of the drive from the ranch and made the wide turn toward Sheridan which was only a short distance up the road. The two former students had dressed to look as much like cowboys as they could and wondered why after only a short distance the truck stopped. Maybe they were at the place to exit already, but they were to make no sound or any effort to get out until the driver let them know it was safe to do so.

The Madison County Sheriff's car was sitting on the shoulder of Route 287 with blue lights on and some traffic flares lit to stop traffic. They were asking for registration and license and observing for any sign of the fugitives.

When the deputy saw the ranch name on the truck, he became very cautious but the Hispanic looking driver spoke good English and was courteous and smiling and when the deputy asked him to open the escape door at the front of the trailer to look inside, he did so with no hesitation. The trailer was full of Angus cows and had some small hay bales and a sack of feed in the overhead storage.

The truck looked to be hauling cows and nothing else. A quick scan underneath with a vehicle inspection mirror and he waved the truck on.

The road into Sheridan was busy and there were cars stopped and waiting when the truck pulled out and it was several minutes before the road cleared and a call came from dispatch for each of the road check points to call in.

When the deputy at Sheridan called in he mentioned the Double Barr Ranch truck and the load of cows. The Sheriff asked the deputy to call in on his cell phone.

"You gave the trailer a good going over I suppose?" said Barry.

"Yes sir. I checked it inside and out as well as underneath with the mirror. I looked in the crew cab as well. The driver was very cooperative."

"Was the driver familiar to you?"

"He was a Hispanic looking guy and I have bumped into him while patrolling the area before. I believe he may be the guy who runs the cattle operation."

Wayne Dunkin had arrived at the office and Debra Taylor came in just as the sheriff was talking to the deputy. Russ was coming in behind from the parking lot.

The sheriff got off the phone and said to them, "A truck from Double Barr Ranch went by a few minutes ago with some livestock on a trailer. The deputy says he checked it inside and out and it was clean."

Russ said, "I wish we could interview that driver if he just left the ranch. We might get him to give us a clue about what was going on this morning out there."

The sheriff raised the unit on the radio, "See if you can overtake the truck in question and detain it until Detective Baker can arrive. He will leave now and I will notify Gallatin County and Silver Bow to be on the lookout."

Russ and Debra were already out the door running to his car. She grabbed her bag from the Jeep and they were moving toward Sheridan.

The deputy, who was already moving with lights and sirens, said to Barry, "I don't know if I can catch them before Twin Bridges and they could take the dirt road over to I-15 or they could go on through Silver Star. That road splits past there a ways. Which route do you suggest I take?"

"Take 55 and hope for the best. Hopefully Silver Bow can help over the other way but I would hope we can get them before they leave the county." Barry hung up.

Then the deputy called in, "Madison County this is Unit Five. The suspect vehicle is still in Sheridan. I just passed it. It is over on the side road by that trailer park and it was coming back toward Main Street! I am pulling over. Hold on a minute."

"10-4 Unit Five. Standing by," said Barry.

"The vehicle is trying to get out on Main and looks like he is trying to head out toward me. That long trailer is hard to make that sharp turn so it's slowing him down."

"Unit Five, stop him and detain him. Unit Eight is on the way to assist. He has another officer with him. I am waiting on a phone call from Boulder."

Debra Taylor came to help out and was loving the excitement. Russ's time as a patrolman showed in his driving of the police car as the car traveled the 20 miles or so to get the Sheridan in short order. The Madison County deputy had the truck and trailer load of cows pulled over and the long rig was barely off the road. The city of Sheridan does not have its own police department so the people in town are accustomed to seeing the Madison County Sheriff handling traffic and domestic calls and the occasional break in.

Russ liked Debra's mannerisms when in the role of police officer. She looked like someone who would watch your back for you.

The Madison County officer, Deputy Kauffman, was on the scene and had the driver out and in front of the truck. He explained to Russ that the truck had been in the area of the trailer park when he spotted it and had returned to the main road to where it was sitting now. The driver did not look too concerned.

Deputy Kauffman handed Russ the license and told him that he had looked at the truck south of town but had not looked at it again and was waiting on Russ to arrive.

Russ started out with a serious but low key tone: "Where are you taking the cows, Mr. Estaban?" The name on the driver's license was Victor Estaban.

"I am taking them to Three Forks. What's the problem officer? I was already checked by this other policeman just down the road."

Russ ignored the question and asked, "Why did you stop at the trailer park, Mr. Estaban?"

"I have a friend that lives there and I stopped to see him for a minute."

"What is the name of the friend, Mr. Estaban?"

"He did not do anything. Why do you want to know his name?"

"I want to know his name so I can go to his house and asked him why you stopped by there this morning. I also want to see just who it was you dropped off up there, Mr. Estaban. I want to see if we can arrest you on charges of aiding wanted fugitives and criminals and maybe put you in jail with them for a long time. What is your friend's name?"

"Xavier Hernandez is his name."

What is lot number of the trailer that your friend lives in?"

"His is number eleven. Can I go now?"

"I would like to look in your truck, sir. That's a nice truck. Would that be alright?"

"Yes, I guess that is alright."

Russ and Debra opened the truck and it was a deluxe rig designed to carry five very comfortably while pulling horses, cows or farm equipment. They saw nothing that looked out of the ordinary.

Russ stepped down and looked at Victor and said, "We would like to look in your trailer, again, is that alright?"

"I have nothing but cows. I showed the other policeman. But, I'll be happy to show you."

The trailer was a thirty foot long aluminum rig. It was the type you might see at a horse show or a polo match and not the usual beat up and rusty utility trailer. Very nice.

The trailer had a compartment that was accessed by an escape door so that if a person was in the trailer and the livestock became excited and panicked anyone in the trailer could get out from the front. This area had a small divider with a sliding gate. Some rigs used the space for a dressing area when going to horse shows, etc. There were a few regular bales of hay on the floor and a bag of feed in the small overhead storage bin.

Deputy Kauffman was looking in and said, "Those bales were up in the bin when I looked in here before."

"Why did you move the bales, Mr. Estaban?" asked Russ.

"They must have fallen down," he replied.

Russ stacked a bale on top of another and stood up on it to look into the overhead area. As he stepped up, the driver lunged and pushed Kauffman backward. This sent Kauffman tumbling and Estaban started to run. Debra Taylor stepped in front of the man and holding her Glock 9MM with both hands, she pointed it at his face and yelled, "Congelo, o disparo en el culo!" in Spanish. Loosely translated it meant to "Freeze or I'll shoot your ass!"

Russ was trying to recover and get out to assist. Deputy Kauffman was also scrambling to get back to his feet. The driver wanted to run and thought about it and Russ yelled, "I don't know what she said but you had better do it! She means it, Estaban!"

They put handcuffs on the driver and Russ looked at Debra. He gave her a nod and a silent, "Well done."

"Debra, you and the officer will recall that the driver granted us permission to search the vehicle. So I plan to see what is up in the storage section."

"Russ climbed up using the hay bales and moved the feed out of the way and he could see the aluminum panel that had been crafted to fit and close off the front nose of the section. When Russ removed it, there was piece of carpet and a blanket and some candy wrappers. Russ climbed down.

"Who did you have in there, Estaban?" He had dropped the *Mister*. Estaban did not answer.

"Did you leave them at the trailer park, Estaban?" No answer.

"Do they have guns, Estaban?" No answer.

"Well then, here's what we are going to do. You are going down to that trailer park with us and you will stand in front and we are going to knock on every door and see what we find. If there is any shooting, you will be the first to be shot."

"You cannot do that!" yelled Estaban.

"Is it two people, Estaban?"

"Yes it is two." Estaban answered with less defiance.

"Do they have guns?"

"Yes, they have pistols and one has one of the goat horns I believe. I did not really see it but I heard them say they had one." Russ knew that *goat horns* is a nickname the Mexican drug cartels have given the AK-47 Russian assault rifle due to its appearance.

"Debra, can you get the pictures from the car? I want to show them to Estaban and let's see who we have down there?"

"Which of these people did you bring?" Debra asked as she showed him the pictures of the four men; the two younger men and the two international terrorists.

"It was these two," he said pointing at the two former students. "Those other men I saw at the ranch but I do not know if they are still there."

"Is anyone else down at the mobile home park with them?" asked Russ.

"Not that I know about. They paid me to bring them out from the ranch and to leave them here so someone could come and get them. That's all I know."

"And they are in the mobile home on lot eleven, is that right?"

"They are in the mobile home on lot nine. My friend lives on lot eleven. That trailer number nine does not have anyone living there right now. My friend does some repair work there for part of his rent and has keys to all the trailers. The men paid him to let them stay there a night or two."

"What is going on at the ranch? Did they know you were taking these men out?" Russ asked.

"I don't think anybody there knew. I did not see anybody else. They got in the trailer before I loaded the cows and I did not see them or anyone. Someone may have known but no one said anything to me."

"How many others are there at the ranch?" asked Debra.

"I don't know. They have been staying hidden since the last raid by all those cops. They do not let me see them. Many left that were there. I only do the ranch work. I don't know their business."

"But you let these guys hide in your truck and brought them here."

"People who come to the ranch sometime want to slip out to Sheridan or somewhere to drink and meet women. Sometimes they want to go to the lake and fish. I take them and bring them back and they pay me. That is all. That is not a crime," Victor said with a shrug. "And, I need to get these cows to Three Forks."

Russ looked at Deputy Kauffman, "What can we do about the cows, deputy? Any suggestions?"

"There is a feed lot down on Kearney Lane. We could probably off load them there for a while."

Russ looked at Estaban. "Do you have a phone number for who you are meeting in Three Forks?"

"Yes."

"You call them and tell them your brakes went out here in Sheridan and you have the cows on the trailer and ask them to come and get them. You will give them a discount on the price. Officer Taylor will listen so there better be no tricks."

"Deputy Kauffman, get hold of Deputy Dunkin and tell him we need someone to manage Estaban and the truck until the cows are transferred. And, we need backup here. Now."

"Okay, Estaban, you show us which mobile home those two men are in. Draw me a picture on this note pad."

The two men were in a double wide at the back of the mobile home park and the mobile home they were in could not be seen from where they had stopped the cattle trailer. But Estaban's sketch showed them where to look.

It was almost a half hour before Deputy Wayne Dunkin, Sheriff Barry Steinbrenner and Deputy Hal Smisson arrived. Once the truck was turned over and the road cleared, they turned their attention to getting the two men from the trailer.

Debra Taylor and Deputy Smisson would go down the back of the park using the mobile homes to conceal themselves and get in position on the back side of lot nine. Russ, Wayne Dunkin and Barry would drive around to the front of the mobile home and announce themselves and knock on the door. Hopefully the men would come out peacefully.

With Barry at the wheel, they pulled in front of the mobile home. Russ and Dunkin approached the door and Russ knocked loudly and ordered the men to come out. His knock was answered with a quick burst fired from inside the trailer from the 7.62 Caliber AK-47 that sent Russ and Dunkin running for cover.

Barry Steinbrenner, who had exited the car and was standing on the other side, also hit the dirt. Being shot once was enough for Barry.

Another burst and the door flew open and the man that had been called Cas jumped down from the top step carrying a handgun and Sam was right behind with the AK-47.

Sam spun around and fired another burst from the weapon at the direction of the car and another in the direction of the mobile home that Russ and Dunkin were behind. The two former students then turned and ran toward the rear of the mobile home.

Debra Taylor was down on one knee with her Glock ready and when the man, Cas, came around the corner, she yelled for him to stop but he turned and fired and Deputy Hal Smisson shot Cas twice. At the same moment Sam came around and fired a burst in the direction of Deputy Smisson. Debra Taylor had never fired her gun at anyone before, but today she shot Samer Mustafa three times.

Both men lay on the ground as Russ, Dunkin, and Sheriff Barry Steinbrenner came running to where they were.

The two men were wounded but still alive when Barry called for an ambulance. Deputy Smisson had been hit twice in the chest and would be very sore for a few days but the Kevlar vest had saved his life. His Kevlar vest and a 9MM Glock in the hands of Debra Taylor.

"Are you alright, Debra?" asked Russ.

"I'm alright. Just a little shaky. I don't know how we got away with no bullet holes. Deputy Smisson was lucky he had on that vest."

"And he is lucky he had you for back up, Debra. You did a helluva job!" replied Russ.

"I guess after I've had time for it all to soak in, I may feel badly about shooting the guy. I hope he makes it."

"Those two had the appearance of two nice young students when they were in Salt Lake and today they look like cold blooded killers, Debra. If you had not reacted the way you did, one of us would have been dead. When you think about that guy, look at Hal Smisson and look in the mirror. That's two lives you saved," answered Russ.

"If my father hears about this, I am going to catch hell from him," said Debra.

Barry Steinbrenner overheard Debra and said, "I won't tell him but at some point you probably should."

When the ambulance arrived the men were carried to Butte since it was about half the distance that it was to Bozeman. It was two down, and at least two more to go. They still did not know who had shot Barry.

"Barry, I have an idea I'd like to throw out," said Russ.

"Let's hear it, Russ."

"Do you think we are going to get that warrant today?" asked Russ.

"I hope the district attorney has it now, Russ. They had gotten the judge on the phone and were working on it before I left," said Barry.

"What if we went down to the holding pens where they took those cows and get that driver from the ranch? Maybe we see if we might cut him a deal for his co-operation? He might be our ticket onto the property."

"What do you have in mind?"

Russ explained: "We get him to call the ranch and say his truck broke in Sheridan and he is meeting the buyers here and will be back late after transferring the cows and he gets someone to fix the brakes. Some of us pile in the trailer and the truck and we just ride right in to the ranch compound after dark in their own truck. We wait out of sight until the people show themselves and we arrest them."

"We position cars on the main road and on the road behind the ranch in case anyone tries to beat it out the back. We arrest these guys and after it's all over, maybe we have the guy that shot you. We keep a low profile at the loading pens and keep our cars out of sight so no one tips our hand or calls the ranch if they see the truck and a bunch of police vehicles."

"I like that, Russ. Let's go talk to the driver. I'll call the DA on the way and see if we have that warrant."

23

At the Double Barr ranch, another meeting was going on between Nabil Mussan, Mahdi Shamah, the security man, Chapelle Robichaud and the Imam. The exchange was heated! Robichaud had just determined that the two young students who had been holding up in the other bunker were gone.

"I had not seen them all day and the camera in their bunker was covered so I called them on the intercom and got no answer. I went down into the bunker and they are gone. I do not find them anywhere on the property. I believe they left some time during the night."

Mussan, who was a very scary man, asked, "How could they have gone. Did they have a car or did they walk out? Maybe we can find them before they get too far. If they get caught, they might well tell the police everything!"

The security man named Hussar said, "They did not have a car. There are no horses or four wheelers missing. I have checked. The ranch manager left early this morning with some cows to take to be sold and had the truck and trailer. The camera at the front gate showed him leaving and accessing the key pad to open the gate. There is no sign of them on the tapes. They could have been hiding in the trailer. There is a place for that."

Mussan asked, "Do you think the driver knew they were leaving?"

"It is possible. Some of those staying here have often ridden on the farm trucks to Sheridan or Alder or the lake and he would allow them to do so when he was going in that direction and they would come back when he came back. It has never been a problem until now," said Robichaud.

Mussan said, "It is a problem now! If they are caught we will have police here to arrest us! We have to leave now! We have to act as if they went straight to the police and we cannot delay!"

Robichaud said, "It is not safe to travel on the road. They may be looking for you and if they are, the road is covered. No matter what vehicle we use they will be checking. It is possible that we could put you on one of the four wheelers with food and extra gas and Hussar could get you to the other side of the Ruby Mountains to the Cottonwood Road. There are some old hunting cabins there that are not used much and you could stay there until I can arrange for someone to come in from Dillon to get you in on one of the mine trucks that go to the Treasure Chest Mine. It is at least a thirty mile trip. Some is roads and some will be cross country. And, you may have to spend the night outside but there are trees to help hide yourselves and the four wheeler."

"Let's go now, then," said Mussan.

"We need to get all of your items together and all that you do not take we will burn. We need to wipe the places clean and have no trace of you here," said Robichaud. "People will take little notice of you on the four wheeler as the people ride over in the mountains all the time."

The men feverishly loaded food, gas, guns and some camping equipment into the large Polaris 1000. The four seat, 100+ HP rig was quite impressive. In a light snow, the three men headed across the alfalfa field to the side road and soon were out of sight. In a little while they would be off the main road onto one of the many tracks that went around the Ruby Mountains.

The Imam said, "At least we have them all away from here now." They set about removing all traces of the men and the two students and hid all the weapons. "Let the cops come. They will find nothing."

Russ and Barry had everything in place for a return to the ranch but they had to get their equipment and that would require going back to Russ's place and to the sheriff's office. Barry would dispatch cars to the road behind the ranch and outside on the main road to be sure that no one came or went. Two young men were hired at the holding pens to wash out the trailer and have it ready for the trip back with its new human cargo. All that was needed now was the go ahead from the judge and it was expected any minute.

Russ and Debra went to his house to get their night vision equipment and Russ said, "Debra, this could get pretty intense. I would prefer that you stay back and not come with us on the truck. I think Barry will agree."

Debra walked up and stood on her tip toes, making her almost as tall as Russ. "Listen, Russ, I did not come here to stay behind like a good little girl. I am responsible for myself. I do not need you to protect me, although it is kinda sweet. I think I have already shown I can perform under pressure. And in more ways than one, if you know what I mean."

He did.

Russ's phone rang. It was Nancy. "Hello Nancy. How are you?"

"Good evening, Russ. Can you come over tonight for a little cake, coffee and sitting by the fire? It will require mingling with my mother and brother and his family? I know its short notice."

"Sorry, Nancy. We are working tonight at the sheriff's office. We're trying to catch some bad guys. But I hope you have a good time. I'll try to see you in a day or so."

"You will be careful, won't you?" she said softly.

"I will be careful."

"I know that wasn't your mother Russ. That must have been a girl friend to be worried about you being careful," said Debra who walked in dressed in her swat team clothes as he was finishing his conversation. "Are you cheating on me?" she said with a laugh.

"I don't know how to answer that," he said. She knew not to push that any further.

They drove back to Sheridan and the team assembled at the holding pens. Russ and Deputy Wayne Dunkin were placing their gear in the trailer.

The sheriff was having a private discussion with Debra Taylor. Russ could figure out what that was about: the sheriff was telling her she could not go on the trailer. Good.

Hal Smisson was putting his stuff in the trailer and the sheriff came to review what was happening. Debra Taylor climbed in the trailer carrying her rifle and her gear. She looked at Russ and winked. "Well," he thought, "Barry couldn't tell her no either!" All he could do was nod and smile back.

The truck driver would drive to the ranch gate, get out and punch in the code to open the gate. He was to drive to the large shed where the trailer was kept, park the trailer and truck as usual and get in his car and go home. That was his normal routine. He would be met on the road and detained once he left the property.

The lights were on in the main house and the motion lights came on as the truck entered the area but there was no one to be seen. The four officers inside the trailer were on high alert with guns ready in case someone was waiting. Barry and his deputies and some back up from Gallatin County had the Double Barr Ranch surrounded. At least as much as you can surround 7500 acres. Now they would wait.

Trying to attack the bunkers did not seem like a good idea since they did not know who might be in them. Maybe there were kids and women. They did not know. They wanted the fugitives to come out and then they would apprehend them. If not, they would try tear gas if they could find the air vents.

The aluminum trailer was pretty clean and did not smell too bad but it was cold and hard. It would be a long night. Debra would have liked to have snuggled up close to Russ but she kept her distance. There would be time for that later, she hoped.

Time was dragging by. Deputy Dunkin eased over to where Russ was leaning against the side of the trailer.

"No one is coming out or moving anywhere. Why don't we go and open that bunker and toss in a flash bang grenade and get those guys out?"

"Do you feel we can do that, Wayne?"

"Sure. Why the hell not? I don't see any reason to wait. Debra can cover the house and take down anyone who comes at us from that way. Hal can cover our backs and we go in and get this over with."

"Call Barry and if he gives the go-ahead with it then we do it," said Russ.

Wayne Dunkin touched the button on his headset and called Sheriff Steinbrenner, "This is unit Two calling unit One."

"One. Go ahead," said the sheriff.

"Request that we go and drop in a flash bang in the bunker and get these guys out, over." Debra sat up on her knees and so did Hal Smisson.

"Are you sure, Two?"

"Yes."

"Is Eight in agreement with that?"

Russ nodded at Wayne and Wayne answered, "That's affirmative."

"Then do it," said the sheriff.

"We go in five."

The four huddled in the trailer. Russ said, "Debra, you cover the space between the lot and the house. You should be able to have a good view from here in the trailer with the yard light and some more will come on when we start moving. Hal, you need to watch from the hay storage where the other bunker is in case anyone comes out of there. I will get the entry door open as soon as I can find the release and lift up that water trough. Wayne will handle the flash bang as he has more experience. Is everyone ready?"

Debra found a position where she could set up her rifle. Hal would have to run some distance to get to where the other bunker was and Russ and Wayne would run as fast as they could to provide as much an element of surprise as possible.

Wayne Dunkin spoke into his headset, "Unit One, we are go here."

"We will come in on your call, Two or Eight. Good luck."

Russ opened the escape door and hit the ground running toward the cattle feed lot where the bunker was located and Wayne Dunkin was right behind. Motion lights came on and the three men could be seen on the security monitors in the bunker as they ran to their places. Debra tried to keep focused on the open area toward the house and see what the men were doing at the same time.

Russ scaled the metal rail fence and got to the trough. Wayne Dunkin was there with gun at the ready as Russ hunted for the release under the trough. When he found the pedal, he pushed it down with his foot and the trough clicked and it popped up and then Russ grabbed the handle. He had expected it to be heavy but was surprised that it raised with little effort. He turned away slightly as

Wayne Dunkin tossed in the flash bang device. The blast from the device and the light erupted out of the stairwell and in a second Dunkin started down the steps and Russ followed. There was little light on in the bunker as Dunkin and Russ were shouting out, "Madison County Sheriff's Department. Face down on the floor. Do not move and put your hands over your head!"

Lights came on in the house and Chapelle Robichaud came running out the front door and down the steps carrying a hand gun. As he started toward the feed lot, Debra Taylor hit him in the face with a beam from her tactical light and yelled, "You at the house! Stop and throw that gun down or I will shoot you! Do it now! I will not tell you twice! This is the Madison County Sheriff's Office!"

Robichaud did as he was told and tossed the gun aside. "Get face down on the ground," she said and he did.

In a few seconds, Russ found a light switch in the bunker and the smoke was clearing. Dunkin said, "There's no damned body here, Russ."

"Let's go to the other bunker," said Russ. Wayne spoke into his headset as he hit the top of the steps, "Unit One the first bunker is clear. No one inside. No resistance, so far. Going to the other bunker."

"Is everyone clear?" asked Russ. Debra reported, "Clear, here. Have one on the ground." Hal Smisson reported, "Clear here. No one in sight."

Russ and Wayne repeated the process on the second bunker as the Sheriff and several other cars came down the drive with lights flashing. The results were the same. Empty.

Frustration was the mood. "I'm damned glad we did not call those FBI and Homeland Security people. It's embarrassing enough to have Gallatin County here. I will never hear the end of this from Charlie," said Sheriff Steinbrenner.

They looked through all the cabins and house and only the Imam was inside so they finally took Robichaud in to the house. "Where are the men who were here, Mr. Robichaud," asked Russ.

"All of our guests have gone. As we have told you before, we are remodeling and are not open at present." His calm manner was enough to make the most even tempered police officer mad.

"You had people in those bunkers a few days ago. Two of them left this place yesterday morning on the livestock trailer," said Russ.

"I don't know who you mean. If there was anyone on the livestock trailer, you would need to talk to the ranch manager. He handles the livestock and the trailers."

"Why do you have those underground bunkers?"

"There are thousands of those in the United States, they are perfectly legal. We had a company build them for the security of our guests. We have recently been repeatedly attacked by the police and that seems to be our most serious threat," Robichaud answered quietly. "You will find nothing or no one here that is illegal. I do not know how you would know anyone has been in the bunkers. Have you had a warrant to search them? Maybe you have been here illegally looking around?"

"You have been harboring fugitives here. We know it and you know it. Either you cooperate or you are going to be the only person going to jail," said Barry Steinbrenner. "And one of those guys shot me just outside your gate and I intend to find him. We have two of your *guests,* as you call them, in custody now. We should have a pretty good case with their testimony. They don't seem like the types that want to spend a lot of years in jail."

"Sheriff, I am sorry that you were shot. But if you have a desire for vengeance, you will have to look somewhere else. Is that clear? Whoever you have in custody would have little knowledge of anything going on here. And I will not be talking to you any more until I have a lawyer."

312

"We have you on state warrants, Mr. Robichaud, but the federal warrants will take precedent and you're looking at life in prison. The only way you have a chance of ever getting back to France, or wherever you are from, is to cooperate with us in finding those fugitives."

Russ left the house and Debra was standing on the porch talking to Deputy Dunkin when he came out.

"Russ, I think we are going to keep this lady and not let her go back to Salt Lake. What do you think?"

"I think if Deputy Wayne Dunkin likes her that well, she must be mighty damned good!"

"Where are those other guys, Russ?" asked Dunkin.

"Let's go look around and see what we don't see. We see what we see, but let's see what should be here but isn't. This place has a place for everything and everything is in its place. Let's see if we can find what should be here that is missing," said Russ.

Tractors, implements, hay cutting and baling equipment along with grain drills and sprayers were all in neat sheds and looked well maintained. There were several small ATV's and even a couple of trail bikes for off road use.

There was a stable with several horses and a neatly organized tack room that seemed to be full of riding equipment. In fact, it looked too full for anything to be out of place.

"Wayne, you probably know this area better than anyone. How could they have gotten out of here?" asked Russ.

Wayne laid out a description of the area behind the Double Barr Ranch. "The Ruby Mountains behind here are good place to hunt elk and deer. Cold Mountain Outfitters has people hunting and trout fishing back there during the year but they close the place up the first of December."

"There are some open pit mines and lots of trails and roads snaking through the area. The East Bench Irrigation Canal is back there and the Canal Road. It's about thirty five miles or more around to get over to Dillon. You could get on the Canal Road and go all the way. Getting to the road from here wouldn't be hard, you just go out down by that hay storage lot where I came in the other night. You would take Middle Road to Silver Spring and hit Ruby River Road. Another turn or two and you are on Canal Road. That is, if you were trying to make Dillon."

"Not easy to try to go over the mountains, especially with snow and its 10,000 feet up in places. But, with a map and GPS and if you have someone that knows the area, you could leave and go around to Dillon and on to I-15 and then it's anybody's guess."

"How would you go around there if it were you, Wayne."

If I were trying to hide from the cops, I'd take an ATV and stay off the likely routes. Another way is to go south and go by Ruby Lake. That has too much local traffic to avoid anyone seeing you, though, I believe. I'd probably go around the north side and come down to Stone Creek. There are some places you could hide a night or two."

"Like where, Wayne?"

"There are a couple of old cabins over there on that road. Hunters use them sometimes. I've spent the night there with my camping stuff once or twice. I don't see these guys sleeping outdoors in the snow, do you?"

"There is a spot here in this shed where something has been kept. I'll bet. Looking at the tracks, it was an ATV of some kind. Let's go around to that hay storage lot and see if we can see anything," said Russ. "Throw your stuff in the sheriff's Explorer, just in case."

They hurriedly told the Sheriff they were taking his car and Debra, Russ and Wayne went to look at the hay storage lot where the ground was somewhat soft with a light snow covering. The hay lot sat outside the fence and a gate opened to allow the hay to be stored there from the field.

When they got to the gate, it was partially open. While there was snow accumulated, it was obvious a heavy tread vehicle had been through recently.

The gate being open would suggest it wasn't cowboys and field hands as they would never leave a gate open. But, someone in a big hurry might!

"Somebody went out in a hurry and left that gate open," said Wayne.

Middle Road was hard packed but the tracks of a vehicle leaving at high speed with wheels spinning and throwing gravel could be seen even in car headlights and snow.

"I'll bet you they went this way, Wayne. Now, where do we go to find them?"

"They've had a head start and probably have been gone several hours if not all day. If they were going straight to Dillon on the Canal Road, they have made it to Dillon a long time ago and are gone," said Wayne.

"So, if we were going on a wild goose chase, maybe we go check out those cabins. I'll bet they left without plans to be picked up. They have to wait somewhere."

"Maybe Robichaud was planning on picking them up when the heat is off," said Russ. "What is the fastest way to get there from here?"

"I'll drive," said Wayne. We are going to Alder, hit the Upper Ruby Road and then Cottonwood Creek Road. That becomes Stone Creek. It'll take a little while, but if they went off road, it took them a good while longer to get there, too."

Russ pushed the button on his headset: "Unit Eight to Unit One."

"Unit One, go ahead Eight."

Units Two and Eight are going to check out a hunch. And that's all it is. We have your car and Deputy Taylor is with us. We are going to Stone Creek Road past Ruby Lake on the way to Dillon. Unit Two knows a place some people could hold up a day or so at some old cabins over there. We think they may have taken an ATV and gone cross country. If they went straight to Dillon, Unit Two figures they are probably long gone. But you might call the sheriff over in Dillon and see if he can put a car on the Stone Creek Road at Highway 41. Just in case. We'll check out the cabins. We have our gear."

"Be extra careful! Watch those guys. If it is the one who shot me, he will not hesitate to shoot. And, Russ, please don't get my car shot full of holes!" said Barry.

"Oh, so it's only the car you are worried about?"

"Yeah. I've seen some of your work before! The car and maybe that officer from Salt Lake. I don't want her father on my case. Out."

Wayne Dunkin had driven enough backroads and dirt roads and ranch roads to be an expert. And he showed it as he wasted no time in getting to the foothills of the Ruby Valley and the place looked dark and lonesome at 3:30 in the morning as they approached the area where the cabins were. It was mid-January and cold.

About a mile before they reached the dilapidated cabin, Wayne pulled the car into a side road and stopped. "I think we should gear up and walk the mile so they don't see us in case they have someone standing watch. We don't really know how many there are, do we?"

"No, Wayne. That's a good point. We don't. I guess at least the two and maybe that's all."

Wayne was putting on his ghillie suit. "I think there is a little creek behind those cabins. I will go around back and see if I can see the vehicle. They would most likely park it in the back out of sight. I'll take up a position on the other side and across the road, unless you have a better idea."

"I don't have a better one," said Russ. "Debra, bring your rifle and night scope. We'll find some cover on this side for you and I'll try going behind and approach from the far side but out of Wayne's line of fire. Let's see if we can detect anything with the night vision from one of the three angles."

"When everyone is set we'll try calling them out. I don't think we have enough fire power to go charging in there without knowing how many there are. I don't think we can risk going up to the door and tossing in a flash bang."

Wayne was off and headed up the ditch behind the cabins. It did not take long until he was not visible as he made his way the mile to the cabins. After waiting for a few minutes, Russ and Debra followed.

Then they heard Wayne on the headset: "The ATV is here! At least somebody's ATV is."

It seemed like an eternity for Debra to get in position and Russ to make his way around. No one could see anything at first. Then Debra spoke into her headset: "I see someone smoking a cigarette. Someone's on guard!"

"Do you have a shot?" asked Russ.

"No. But do we know who we are shooting at?"

"No. Good thinking! I guess it's time to find out," said Russ. "Are you guys ready?"

"Russ, we could wait till morning and get Barry and them over here to help," said Wayne.

"Do you want to wait, Wayne?"

"Hell no," said Wayne. "Just throwing it out."

"I guess its time then. Let's do this," said Russ. "Don't give your positions away until you have to."

Russ lit up the window of the house with his high intensity flashlight. Then quickly turned it off.

They could hear someone yell inside in Arabic and they could not understand what was said but they knew there were at least two people in the house.

"This is the Madison County Sheriff's office! We have you surrounded! Come out with your hands over your heads or we will start shooting! You have thirty seconds!"

There was more talking and yelling in what Russ thought was Arabic.

And then one of the people inside ran out the back and toward the ditch. Russ fired at the runner but did not feel he had hit him. The runner fired a burst back in Russ's direction from what Russ took to be an AK-47 or some automatic weapon.

A second man got to the ATV started it up in the back and went out the other side of the cabin toward where Debra was positioned. Debra pointed her light in the guy's face and blinded him for an instant and she yelled for him to stop. He leaned out and fired his automatic weapon at the direction of Debra and her light went out.

"Oh, hell!" thought Russ. "He's hit Debra."

Debra Taylor was positioned looking through the night vision scope on the Remington 700. She had the crosshairs on the driver of the ATV when he fired at her. She had no time to be afraid, she pulled the trigger on the .308 Cal sniper rifle. The first time she had ever fired it at a living target.

Russ had panicked thinking Debra was hit by the automatic weapon fire. But the shooter had not actually seen Debra and was using the "pray and spray" method and was shooting blindly.

Russ heard the sound of Debra's rifle. It was all over for the driver of the ATV. The vehicle lurched to the right and off down into the creek and stopped. It was not going any farther. And neither was the driver.

Russ started running toward the direction of the ATV and Debra, and was almost to the cabin when a figure stepped out of the doorway. It was the third man and Russ was suddenly caught in the open and under attack from another shooter and another automatic weapon. He tried to return fire but was no match for the firepower and the shooter was firing and running toward Russ. Russ went diving toward the ditch trying to find cover in the dark roadway.

Wayne Dunkin was crouched behind a large rock and looking at the shooter through the night scope on his Barrett rifle. He pulled the trigger on the .338 Magnum and the shooter was knocked off his feet and the gun fell to the ground. His days as head of security for the Double Barr Ranch were over. He was dead when he hit the ground.

"Are you two okay?" Russ yelled into his headset. Both Wayne and Debra said, "Yes."

"I'm going back after the other guy. He went up the creek I believe."

Russ started back in the direction he had just come from and looked with his night vision goggles to see if he could spot the last shooter.

He thought he saw the man move in the small trees, headed to the creek. Russ moved quickly in that direction. Wayne Dunkin was coming in a trot to back up Russ.

The man was about a hundred feet away darting in the dark from one tree to another. Russ, being able to see better, was gaining but was out gunned.

Then Russ could not see the man through his goggles. He had apparently gotten behind a thick growth of the low growing trees.

Wayne Dunkin was running up the road and Russ could hear him coming. As Russ moved forward he suddenly saw the figure moving around the bush and headed back in Russ's direction. Russ pointed his Beretta at the figure in the dark ditch and fired. One. Two. Three. Four. Five. And then he did not see the man.

Wayne Dunkin dropped down beside Russ. "I think you hit him, Russ. He fell and rolled down in the creek."

Russ was looking with infrared and could not spot him.

"Stay down, Russ, and put your bright light down in that ditch. If the guy stands up, it'll be the last time he does."

Debra Taylor had taken a prone shooting position in the road, also. This was going to be the end of the line for the gunman.

Russ turned on the light and pointed it toward the creek from behind the bush. With the intense light they could see the man's legs and feet. He was face down in the creek. Nabil Mussan, who had shot Barry Steinbrenner on the side of the road and left him for dead over a month ago, was now lying beside a road himself.

It was still not sunup in Montana, but the lights of the three gunmen were out for good. They had no more sunrises or sunsets to look forward to.

"I'll go get the car and radio the sheriff and get some ambulances out here, said Wayne." He jogged the mile back to where the car was parked.

Debra Taylor came to Russ and embraced him and he could feel her holding back the sobs. She was glad to have Russ to hold on to. He was glad to have her holding on. She was one tough lady.

Wayne Dunkin got back with the car and they sat for a moment with the engine running trying to gather their emotions and get warm. The radio was alive with ambulance calls and the sheriff's office dispatcher giving directions and it was now almost 5:30 AM on a January morning in Madison County Montana. The three officers suddenly realized they were dead tired and drained.

"I'm going down and confirm the condition and location of the suspects and put a flare so the EMT's can find them," said Dunkin.

"I'll go with you," said Russ. "Debra, if you would you can monitor the radio in case Barry calls. The car should be warm by now."

She did not seem to mind that suggestion.

They walked back to where the ATV had come to a stop in the creek. The lights were still on and the motor was idling.

The driver's blood covered the front seats and he had fallen out on the passenger side. There was a gaping wound on his back where the .308 round had hit him from Debra's rifle. Russ was glad she had stayed in the car. As tough as she was, this might have been too much tonight. This was the second person she had shot in two days and this one would not need medical attention. There would be no trial. No deportation. No prison time. No more car bombs.

Wayne Dunkin switched off the engine and there was a strange sound. The sound of no sounds at all except for the low idle of the Ford Explorer just a few steps up the road.

The man at the front of the dilapidated cabin was in no better shape. The .338 Cal Lapua Magnum had instantly removed the life from the would-be attacker. Wayne Dunkin had been trained by the best: The United States Army. He had learned his skills well.

As Russell Baker looked at the man on the ground and the AK-47 lying on the ground nearby, he remembered something Sheriff Barry Steinbrenner had said to him a year or so before. "If you are in a serious situation, Wayne Dunkin is a man you want watching your back." He'd saved Russ's back tonight and more!

On up they found the last of the three. He had been hit twice or three times it appeared when Russ had fired and had collapsed into the creek with his face just touching the cold shallow water. Russ turned and walked away. He had seen enough.

"Russ. Look at this," said Dunkin. Wayne was holding up a semi-automatic pistol by his fingertips. "He had this in his waistband. It's a Glock 22, .40 Caliber. I believe we may have found the weapon used to shoot Barry."

That brought a slight smile to Russ's face.

"I think you finally got Barry's shooter, Russ!"

Lights and the sound of emergency vehicles started to be seen and heard as first one and then another of the Madison County, Gallatin County, and the Beaverhead County sheriff's cars and ambulances arrived at the scene. Barry Steinbrenner arrived and stopped one of the EMT crews that was headed to one of the downed perpetrators: "Come with me," he said. He went to where the three deputies were standing by the Explorer.

"Is any one hurt? Does anyone need medical attention?"

"We are fine," they all agreed.

Barry walked to where each of the three dead fugitives was lying and looked at each man for a minute and then walked back to the deputies. Uncharacteristically, he hugged Wayne, then Russ, and Debra. Wayne handed him a plastic evidence bag containing the Glock .40 Caliber pistol. Barry looked at it and nodded and then he turned to walk away, finding it difficult to look them in the eye at that moment. He was caught up with the emotion. He stopped and turned back toward them.

"Thank you for all the work and for taking the risks. You did a damned good job here tonight. I am glad you were not hurt. Russ, you take my car and go home. Debra can ride with you or Wayne. Wayne, take that Dodge I came in and you all go home. We can meet for a short briefing at the office about noon and try not to work all day on this. I have to get the Feds their updates." That would be something he would savor.

"I left my car at Russell's so I will go back there with him to get it. Thanks," said Debra.

They got in the Explorer and made the drive on the lonely Montana road in silence as Debra curled up on the seat and looked to be asleep as Russ drove the rough and curvy road back to Alder.

When they got to Russ's house and got out of the car, Debra said, "May I take a quick shower and stay here? I really don't want to be by myself tonight."

"Of course, Debra," Russ said as he gave her a hug with his arm around her shoulder.

In a few minutes Russ almost collapsed onto his bed. And moments later, Debra was under the covers beside him. And they were both asleep.

24

The next morning they struggled to get to the office and they drove in separate cars. There was a full jury room of people and some reporters were outside that had gotten word of the events of the past two days.

Russ simply gave them a "No Comment, you will need to talk to the Sheriff," reply.

It was clear that Barry Steinbrenner had not been home or to bed. He had spent all night doing paper work and phoning the agencies that were in some way involved with the case.

They were working on what charges they could file against Chapelle Robichaud and the Imam and the two former students. Maybe RICO charges could be brought against the Double Barr Ranch. That would mean a tidy sum of money for the Madison County Sheriff's office.

"The two men from the trailer park shootout are both going to survive. They will stand trial on a variety of State and Federal charges and I hope they will tell us for sure which of the men shot me. I guess it doesn't matter too much now, unless it was one of them, but I would like to know," said the sheriff.

After the meeting, Debra asked Russ to step in the small interrogation room and closed the door. "I have to go, Russell. My dad is sending the plane for me. I have to get home or be disowned. There is plenty of room on there for you to come with me."

"I don't think I can come today, Debra. But maybe I can get out there soon," said Russ. "I need to take care of some things here and call my in-laws and get with Miriam Alexander and let her know what has been going on."

"I have actually been considering moving back to Georgia, Debra. I have to make a decision on that. No one here knows about that so please don't mention it to anyone."

That was like a punch in the stomach to Debra, but she maintained her composure.

"I don't want to put you on the spot, Russell, but I would love to see you again. I think you know that I don't just sleep around. I am very fond of you. I can come back here, or to Atlanta; it doesn't matter to me. I guess we'll talk more later. I sure hope so, anyway. And I may have to come back here regarding the case."

Before Russ could answer, she stepped up to him and kissed him passionately, and then she turned and walked out the door to her rented Jeep and did not look back. She did not want anyone to see the tears on her face.

Wayne Dunkin, the least romantic guy in the world, Russ thought, came over to the window where Russ was watching Debra leave and put his arm on Russ's shoulder as he watched Debra drive off.

"That is one fine woman, Russ. And I don't mean that she is just good looking. She has it all. The fact that she is rich, well, that's a bonus! I would love to be on her list. Of course, my wife would not like that too much! Have a good evening."

Wayne Dunkin turned and walked out to his truck and left. There were no tears in his eyes.

Russ walked to his car and his cell phone rang. It was Miriam.

"Hey, handsome. I hope I did not call at a bad time but I wanted to see how things are going and let you know I will have a lot of time on my hands if you ever want to come out here to see me. You *could* come tonight, of course. But you probably are booked up with Nancy. Russ, I'm sorry. I should not have said that!"

"Miriam, that is very nice of you. I have had a rough couple of days. First, we had a shootout two days ago with Kasim and Samer."

Before he could continue, she interrupted, "A shootout! You are not injured, are you? I can't believe this! Where are they now?"

"They are in the hospital in Butte and both will survive to stand trial. We were involved in another shoot out early this morning with the two other guys and some third man. We are all okay here. I have had no sleep in about three days now."

"Who was involved with you?"

Deputy Wayne Dunkin and Sergeant Debra Taylor and me."

"Debra Taylor was there?"

"Yes. She volunteered to help and Barry put her on the case."

"What about the three men you were in the shootout with?"

"They are all dead."

Miriam just fell silent. It took a moment to compose herself. Then she whispered, "I am so sorry Russ. I hate you had to go through that again. What are you going to do now?"

"Go home and get some sleep. That's my plan right now."

"I'm so happy none of you got hurt. Call me when you feel up to it. I love you, Russ. Take care."

With that she was gone before he could answer. He could not see the tears and hear her crying now.

Russ got home and lay down on the bed. He fell asleep and it was almost 5:00 in the afternoon when his cell phone rang. It was Nancy Freeman. "Hi, Russ. Are you busy?"

"No, I just woke up from a nap. I had several late nights in a row."

"Just party, party, party I guess," she joked.

"Something like that. I had a get together with some deputies from the Madison County Sheriff's Office last night," he replied. He decided not to mention the shootings. She would find out about those soon enough.

"Would you like to come to my house tomorrow and have lunch? It will be just you and me. Mom has gone over to my brother's house to be with the grandkids and is spending the night. I have wine and the fireplace is working fine. I haven't opened the Christmas present you sent me and I have one for you, so you need to come and get it. We'll have a late Christmas, just the two of us."

"I'll be there, Nancy. I'm looking forward to it. What time should I be there tomorrow?"

She hesitated for a moment, then she said softly, "I guess there is no reason you could not come on over tonight if you wanted to."

"In that case, I'll be there in an hour."

It might be a good year after all! For Russell Baker and Nancy Freeman. And, Sheriff Barry Steinbrenner.

Russell Baker
The Drift Boat Detective
Subsurface 2017
©H Jerome Chapman

CPSIA information can be obtained
at www.ICGtesting.com
Printed in the USA
LVOW13s1202270318
571287LV00009BA/181/P